"I must say," T'Rena said at last, "that in fifteen years in the Federation diplomatic corps, I have never seen a single interview cause so much furor and delight."

Vulcans, thought Pulask⋯ ⋯ *⋯ou were being praised.* ⋯

"Speakir⋯ ⋯ading between the ⋯ ⋯ation I received fron⋯ ⋯ve to say that it's something ⋯ ⋯u familiarized yourself only with the in⋯cies of the hound-racing."

So the castellan hadn't liked hearing the truth? That was his own damn problem. "Even if I was up to speed with every damn story happening right now across the whole damn Union, I would've said the same thing," said Pulaski. "War crimes should be prosecuted and their perpetrators punished. I don't think I'm saying anything too outré here. I bet the Cardassian people agree with me."

"Many do," conceded T'Rena. "Although there is some considerable opposition from parts of the military."

"I bet," Pulaski muttered.

"And may I remind you as a Starfleet officer you are bound by the Prime Directive, which forbids involvement in the affairs of other civilizations?"

"Rubbish," said Pulaski firmly. "These crimes were committed on Bajor. Bajor is a member of the Federation. We're already involved."

STAR TREK
DEEP SPACE NINE®

ENIGMA TALES

UNA McCORMACK

Based on *Star Trek*®
and *Star Trek: The Next Generation*®
created by Gene Roddenberry
and
Star Trek: Deep Space Nine
created by Rick Berman & Michael Piller

POCKET BOOKS
New York   London   Toronto   Sydney   New Delhi   East Torr

Pocket Books
An Imprint of Simon & Schuster, Inc.
1230 Avenue of the Americas
New York, NY 10020

This book is a work of fiction. Any references to historical events, real people, or real places are used fictitiously. Other names, characters, places, and events are products of the author's imagination, and any resemblance to actual events or places or persons, living or dead, is entirely coincidental.

First Pocket Books paperback edition July 2017

POCKET and colophon are registered trademarks of Simon & Schuster, Inc.

For information about special discounts for bulk purchases, please contact Simon & Schuster Special Sales at 1-866-506-1949 or business@simonandschuster.com.

The Simon & Schuster Speakers Bureau can bring authors to your live event. For more information or to book an event, contact the Simon & Schuster Speakers Bureau at 1-866-248-3049 or visit our website at www.simonspeakers.com.

Manufactured in the United States of America

10 9 8 7 6 5 4 3

ISBN 978-1-5011-5258-0
ISBN 978-1-5011-5259-7 (ebook)

For Ina

HISTORIAN'S NOTE

This story takes place in late 2386, seven years after the *U.S.S. Enterprise*-E's confrontation with the Romulan praetor Shinzon (*Star Trek: Nemesis*) and one year after the *Athene Donald* visit to Deep Space 9 (*Star Trek: Deep Space Nine—The Missing*). These events unfold only weeks after Julian Bashir's mission that aided the Trill journalist Ozla Graniv's bombshell exposé of Section 31 and its numerous clandestine activities (*Star Trek: Section 31—Control*).

*A novel about the past, the future,
and everything in between.*

ENIGMA TALES

ENIGMA TALES

My dear Doctor—

I often imagined what your first visit to Cardassia Prime might be like. When first we met, I pictured us strolling through the capital, finding shade under the great and ancient ithian trees that lined the boulevards of Tarlak, stopping to drink hot bitter gelat in the corner houses of Torr, and climbing the heights of Coranum to look down upon the splendor of my city, the heart of the empire that I have loved and served. I imagined a journey into the country, to a grand house where you could see our world in all its stark beauty, and understand how the land had formed us, and the nature of the demands it put upon us.

A pleasant fantasy, and one that sustained me considerably during the early years of my exile, when Cardassia seemed lost to me forever, and you were a rare friend. Over the years I revised the tale, not least as Cardassia became more and more fantastical to me, a place that I could scarcely believe ever existed, never mind be one to which I could possibly return.

And I did return, in the end, but not to the Cardassia I knew.

I was glad you did not come then. I did not want you to see our ruin, and our shame. I did not want you to see us holding out a begging bowl to the rest of the quadrant. And I knew that if you came you would not hold back from seeing all that was there. You would not hold back from trying to help; you were constitutionally incapable of that. But I did not want you to see hunger, privation, and fear. I did not want you to see us suffer through the dust storms, stand in line for water, dig up bodies with what strength we had, and then have to find the strength to bury them again. I did not want you to see. I did not want you to help.

Then, one day, I woke up and it was spring. The sun was shining. The children were living, not dying. The buildings were tall and busy, not ruined and empty. There was life. There was hope. People change, the poet says, and smile. I hoped that you would come, and see us smile.

You are here now, Julian, and it is not how I imagined it would be. Still, I wish that I could show you Cardassia. I wish that I could show you anything at all.

> Your friend,
> Garak
> [unsent]

One

There is nothing quite to compare with arriving on a new world. As the ship comes into orbit, even the most seasoned traveler cannot help but stop their reading or their moss-gathering and peer at the planet moving slowly into range. Questions form in the mind: *What will I see that is new? Will I learn something? Will I be surprised? Will my visit here change me in some small but significant way?* When the time comes, you board the landing shuttle and, for a while, you see little more than its sealed interior, and hear little more than engines thrumming as you are brought planetside. But soon enough you're down, and safety harnesses are released, and you rise and stretch, and fumble around for your bags, and at last you come out into the spaceport, into the whirl and noise of a thousand alien strangers, busy about their lives, caring little for your concerns, anxious about missing connections or finding friends or simply getting home. You begin to find your bearings. Your journey on into the new world begins. You have arrived.

No, nothing quite compares. You are weary. You are disoriented. You are excited too. You are struggling to get your bearings. And when the world in question is Cardassia Prime, mystique shrouds your arrival. You know that Cardassia has been at peace with the rest of the quadrant for over a decade, and all the signs are positive that the peace is lasting. You know that there is an alliance in place now, a special relationship between these people and yours, but this is an alien world after all, and one can never be too careful. You are aware of all of this, but the war still lingers in the memory, and behind it lurks the Occupation, a scar that has never quite healed. You are aware that Cardassia's legal and judicial system is now considered second to none within the quadrant in terms of transparency, equity, and efficiency. You gather that the police service too these days is a byword for honesty and fairness. Education, healthcare, social care—all flourishing, all nurtured, and with a philosophy that prioritizes care ahead of cost. Most importantly, nobody *starves* in the Cardassian Union these days, and while remoter regions of Prime and some of the outer worlds might still require the more rugged and self-denying sort, nobody is thrown to the wolves. You try to shake off your doubts. This is a new world. But there remains some dark glamour to Cardassia Prime, some continuing sense that something cruel may still lurk in the shadows. Perhaps you are wondering if you are safe here. Perhaps you are wise to wonder.

Katherine Pulaski was not immune to glamour, but like most things it had to work fairly damn hard to cast any kind of spell on her. This morning, Cardassia Prime, as if sensing a worthy opponent at last, was pulling out all the stops. The spring sunrise unfolding beyond the transparent-aluminum walls and ceilings of the spaceport was a veritable symphony of color. A bass line of rosy pink warmed the sky. Gentle arpeggios of yellow rippled through, counterpointed by sharp and sudden purple leitmotifs. The whole opened out into a faultless final movement: the vast unbroken blue of spring over the Cardassian capital. *Welcome, Katherine Pulaski*, Cardassia Prime seemed to be saying. *Ta-da! This world is like no other. Enjoy your stay here. We promise you the trip of a lifetime.*

Pulaski yawned, stretched, and scratched. "Look," she said to her traveling companion, pointing ahead. "Coffee. Goddammit, Peter, they really are civilized here after all."

Her companion, a lean man in his midthirties with black hair and space lag, peered above the rims of his dark sunglasses, and muttered, "Praise be." His name was Doctor Peter Alden, and he and Pulaski were colleagues and, sometimes, such as in meetings, archenemies. Grabbing their in-flight bags, they shambled across the arrivals hall to the small café that Pulaski had spotted. She sat Alden down with the bags, and put in their order with a friendly young Cardassian male who was excited to see two humans and chattered about the human teacher he'd had at his school as a kid. Pulaski smiled and nodded and managed a facsimile of friendliness: no mean feat for her. When their order arrived, she and Alden sat in silence until Alden had finished his coffee, leaned back in his chair, and taken off his glasses.

"Of course," he said, "the reason that there is coffee is down to us."

"What?" Pulaski said. "I'm willing to take credit for a lot of things, but I can't see how I can get away with that one."

"Starfleet—the Federation—we were here for years. The reconstruction effort. All mixing with the locals—like that young man there who brought us our drinks. I bet we won't struggle to find human food and drink." He looked thoughtful. "I could murder a curry."

Pulaski smiled. "If you're offering analysis *and* feeling hungry, I'm going to guess that your space lag is better."

Alden stretched and looked up through the ceiling. "Well," he said, "it's a nice morning."

"It's beautiful. Who would've expected it from Cardassia Prime?"

Alden grunted. "I gather it has its charms."

Pulaski contemplated her companion as he leaned forward and started making short work of the pile of small iced buns that she had brought with the coffee. Pulaski's current assignment was on board a scientific research vessel, the *Athene Donald*. Scientific research vessels were plenty in the Federation, sure, but the *Athene Donald* was special. Its crew was the most diverse yet assembled, drawing as it did not only from Federation species, but from allied and not-so-allied worlds. Ferengi, Cardassians, even a Tzenkethi, mingled freely with the humans, Trill, and Vulcans. The idea was that a untrammeled scientific community would find ways of working together that were not bounded by diplomatic needs or constraints. It was a truly utopian vision. There had been numerous complications, but one of the most irritating, to Pulaski's mind, had been the appearance at the very start of the ship's mission of Starfleet Intelligence, in the form of Peter Alden.

Pulaski didn't want spooks aboard her ship. She didn't like their games, and she thought it made a mockery of their mission. Alden came anyway. By the end of that first voyage, however, Alden had been what Pulaski called "cured." He quit the intelligence service, signed up on the *Athene Donald*, and had completed his doctoral studies in xenosociolinguistics in record time, working with Ferengi and Tzenkethi advisors. Since then, Pulaski and Alden had enjoyed sparring with each other whenever they could. When she had been invited to Cardassia Prime, she told him he should come along. Alden agreed immediately, to the vast amusement of their colleagues. There was a pool on the ship (neither of them knew this) as to how soon she would make him the fourth Mr. Pulaski. There was also another pool (they perforce knew nothing about this either) as to how quickly she would divorce him.

Their quiet, restorative breakfast was interrupted by the sudden arrival at their table of a rather harassed-looking young Cardassian male. He was breathless from hurrying across the concourse, and he was waving a piece of cardboard on which PULASKI had been written in big block letters.

"Doctor Pulaski!" he cried. "Doctor Pulaski!"

"Watch it, Kitty," Alden said. "I think someone wants your autograph."

The Cardassian screeched to a halt at her elbow. "Oh, thank goodness!" he said, between gasps of breath. "I thought I'd missed you."

"Well, sonny, don't worry," Pulaski said. "You're back on target."

"Oh, thank goodness!"

She smiled at him. "Who are you, exactly?"

"Me? Oh, yes, my name is Metok Efheny. I'm from the chief academician's office at the university. I've been assigned as your aide during your visit, and I'm here to take you into the city. We have everything . . ." He looked anxiously into their cups. "Oh my goodness, I'm sure we can find you something better to drink than that noxious brew . . . Anyway, I'm so glad I've found you! Professor Therok would've been furious if I'd missed you!"

"Hanging offense, huh?" said Pulaski.

Efheny blanched. Quickly, he said, "I must assure you, Doctor, Cardassia is nothing like that these days—"

Alden covered a laugh. Patiently, Pulaski said, "It's just an expression. I wasn't expecting to face the death penalty—not this early on in the trip, anyway."

"Really, we don't do anything like that, not anymore—"

"Sonny," said Pulaski, "stand down. This is a great welcome, this is great coffee, and you're doing just great."

That did the trick. Efheny looked relieved and very grateful. Pulaski stood up, Alden close behind. There was some fuss and bother while Efheny found their luggage, and then he led his guests out into the bright morning. Alden put his sunglasses back on, but Pulaski enjoyed the heat of the sun upon her skin. She'd been on board ships a lot the past few months.

"What a great morning!" she said, and Efheny smiled happily. Nice kid.

With some further hustle and bustle, Efheny got them to their skimmer, packed in the luggage, and settled them into the back. It was a very nice skimmer, Pulaski noted, with some satisfaction. Plenty of room for the three of them to sit, with Alden and Pulaski facing Efheny, and a driver up front beyond a barrier. Being a very important person was very fine, Pulaski thought. Alden nudged her, and she saw that Efheny was looking at her anxiously. "Say something nice," Alden muttered.

"Gorgeous skimmer," Pulaski said. "I feel like a star."

Efheny went pale with pleasure. "You really are

an extremely honored guest. What you did to solve
the Andorian genetic crisis . . ."

Pulaski was embarrassed. "Well, it was a team
effort," she said gruffly. In all honesty, she wasn't sure
why she had landed this gig on Cardassia Prime. But
the University of the Union wanted to pin a medal on
someone, and given that Julian Bashir was . . . Well,
Katherine Pulaski was always ready to take one for
the team. One keynote speech on biomedical ethics,
one medal ceremony, a few receptions and dinners—
she was happy to oblige. Though she knew it was
Julian Bashir who really deserved this accolade.

"The Distinguished Impact Medal is the highest
honor that the university can bestow," Efheny said.
"I hope we are able to do you and your work justice."

"I know you will," said Pulaski. She flicked
through the itinerary that Efheny had sent to her
padd. "I was hoping to see Julian Bashir," she said.
"See how he's doing."

She looked up. Efheny's mouth was opening and
closing like a gasping fish. "I'm afraid that I . . . I'm
not sure that I . . ."

Pulaski became aware of Alden's hand upon her
arm. "I suspect," said Alden, "that this is something
that we can take up with the chief academician. Or
perhaps the castellan himself, when we meet him."

Efheny gave Alden a grateful look. Alden gave
Pulaski's elbow another nudge.

"Of course," she said. "All right, sonny. Let's see
what you've got lined up for me."

*   *   *

Professor Natima Lang looked up from her padd and began wrapping up her lecture.

"And so we see," she said, "that the enigma tale is a more complex, more disturbing form than perhaps we are in the habit of thinking, and one that is surely standing on the verge of significant transition. A form that, like no other, deals with that peculiarly Cardassian trait—guilt."

Her audience laughed knowingly. Lang smiled out at them. This was the last in her series of lectures on contemporary literature and, as usual, she had filled the hall. Lang's lectures attracted interest from well beyond her immediate students. She saw colleagues here, people eminent in their own fields, who had come week after week to hear what Lang had to say about the books she had been reading. Her heart filled with joy to think that her civilization was now one where reflections on literature could attract such interest and lively response, rather than suspicion and outright hate. Her heart burst with pride to think of the transformations her people had wrought upon themselves.

"In the enigma tale as we have known it," she said, "we have evidence that literature—that art—encodes into itself, despite all attempts at extirpation, critiques of the world in which it is created. In the enigma tale, these authors tried to address—through the medium of the puzzle, the riddle—what we could not discuss in public: the nature of our guilt, its role in our past, and its impact on our future."

She paused and took a small sip of water. Nearly done. But she wanted them to listen to this final part—really listen. So she paused, and quietly cleared her throat. When she knew she had their full attention, she continued.

"Literature such as this creates within its bounds a microcosm for society. In the country houses of the Second Republic, the mansions of Coranum, or"—she gestured around puckishly—"the lecture halls and committee rooms of the university, we see our world writ small. The crimes and misdemeanors of the wider world, the perpetrators and offenders, were concentrated and offered for our consideration."

They were smiling. They were with her.

"But Cardassia has changed—changed almost beyond recognition. Some of us old villains are still around, yes"—she tapped her chest and they laughed—"but my question now is—what might the enigma tale look like under our new dispensation? We have seen how, in the past, the question was not *which* of the characters was guilty, but *how* were the characters each guilty? Is it possible that in the future an enigma tale might contain a character who is—I can hardly imagine it—*innocent*?"

More laughter. Good.

"The Cardassian way of life has for a long time meant that we have all felt ourselves tainted in some way by guilt, by our treatment of each other, our actions on Bajor, our perfidy during the Dominion War. But will that be the case in the future? And to have dealt so successfully, so *honestly*, with our past—where might that lead us? Where might it lead our culture, our stories, ourselves—and our Union? Where does the enigma tale—where does the Union—go next?"

She turned the last page and rested her hands upon her padd. "As yet, I have no answers to these questions. I can only put them to you." She looked out at her audience—most of them so young, with bright and constructive futures ahead of them, and she smiled. "They will, I think, be questions for you to answer. In the meantime—thank you for listening."

The applause that followed was rapturous. Lang was almost embarrassed. This was good work, she thought, but by no means her best. That had been done years ago, under the shadow of the old Union, when every day she had feared the knock at the door, arrest, torture, hard labor, perhaps even execution. She would not go back to those days, by any means. But she knew that she had done her finest work then, desperation at the plight of the Union and what she knew would be its inevitable self-immolation driving her to write as if all their lives depended on it. Those writings, those words, had been read by many, and moved many. She gathered even the castellan had her work on his shelves—but then, he was rumored to be a great reader.

Lang lifted her hand to quiet the applause and glanced up at the chrono on the wall. Nearly midday. She had kept these young people here long enough.

They must be tired, and they must be hungry. She knew she certainly was. But a few hands were hovering, ready to go up. "Just a couple of questions."

Eight or nine hands shot up, and she took each one in turn, running on slightly over her time. Nobody left. The thoughtfulness behind the questions, the genuine engagement with her words and ideas, humbled Lang. She thought back to her own time at the U of U, struggling to find ideas within the allowed orthodoxies, and she was proud to be part of this new flowering of ideas and freedom. *This new generation*, she thought. *We are hardly worthy of them.*

At last they were done, and Lang wrapped up the session to more rapturous applause. A few of the shyer students lingered to ask questions, and she answered these fully and with courtesy while gently guiding them toward the door. Soon she was done, running down the steps of her department building, and out into the main square of the campus. It was a fine spring day, one of the last days that people would be able to bask outside before the summer dust storms rolled in from the mountains. The midday sun was high, and the students were out enjoying their lunch and each other's company. On one side of the square, a big screen was showing the rolling news. More than anything—more than the weather report, more even than the hound-racing—Cardassians loved rolling news. The novelty of a free press hadn't worn off yet.

The campus was of course completely different from when Lang had studied here. It occupied a slightly different part of the city, for one thing. In the last days of the Dominion War, the student body had mounted a courageous if foolhardy defense of their university against the advancing Jem'Hadar. The Jem'Hadar had been instructed to carry out a particularly vicious reprisal. The result had been a terrible massacre, made all the worse by the fact that so many of those who died were so young. More than that, most of the university buildings had been flattened, and the use of chemical agents had left a large part of what had once been the campus unusable. Lang, who sat on the relevant committee, knew that the detoxification process had been going unexpectedly well, and the land should be available again for the university within the next couple of years. It would be a welcome site for expansion and would be soon needed. Cardassia's birth rate had been shooting up in the past few years, further evidence that people felt optimistic again. The future looked bright for the U of U. It was a future Lang sincerely hoped to shape.

She took her usual route to the skimmer park. This took her to a high hedge. She followed this around until she reached a gate in the hedge, which led in turn into a small quiet garden. She went through the gate, softly closing it behind her. The garden was full of spring flowers: *isca* with its tiny star-shaped flowers; pale blue *caroci*, bunched in clusters; and a few remaining *nhemeni*, whose bright yellow flowers were the first sign that winter was ending. At the heart of the garden was a pool, the water still and covered, right now, in a blanket of *meya* lilies. On a stone stand in the center of the pool was a memorial to the students who had been murdered by the Jem'Hadar.

Lang stopped to look. It was an unusual piece, two solid blocks of black stone, taller than head height, each one covered in symbols representing knowledge: equations, formulae, fragments of old scripts, Hebitian figures, well-known quotations. Resting on top of the blocks, connecting them, was a piece of gray metal fashioned into an infinity symbol. Etched around this were the words from the dissident student poet Lim Pa'Mar, who had died in a labor camp on Cardassia IV:

They will not grow old, but the memory will never fade
Of their never-ending sacrifice.

Lang had known Pa'Mar. She had taught her. She had nearly saved her, but had come too late. She thought of her daily, and she had lobbied for her words to be put on this monument. Cardassia had sacrificed its youngest and brightest for many years. It would never, she hoped, do such a thing again. Lang placed her hand upon her breast and bowed her head. Lang was not religious—few Cardassians were—but she was steeped in her own history, and this quiet grave garden moved her like few other places. Most days she spent a few moments here, remembering the past, hoping for the future.

A tiny *londub* bird, black and bright-eyed, hopped

past, glancing up at her. She smiled at it and then left the garden, carrying on down the path that ran alongside the memorial garden to the skimmer park. As she walked, she heard footsteps behind her. She looked back over her shoulder to see a figure hurrying toward her. "Professor Lang!"

Lang sighed. She really wanted her lunch. But it was a matter of principle always to take the time to speak to a student. It was her work. She stopped walking and waited until the young man had caught up with her.

"Thanks!" he said. "Phew! I thought I'd missed you."

She waited patiently while he sorted himself out, and next thing she knew she had a holo-recorder shoved into her face.

"Student news," he said. "We heard this morning that Chief Academician Enek Therok intends to resign his post at the end of this term. Is there any truth to the rumor that you're intending to put your name forward for the position?"

Lang looked down at the recorder. "That's a very nice piece of equipment," she said, "for the student news."

He looked at her shiftily. "Well, I'll do an item for them too. Probably."

She smiled, nodded, and turned to go. This young man was on assignment from one of the mainstream news channels. Probably hoping for a job after graduation. But he would have to do it without turning her into an exclusive. "No comment."

"But Professor Lang!"

"Young man," she said, "I admire your initiative, your commitment to the fourth estate, and your desire to build an impressive curriculum vitae. But do you really think that university politics are of the slightest interest beyond this campus?"

"With great respect, Professor Lang," said the young man, and his serious tone stopped her in her tracks, "do you really think they're not?"

She turned to face him. "What do you mean?"

He gestured back over his shoulder. "That memorial. People don't come past it much, but they think about it all the time. People who never come onto this campus—that's the single thing they know about U of U. The massacre. And it breaks their hearts. One hundred and forty-nine young people, at the very start of their adult lives, murdered by the Jem'Hadar. People *love* the U of U, Professor Lang. They love seeing its students on the streets of this city. They love our freedom and our enthusiasm—they even love our stupidities! We're proof that things really have gotten better. Oh yes," he said with a smile. "People will want to know who's going to be in charge."

Lang looked back to the hedge surrounding the memorial park. She could just see the top of the statue, the great swirl of infinity. She felt the prickle of tears in her eyes. She was glad, she thought, that she had stopped for this young man. She had loved this university her whole life, but had always feared it was self-indulgence on her part. Now she knew that more people than she had ever imagined felt the same way.

All the more reason not to show this young man her hand at *kotra*. "Thank you," she said. "That was lovely to hear. Truly. But I still have no comment."

She walked on. He kept pace alongside her. "How about if I gave the exclusive to the student news?"

Now that, she thought, was almost tempting. But not quite tempting enough. She walked on to her skimmer. "Thank you for your interest! Good luck with the story!"

He wasn't following her, but he did call out one last time. "You're a public figure, you know, Professor Lang. Whether you like it or not! People are *interested*!"

Horrific thought, but Lang didn't let it spoil her lunch, nor her afternoon nap, nor her early evening writing session.

Doctor Elima Antok had spent the day in the blissful isolation of the university archives. The place had a somewhat sacrosanct air: the destruction of the capital city that had happened in the very last days of the Dominion War meant that the great cavernous libraries and sealed archives of old had been leveled to the ground, and the new small archives that were being built—while beautifully appointed and spotlessly kept—sometimes had an empty, regretful feel about them. Records from before the war were scant, and whatever had survived was precious. Still, Antok easily became lost in her work here, and the fragmentary nature of the material with which she was working only made her task more absorbing. She treated it like a puzzle, a great riddle, piecing together what was left, trying to weave a story from the fragments salvaged from the ruins.

Antok checked the time. The afternoon was wearing on and she was particularly keen to get home this evening. She made a few sketchy notes for what she would do during her next visit, then saved and closed her files. She stood and stretched, thinking about the evening celebration that lay ahead and smiling in anticipation of her boys' excitement. Then she realized, with some annoyance, that she had left her bag back in her office. It contained most of what they needed for the evening (well, apart from the food, which had been organized some days ago and was already prepared at home for the family to break their day's fast), but there were the candles, the lights, the last decorations. She hurried out of the archive building and across the northern edge of the campus to her department building.

Elima Antok was a historian, an expert on the Occupation of Bajor, and specializing in how the Occupation had affected life back in the Cardassian Union. Her doctoral thesis had documented the lives of the small but significant number of Bajoran comfort women and their children who had been brought to Prime, and the book arising from that research had won an important award within her field. Altogether a most auspicious start to her academic career, and the success had brought an appointment at U of U. She was lucky that her subject matter not only attracted attention, but was considered vital work in postwar Cardassia, where examination of the past was considered as important as reconstruction of the buildings. Nobody quite wanted to close the book yet on recent history: there was a definite sense that there was more to be revealed. So Antok, who did good work, was in the enviable position of doing work that had mainstream interest and, more importantly, funding. She had provided evidence to a recent Assembly report looking into Bajoran Occupation war crimes. She had received a substantial grant to investigate the university archives and discover what role the institution had played during the Occupation. On top of all this, one of the big three news 'casters had been sniffing around. There was talk of a documentary series. Antok had a pleasant, informative, and nonconfrontational lecturing style that also managed to be authoritative. Altogether, she thought, life in the new Cardassia was good.

She dashed into her office, hoping not to bump into anyone who would keep her talking, and grabbed her bag from the chair by her desk. As she turned to go, she heard the comm on her desktop chime. Antok groaned. Wasn't it always the way? Just as you were walking out of the door, another message would arrive and demand attention. She considered pretending she had already left, but the chime, while soft, was insistent, so, with a sigh, she put down her bag and went across to check, promising herself that she would not get absorbed in any other messages she had missed during her day's isolation.

The message turned out to be from Chief Academician Enek Therok. It had been marked URGENT and ALL STAFF MUST READ, so Antok dutifully read. There was a lot of sentiment and braggadocio, which was par for the course for Therok, but the upshot of the message was that he was retiring. Antok marked the message as read, closed her comm, and smiled. This was undoubtedly big news for Therok, but Antok could have gone uninformed until the morning. She grabbed her bag and dashed out. Already she was thinking about how she could make this work for her. There would be lots of people wanting to speak to experts on the U of U staff to give Therok's career context. He'd been here *forever*.

She found her skimmer and began to ease her way off campus. With luck, she would be on the main city circular before the rush hour began in earnest. She drove, like all Cardassians, with one of the newscasts muttering away in the background. The national addiction. There was a short piece about Therok, of all things, and some conjecture about who would be his successor. Natima Lang seemed to be the front-runner, thank goodness, and Antok nodded. If anyone deserved the honor, it would be Lang, who had been steadfast in her defense of freedom for years before the Dominion War. The story moved on to discuss the arrival of some Federation VIPs, and her attention drifted. Tonight, she and her family were celebrating Ha'mara.

Ha'mara: the Bajoran festival of light that celebrated the arrival of the Emissary. A festival of gratitude, of thanks to the Prophets for their special love for the Bajoran people, and their gifts and aid during a long, dark history. Antok stopped to allow pedestrians to stream past, and she stared, as she often did, at their faces, wondering who else shared a background like hers, who else on Cardassia Prime would be celebrating tonight?

She pulled up outside the school and waved to the two small figures standing at the gate. They waved back and hurried to meet her. Her boys. One-eighth Bajoran, as she was one-quarter. Antok's paternal grandmother had been brought to Cardassia as the mistress of a gul toward the end of the Occupation. She was hidden away, but important, because she was the mother of a son—a son who looked unquestionably Cardassian. They all looked Cardassian: Antok, her two sons; her brother, his three daughters. Nobody would ever guess. The question was, these days—would anyone even care?

The boys scrambled into the back of the skimmer. "I did it, Ma!" said Evrek, eight years old and senior. "I fasted *all* day." He looked scornfully at his little brother, who was strapping himself carefully and methodically into his harness. "Velek had lunch," Evrek said darkly, as if at some great betrayal. Velek, now securely fastened in, looked calmly ahead. "I was hungry," he said.

Elima Antok nudged the skimmer back onto the road. "Well, you know," she said, "children don't have to fast."

"Bajoran children didn't have the *choice*," said Evrek, glowering at his brother. "Bajoran children didn't have enough *food*."

Velek was unperturbed. "I'm only a bit Bajoran," he said. "And I was *hungry*."

"I'm proud of you, Evrek," she said. "And of you too, Velek, for knowing you should eat." She saw Evrek roll his eyes at this maternal even-handedness, and quailed a little at this brief presentiment of adolescence. "Dinner for everyone when we get back," she added, and a big cheer erupted from behind her. "And cakes."

She eased the skimmer onto the circular. As soon as she and the boys were back, she and her partner, Mikor, would close the shutters, chill the room and darken the lights, and make the whole house cozy. Then they would light candles and give thanks and eat their strange home-cooked food until they were sated and happy and suffused in love. Mikor was Cardassian, wholly, but he had embraced these celebrations. In fact, he was grateful to be admitted to them.

Elima Antok glanced behind her and her heart swelled. These two creatures, she thought, how unlikely, how impossible they were. How astonishing that her grandmother had survived. How astonishing too that her son—Antok's father—had produced a daughter before war took his life. And how grateful she was that she, Elima Antok, had been spared the last days of the Dominion War to produce these two boys, and live to see a Cardassia where they could explore their Bajoran roots without fear of reprisal. Truly, Antok thought, she had much to be thankful for. And as she drove along, she gave thanks to the Prophets for all their gifts.

The day was nearly over, and Elim Garak had not yet started work. To be sure, his day had been busy. There had been a ceremony in a remote northern province celebrating the opening of the first technical college in the region in its entire history. He had transported back to the capital in time for a pleasant working lunch with the leader of the largest party in the Assembly. There had been a private meeting with a deputation of vedeks about the Bajoran temple they were opening in the city. And then, late in the afternoon, there had been a satisfying conclusion to a small trade dispute that had been simmering for several months with the Ferengi (everyone had saved face and nobody had been out-of-pocket). But he had still not even started the main task that needed to be done that day. The report—which had arrived at his secure padd sealed and thoroughly encrypted—had not yet been opened. He dreaded to see what was inside, and the thought of its contents had loomed large even over the day's successes.

After three years, Garak wore the castellanship lightly and with considerable style. He had taken to the job like a riding-hound released onto the wide Veletur plains, savoring the theatricality, the busyness, and what he called the "varied and variable reading." He had thought when he embarked upon this project that he might like aspects of the job—certainly he believed he was duty-bound to take it on—but he had never expected to enjoy it quite so thoroughly. Moreover, people seemed to like what he was doing. His advisors—an achingly young and committed set of individuals—were constantly saying things like "Great job!" and "Stunning!" and "Castellan, you are *unique*!" and had a vexing habit of using slang that made him feel old. Commentators on the 'casts sometimes muttered phrases like "new Golden Age imminent," and his popularity was high. And sometimes, sometimes Kelas Parmak said, "That was well done, Elim," and Garak would smile and be content.

This evening, however, the castellan did not like what his job entailed, and he was doing all he could to put off the moment when he began work. He wandered around the room, a private office-cum-sitting room on the second story of the castellan's official residential complex, and located a bottle of *kanar*. He poured a measure, took a sip or two, then abandoned the drink and resumed his pacing. He flicked through books. He adjusted cushions. Eventually, he came to a rest standing looking out of the window. The sunset was very beautiful and very melancholy.

Garak fiddled with the curtains. He had chosen the color and the fabric, of course, but he was no longer sure about it. He had not been keen on the move to this new residential complex. His private home was in Coranum, a district up in the hills that had once been the location of the mansions of the wealthiest people in the Union. After the war, Garak had gone there and found the ruins of what had been his father's home, and he built a sanctuary from the rubble. He had raised memorial stones, too, where history had happened, and grown a garden that made him proud. But the security teams were having none of this sentimental nonsense about attachment to one's home. Garak was head of state now—head of state of a major power in the quadrant—and a ramshackle set of rooms perched on a hillside was not secure enough in their judgment, no matter how safe Garak felt there.

He remembered the meeting with the security officer assigned to head the team when the topic of his potential assassination had been broached.

"Nobody," said Garak firmly, "wants me dead. Certainly not among our allies. In fact, I doubt you'll find one of our enemies who wants me dead. I'm not flattering myself when I say that Cardassia would be thrown into chaos. Look where that got us last time. No, I must be the least uneasy head wearing a crown in the whole quadrant."

The security officer, give him his due, stuck to his guns. "There is also the matter of *personal* animosities toward you," he said. Rather forward, in Garak's opinion. (Manners were not what they once were, but then one no longer had the weight of the Obsidian Order by which to enforce them. Nobody is rude to the secret police.) But he had to admit it was true. Over the course of his life Garak had met many people who had ended up wanting to kill him, and regretfully most of these had extremely good reason. So, dutifully, Garak had packed his rather slender possessions—books and pictures, mostly—and moved into the new residence. One day, he thought, he would leave it behind—leave the castellanship behind—and go back to his garden, where anyone still alive and desperate enough to take a pot shot at him would at last have their chance. If they'd waited that long, they probably deserved it.

The sun had almost faded when Parmak came in. With one glance, Parmak took in the situation—the closed comm, the glass of *kanar*, and the brooding head of state by the window, and said, "You've still not started, have you?"

Garak, who had of course heard him come in and known exactly who it was, said, "By this time of day I would prefer a lighter read. Did you know that Sayak has a new collection of enigma tales? I've been sent a copy prior to publication." He walked over to a nearby table where a slim and handsome dark-green volume lay, picked it up, and began to flick through the pages. "I do like the perks to this job—"

"Enigma tales are *not* light reading," Parmak said, extricating the book from Garak's hands. "Guilt, more guilt, death. Murders. Trials. Executions. More guilt—"

"But the *settings*!" Garak's eyes sparkled wickedly. "Always so *baroque*. That's what makes enigma tales so delicious, don't you think?"

"I don't agree, and I don't think you believe it either—"

Garak opened his mouth to protest.

"I'm prepared to admit that you like reading them," Parmak said. "You have some strangely low-brow tastes."

"I was not quite as expensively educated as you."

"But I'm not prepared to admit their excellence."

"Popular culture," said Garak portentously, "can tell us a great deal about a society. I know that because Natima Lang says so. Said so this very day, in fact."

"Perhaps they can. But so can an important report into the actions of the military on Bajor during the Occupation. Which you have not yet read."

Garak sighed. Gently, Parmak maneuvered him over to his chair.

"I already know what's in it—more or less," Garak said bitterly.

"You might know the gist," said Parmak, "but you don't know the details."

"I don't need to know the details," said Garak. "I can imagine them."

"You also don't know the conclusions of the committee," said Parmak.

Garak gave him a narrow look. "You think I can't guess?"

"You won't know for sure until you look."

"What do you think their conclusion is, Kelas?"

Parmak rubbed his eyes and sat down opposite him. Quietly, he said, "I think they're going to say that there should be prosecutions."

"That," said Garak, "is what I both hope and fear."

They sat in silence for a while. At last, Parmak said, "It has to be done. It's the last part of the reconstruction, isn't it? Everything else—the rebuilding projects, the education and judicial reforms, the work done with the constabularies and the civil service, the Assembly, the press. It'll all be worth nothing if we don't confront this and make amends."

Garak cradled his *kanar* glass between his hands. "When you say it altogether like that, it's quite a legacy, isn't it? This chapter, in the history book of my life, might not be as appalling as the blood-drenched pages that precede it."

"Not if you don't read that report." Parmak frowned. "What's worrying you, Elim? What is it, really? You know what the subject matter will be, and you must be fairly certain that the committee will recommend prosecuting to the full extent of the law. Are you frightened about what the military might do?"

Garak snorted. "I am in the enviable position of

being a rare head of state of this Union not to serve at the pleasure of the guls. No, I'm not afraid of having a few guls or legates come to my office and shout at me."

"Don't underestimate the guls and the legates," said Parmak. "They might not try a *coup d'état,* but they can probably marshal significant public opinion against you."

Garak narrowed his eyes further. "They can certainly try," he muttered.

"So what is your worry?"

Of all people, Garak owed Kelas Parmak the truth. So he swallowed and took heart. "I know there are political risks. I am concerned that I might not be the man to take them."

Parmak frowned. "What do you mean?"

"I mean that to bring prosecutions successfully might require a castellan with significant moral capital. I am the first to admit that I have something of a weak position when it comes to the moral high ground."

"Perhaps there is nobody better placed to scrutinize the past," Parmak said softly.

Garak picked up the padd and held it lightly between both hands. "Life as an act of atonement? There are worse fates for an ex-spy, I suppose."

Suddenly, the specter of another doctor loomed large: Julian Bashir, here, in this very building, but lost; in a catatonic state where not even Elim Garak could reach him. Parmak, eyeing Garak carefully, said, "Will you go and see him this evening, Elim?"

Garak shook his head.

"It's some time since you've been to see him," Parmak said.

Garak opened the file, but he did not read. The letters swam before his eyes. "There's no reason to see him, Kelas. There's no one there."

My dear Doctor—

Let us take a tour of the city. We shall leave your room, which—while pleasant and offering a fine view and designed to be a great balm to you—is ultimately, like any sick room, hardly the most uplifting of environments.

So let us leave your room behind. We are still in my official residence, and I should confess that I am not fond of the place. It is quite new, which has benefits in terms of comfort and convenience, but I am afraid that it is increasingly starting to feel rather like a prison cell. You will recall I have some experience of prison cells, and therefore I am placed to make this comparison, although I admit that it could be considered rather fanciful. Still, the walls, at times, feel very close . . .

At this point, you would no doubt remind me, as Kelas often does, that I chose this role, and that if I do not like it, I can always give up and go back to reading bad books and pottering around my garden. You would no doubt also remind me that the scrutiny under which I have placed myself is crucial to my successful performance in this role. There are brakes on me, checks and balances, which do not allow me . . .

Do not allow me to indulge my excesses, as I have done in the past, and so many of our leaders have done in the past. Do not allow me to become cruel. Do not allow me to forget that I am not in this role for self-aggrandizement, but to do what I can to make up for the harm that I have done in the past. I, and those who ran Cardassia for generation after generation, repeated in one long blood-drenched repetitive epic.

I digress.

I wish you could meet Kelas. I think you would like each other. I think you would admire each other. Besides, you both have—had—a habit of lecturing me.

I do not mind. Not much. I deserve it. In some respects, I am touched that someone, somewhere, has my spiritual well-being at heart. It is nice to be loved, for what one is.

I did not mind your lectures. I wish I could hear them again.

Garak
[unsent]

Two

"**A**re you ready to see them, sir?"

Garak rose from his chair. He walked around his desk, and stood, rubbing his palms together. Then he put his hands behind his back and braced himself for what was about to come. "I'm ready."

"Then I'll bring them through."

Garak's aide, Akret, was a small and rather nondescript woman of middle age, whom people had a tendency to overlook. A mistake on their part. Akret had an eye and a memory for detail that even Garak envied, and an ability to read his mind and his mood that he found uncanny. He would often ask for files that were already on his desk, or find himself the recipient of a soothing cup of *rokassa* juice before the headache had a chance to start. Now she gave him a moment to settle, nodded her satisfaction at his demeanor, gave him a welcome sympathetic look, and went back out to the anteroom. Garak checked that his jacket was smart (of course it was; it always was) and arranged his features into his calmest and blandest expression. Outside his office, he heard the bark of Legate Renel: "*About time!*"

Legates, thought Garak. *Do they ever change?* He noticed the padd on the desk, and mentally reviewed once again the main points arising from the report. A summary of over two years' work but plain enough in its findings and recommendations. Assemblyperson Carnis had proven a meticulous and methodical investigator, as Garak had hoped when he commissioned this inquiry and put Carnis at its head. When he had, at last, at Parmak's insistence, gone through the report he had asked her to write, he'd found that he approved of her prose style: plain and unadorned, although its sparseness had the unfortunate effect of making the atrocities she described even more appalling.

The door swung open and Renel marched in, followed by a couple of guls. "Garak!" he cried. "I didn't expect to be kept waiting!"

Garak smiled and stood his ground. "My apologies, Legate. Sometimes small crises arise that demand immediate attention. I hope you've not been too uncomfortable?"

"Uncomfortable?" Renel scowled. "What's that got to do with anything? Now listen to me, Garak, I want to know what you're intending to do next—"

Garak turned to his aide. "Some tea, perhaps? Akret?" he said, in measured tones.

"Already on its way, sir."

"*Tea?*" Renel looked ready to explode.

Garak turned his bright blue eyes upon the legate. Most of his life he had devoted to keeping himself out of sight, but he could, when he chose, impose himself on a room, and on any gul or legate who happened to pass his way. The Order might be extinct, but the memory remained, and the training had been thorough. Renel stopped talking. One of the guls swayed back.

Garak smiled brightly. "It's good to see you, Legate. How is your lovely wife?"

Renel collected himself. "I've not come to talk about my family," he said, but his tone was now considerably less combative. Garak led him and the guls across the room to an arrangement of comfortable chairs and sofas. He liked the coverings on these: broad vertical stripes in purple, white, and green. Parmak had chosen the colors. Parmak had good taste, although he was a terrible gardener. Garak, as was his custom, sat down in the chair that put his back to the window. This, in turn, put his face somewhat into shadow, which was always an advantage. Renel took the other chair and the two guls, both big men, perched awkwardly together on the sofa. Garak had asked for the sofa's dimensions to be just slightly too small to comfortably seat two adult males. His cruel streak always found expression somehow.

"Give her my regards nonetheless," Garak said. "I remember her as a charming dinner companion."

The tea arrived. Garak poured. Renel's leg bounced

up and down with impatience. At last he said, "Garak, what do you intend to do?"

With great, almost dainty, ceremony, Garak handed Renel a teacup. "What do you think I'm going to do?"

The three soldiers looked at one another uneasily.

"Carnis isn't a friend to the military," said Gul Telek. Garak reviewed what he knew of the man. Telek hadn't quite been old enough to serve on Bajor—although his father had. Gul Telek senior had been prefect of Rakantha province. Was the son concerned for the family reputation, perhaps? Garak couldn't blame him, and indeed he was rather sympathetic. It was hard coming to terms with the fact that one's progenitor was a monster. Denial was much easier. But it was not Garak's job to spare the feelings of the powerful, particularly the guls.

"Carnis is a fine assemblyperson," Garak said. "Her career as a senior public nestor has made her thorough and scrupulous."

"She knows nothing about the military," Renel said.

"Right now," said Garak, "she probably knows more about the military than anyone else in the Union." He sipped some tea. "It must be clear to you that I intend to accept all her recommendations."

The legate and the two guls looked at one another with alarm. "But that means—"

"Follow-up investigations, yes. Closer work with the Bajoran and, indeed, the Federation legal system."

"And?" said Renel.

"And, if necessary, prosecutions." Garak lifted his hand to quell Renel's dismay. "It *has* to be done, Legate. We've waited too long."

"It was all a long time ago!" said the other gul, Feris. Now, he *had* been on Bajor, Garak knew. Perhaps he didn't want his own record scrutinized? "Sir, I am a great admirer of yours. I voted for you—"

"Thank you very much."

"But I want to know—what is served by all this? Raking over old crimes? We know—we *all* know—that the military on Bajor did not always act, well, wisely—"

Garak's eye ridges shot up. "Wisely?"

Renel intervened. "What Feris means is that of course there were mistakes on Bajor. Many of those people are dead now—dead defending Cardassia against the Jem'Hadar—"

"But some are still alive," said Garak.

"Having given exemplary service at the end of the war—"

Garak picked up the padd. "Did you read the whole report?"

Renel glowered. "Of course I did."

"Forced labor. Torture. Destruction of settlements and towns as punishment for minor infractions. Rape. Shall I carry on?"

"We all know that terrible things were done on Bajor," Telek said. "But the past is the past—"

"Sadly not," said Garak. "Our continued delay in

bringing prosecutions casts a significant shadow over our alliance with the Federation, of which Bajor is now a member—"

"Ah," said Renel. "Now we get to it. Your precious alliance. Some people say, Garak, that you went native during your exile. That you're more than half Federation."

Garak laughed out loud. "My dear fellow! I can assure you that I am about as Cardassian as they come!"

"A true Cardassian would respect what the military has already done to come to terms with its past, and not paint us as monsters," said Telek.

"I am doing no such thing. Monstrous behavior speaks for itself."

"But what you're planning does the current military a great injustice," Feris said. "Not all of us were Dukat's men, you know. Some of us backed Damar as soon as we could. I was there!"

"So was I," said Garak. "I know your record, Feris. Your courage at the end of the Dominion War is not in dispute."

"Neither is yours, sir," Feris said. "And neither is all that you have done since. But, sir, I was on Bajor, at the very start of my career. My first command. I would have allowed nothing like this—"

Garak believed him. There had been places where the Occupation had been almost transactional. Even then, it would not have worked to the benefit of most of the Bajorans. One or two might have made a small profit; not all. Still, he said, "I don't doubt you, Feris."

"And the work my Order has done since then," Feris said. "First into Culat after the war. Burial details. Cleanup. The work we did rebuilding towns and cities—"

"There has been good service, Castellan," Renel agreed. "Fine service. But this—this will blacken our reputation. Rest assured, the military will not appreciate it—"

"The castellan does not serve at the discretion of the military, Legate," Garak said softly. "He, or she, serves at the discretion of the Cardassian people. There is plainly a desire on the part of the Cardassian people to understand fully the nature of the Occupation and to make appropriate amends. This was part of the manifesto on which I was elected. It was and continues to be a significant concern of the people. We have rebuilt, Legate, more quickly and successfully than we could have thought possible—yes, yes, with the military central to that effort! But we must confront this. Only then can the people of this Union go out into the quadrant and be able to hold their heads high. Proud of being Cardassian. Not ashamed."

Renel went stiff. "I have *nothing* to be ashamed of," he said. "I am not a murderer, or a rapist—or a torturer," he said, rather pointedly.

"I don't doubt that for a second," Garak said, and he did believe it—of Renel, of Feris. Of Telek too. "But some people were, and they remain unpunished. It has to be done. Nobody is above the law."

Renel's eyes gleamed. "No indeed. Not even castellans."

Here it was at last. Garak put down his cup and
leaned back comfortably in his chair. His face would
now be completely in shadow. "If I didn't know better," he said, from the dark, "I might think that was
a threat."

There was a pause. Eventually, Renel said, "Not
a threat—"

"Good," said Garak. "A threat from a legate to the
elected leader of the Union might be considered . . ."
He leaned forward and gave Renel his bright blue
stare. "*Unwise.*"

It could, in fact, be considered treason, of course,
but Garak didn't have to hammer the point home.
Renel stood up. "I think we have nothing else to say."

Garak rose. "It seems so. Thank you for coming,
gentlemen. Rest assured that I am not looking for
heads to roll. But I *am* looking for justice."

The trio left. Garak sat back down in his chair
and brooded. Akret came in and began to clear away
the cups. After a little while, there was a polite cough.
Garak looked up. "Yes?"

"These prosecutions, sir," she said. "Could the
military force your resignation? If they found something in your . . ." She trailed off.

"In my what?"

"Your past, sir."

Garak, standing up, helped pile the cups on the
tray. "Yes. They could."

He passed Akret the tray and she headed for the door. "Is it serving the Union, sir, to back yourself into a resignation?"

"I don't know," Garak said. "What do you think?"

"I think we could do a lot worse than you."

Garak opened the door. "Thank you, as ever, for that vote of confidence."

A lazy day of acclimatization followed Pulaski's arrival. She took the opportunity to flick through the holo-channels. To her astonishment, and horror, she counted over thirty news channels. These she went past quickly. Nothing good came of keeping on top of the news. If there was something she needed to know, someone would be bustling about ready to tell her. She enjoyed a few soaps, as outrageous here as they were throughout the quadrant, flicked through some history channels, and then settled on the hound-racing while she wrote the last of her medal acceptance speech. In the evening, Alden arrived after a day's sightseeing, and they had a quiet dinner together. She spent a comfortable night alone in her suite. The following morning, Efheny arrived, bright and early, to take her on a tour of the campus. Alden went off again on his own to investigate more of the city.

Pulaski liked what she saw of the campus. The architecture throughout the city, she had noticed, had a distinctly hybrid flavor: she recognized standard Federation materials in their ubiquitous gray,

but their shapes had been bent to Cardassian tastes—
twists and curves and spikes and spires, arranged in
triads, often with intricate mosaic work. The buildings throughout the capital were of course rela-
tively new, and here on the campus were even more
recent—a great deal had been spent on the university in the past five years, under the stewardship of
the current chief academician, and, more recently,
with the explicit support of the castellan. These new
buildings were more distinctly Cardassian. Efheny
explained that there had been a number of compe-
titions to encourage a new generation of architects,
tasked to experiment with form and function and
materials to create some striking and very beautiful
buildings. There were green spaces too. (They, surely,
couldn't be easy to maintain on this dry world, which
led to a detailed explanation of water management
on Prime—a favorite topic of the inhabitants of the
world.) The students were out in the warm spring day,
enjoying being outside before the dust of summer
arrived. She wholeheartedly approved of the crèche
for the children of staff and students. This was how a
university should be—woven into the warp and weft
of daily life, not imagining itself separate. The *Enterprise* had been the same. People didn't need artificial
barriers erected to prevent them living their lives.

But there was one area that puzzled her as they
walked through the campus: a deep ditch, beyond
which a high fence had been raised, covered with
KEEP OUT signs.

"What's that, Metok? Is there some secret work going on there?"

He shook his head. "That's where the Jem'Hadar dropped biochemical weapons. It's not toxic anymore, not to dangerous levels, but the land isn't ready yet for building."

Pulaski felt ashamed. "I'm sorry," she said. "But this city! This campus! There's so much here that's so good, so beautiful. It's easy to forget how recent the war was."

"We don't forget," Efheny said quietly. "We'll never forget."

After the tour, Pulaski enjoyed a working lunch with colleagues from the new exomedical school and then an entertaining afternoon exploring their facilities (outstanding) and talking to some of their advanced students (brilliant). She fielded questions about her own work (and attempted to get some of them to sign up with the *Athene Donald* when they had their doctorates). By late afternoon, however, Pulaski was glad to go back to her suite and relax for a while with the hound-racing, before dragging on her dress uniform and heading off for the welcome reception in her honor. She sat in the back of the skimmer while Efheny chattered. The reception was a glittering affair, hosted by the chief academician, and with the castellan himself in attendance. Pulaski was glad about that. She had a couple of questions for the castellan.

Congregation Hall, at the center of the campus,

was another fine piece of contemporary Cardassian architecture, and its current lord and master, Enek Therok, the chief academician of the University of the Union, was waiting to welcome Pulaski. He was a big man, cheerful in the way that people are on the verge of a comfortable retirement, and he greeted Pulaski with great enthusiasm and bonhomie. "An honor, Doctor, an honor," he said, grasping her hand and shaking it.

"You have a fine university," she said. "A beautiful place."

Therok was delighted by her praise, as she had intended. They went into the main hall, and he asked for quiet and made a short welcome speech. He talked a fair deal about himself—Pulaski had found that people in positions like this were often their own favorite subject, even more so than their discipline, which they probably hadn't practiced for a while—but he also gave her a very full welcome, so she couldn't complain.

"Glad to be here," she told the room. "I'll skip the speech, if you don't mind, and get on with meeting you all one by one. That way I can start drinking sooner."

They laughed. They applauded. They liked her. Therok led her around the room, introducing her to various eminent people, most of whom she liked very much, which wasn't always the case at university gatherings. Many drinks were pressed into her hands, and she didn't refuse them. After a little while, she caught sight of Alden across the room, and she took advantage of the opportunity to take a break from socializing and went to say hello.

"Nice day?" Alden was no longer a Starfleet officer, so he was wearing civvies. He cleaned up well.

"Good," she said. "Long. How about you?"

"Did the tourist thing in the morning," he said. "Then wandered around East Torr."

"What's that?"

"Bohemian end of town," he explained. "Galleries, markets, *geleta* houses. Found some nice pieces. Ate some good cake."

She laughed. "Sounds like you're having a good vacation!"

"Going to meet some people at xenolinguistics tomorrow." Suddenly, he went tense and started scanning the hall.

"What's the matter, Peter?"

"The room," he said.

"What about the room?"

"It's fuller, all of a sudden, and contains more weapons."

Pulaski looked around. Alden was completely right. Quietly, stealthily, the hall had been infiltrated by almost a dozen plainclothes security personnel. They were covering exits, windows, every single part of the room. Pulaski grasped Alden's arm in alarm. "What the hell's happening? Is there going to be a coup?"

Alden laughed. "Those days are over on Cardassia

Prime, Kitty! No need to worry on that score. I think someone important is about to arrive. Someone you were hoping to meet."

A man came through the door, halting on the threshold to take his own look around. There was no formal fanfare, but everyone stopped what they were doing to turn and see. The man was of middle height and indeterminate age; he was also extremely dapper, and when he realized he was the focus of everyone's attention his bright blue eyes widened slightly, and his mouth twitched in amusement. Behind him, slightly tucked behind in the shadows, was another man. He had a slight stoop, graying hair, and a thoughtful expression.

"The castellan," murmured Pulaski. Now she understood. Of course the room would fill with security. "Who's the other guy, behind him?"

"His name is Kelas Parmak," said Alden. "Garak doesn't go anywhere without him."

"Parmak, huh?"

"He's a doctor, Kitty. You might want to talk to him at some point."

Pulaski eyed him thoughtfully.

Alden smiled. "I do my research."

Therok went forward to greet the castellan. People in the room began to turn back to chatter eagerly to each other about his presence, but Pulaski watched the meeting between the castellan and the chief academician with interest. Effusive on Therok's part; friendly neutral on Garak's. She wasn't sure what to make of that. Friendly but neutral was probably the default for any head of state. She thought she saw Therok say her name, and then, suddenly, Garak's bright blue eyes were turned on her. She met his gaze with equanimity. Garak smiled at her broadly. Therok spoke again, Garak nodded, and Therok led him and Parmak over.

Up close, the castellan's style was reinforced. His clothes were insanely well made (she wondered if he made them himself); his shoes gleamed. Everything about him had a slight gloss, Pulaski thought, like he had been varnished, or was coated in a thin and invisible protective shell. Even up close, she couldn't guess his age. Older than he looked, she suspected. As they were formally introduced—and Garak offered his hand to shake, rather than raising his palm—Pulaski had the sense that his attention was simultaneously on her and on the entire rest of the room. This was definitely someone who knew exactly what was happening behind him. Therok introduced Alden, and then Parmak. There was a brief pause as Pulaski and Garak observed each other further.

Garak spoke first. "The famous Doctor Pulaski. Welcome to Cardassia Prime, Doctor. How has your visit been so far?"

"Extremely welcoming, thank you," said Pulaski. "The young man assigned to us, Efheny, couldn't have been more attentive if he'd tried."

Garak seemed to catch a little of her meaning. His eyes sparkled, and his manner softened slightly.

"Ah, the tyranny of the tight schedule! May we all one day be released from its grip!"

They smiled at each other. He greeted Alden warmly and showed himself familiar with Alden's research. ("I always take an interest in the work of a visitor.") He asked about Alden's sight-seeing and recommended an exhibition of Cardassian-Bajoran art that was about to open in Torr. Pulaski gave her impressions of the campus, and Garak admitted, when pressed, that he had indeed been involved in selecting some of the winning buildings. Altogether, the conversation was . . . well, friendly but neutral. Parmak spoke only a little. At last a brief lull allowed Pulaski to ask the question uppermost on her mind. "How's Julian?"

She saw Parmak start, heard Alden mutter, "*Oops*," and, to her surprise, the castellan visibly hardened. Or was it that the shell became more brittle?

"Quite comfortable, thank you," Garak said.

"I'd really like to see him while I'm here. As a doctor, and as his friend."

Alden tugged on her sleeve. "Kitty," he muttered, "leave it."

"Do put a request in via my office." Garak turned to Therok. "Is Ventok here? I'd like a word with him."

Therok, somewhat on the back foot, murmured, "Yes, of course, over here," and began to lead the castellan away.

"I put a request in *weeks* ago," said Pulaski, but Garak had his back to her and was on his way. She turned to Alden. "Did I just get the brush-off?"

"Kitty . . ."

There was a polite cough beside them. Parmak was still there. "I'm sure the castellan wouldn't want to offend a guest."

"That's not a 'no'!" Pulaski said.

"No," said Parmak simply. "It's not. Allow me to repeat what the castellan said. You're very welcome here. The Distinguished Impact Medal is not given often and not given lightly. I know that Castellan Garak was particularly pleased to hear that it was going to a friend from the Federation." He glanced across the room. "Have you met Professor Lang? You really should meet Natima Lang." He took a step or two across the room, signaling to a tall woman dressed in a long white gown to come and join them. "Let me introduce you."

"Who's Natima Lang?" Pulaski muttered to Alden as Parmak crossed the room.

Alden rolled his eyes. "Really, Kitty, you need to watch the news more often."

"Why the hell would I do that?"

"She's one of Cardassia's most respected public figures—"

"She's written books, hasn't she?" Pulaski said mournfully. "You're going to tell me she's written a stack of important books."

"Yes, a *massive* stack. She was also Cardassia's ambassador to Bajor just after the war, and a fearless campaigner for democratic rights under the old regime. She ended up in exile for a while."

"Has she ever helped save a species from extinction?"

Alden laughed. "Some would say she saved the Cardassian soul."

"Good for her. Bring her on."

Parmak returned with Lang. She was elegant, poised, and she greeted Pulaski with great warmth. Pulaski took to her at once.

Parmak said, "Forgive me, Natima, and I'm sure you've been plagued by this question all day, but—"

Lang lifted her hand and laughed. "No comment, Kelas!"

Parmak turned to Pulaski and Alden and said, "I don't know if you're aware, but Enek Therok has recently announced his retirement—"

"Ah!" said Pulaski. Some of Therok's jokes from earlier now made sense.

Alden said, "Are you intending to put your name forward, Professor, if that's not too intrusive a question?"

"Certainly that's what some people are assuming," said Parmak. "But Natima, it seems, couldn't possibly comment."

Lang gave a bland smile. "I have plenty to keep me busy already," she said. "I have teaching, I have research—"

"Garak liked the recent lecture on enigma tales," Parmak said.

"Did he?" Lang glanced across the room, to where the castellan was in the midst of a jovial conversation with Therok and one or two others. "I bet you didn't."

"You know me," said Parmak. "My tastes are very particular."

"What's an enigma tale?" said Pulaski.

"It's a kind of Cardassian murder mystery," said Alden, unexpectedly. "Don't look at me like that, Kitty. Some of us read beyond our immediate research interests."

"I read beyond my immediate research interests!" protested Pulaski. "I read the parrises squares results."

"A sport," said Alden, seeing Parmak's and Lang's baffled expressions.

"I'm not closed to new information," Pulaski said. "Murder mysteries, huh? So what makes these enigma tales particularly Cardassian? Is everyone guilty of something?"

Alden winced, but Parmak and Lang both burst out laughing. "You've got it in one!" said Parmak. "And they're *terrible*. Potboilers. So predictable!"

"They're more interesting than that," Lang said. "They offer a microcosm for society and, I think, the means to diagnose its ills—and, perhaps, the method to bring about its cure."

"I think you see more deeply than the average reader," said Parmak. "But I have come to believe that this is what literature always does—reflects back some part of the reader. You see a means to reform society. I see melodrama in country houses." He leaned in confidentially. "The castellan adores enigma tales, but I think it's mainly to do with the frocks."

Lang laughed. Pulaski noticed that Garak, still talking to Therok and another man, flicked his head around slightly. Meeting Parmak's eye, he smiled, and with unexpected warmth.

"Take this place." Lang glanced around. "The University of the Union. A more perfect setting for an enigma tale I cannot imagine. A closed environment. A limited cast. Small stakes, but stakes upon which reputations stand and fall. And most of all, an institution that resonates deeply within its wider context. One may detach it for the purposes of a story, but in reality it is deeply intertwined with the society in which it operates." She smiled. "Of course, it could simply be that I'm trying to give academic credibility to my comfort reading. But I think I've earned a little comfort reading. I've spent many years reading things that left me feeling considerably less comfortable."

"I confess I haven't read your work," Pulaski said frankly. "I'm going to. But I have to say—I'm more optimistic about the nature of academic work and the context in which it happens."

"Spoken like a true Federation citizen," said Parmak, with a smile.

"Spoken like a scientist," said Pulaski. "The ship I'm assigned to these days, that's its mission. Create the conditions whereby the science comes first. I'm working with Cardassians, Ferengi, a particularly interesting Tzenkethi. We have our ups and downs, but at the end of the day—the work is what pulls us together."

"Kitty's right," Alden put in.

Pulaski took a step back and mocked surprise. "Somebody call for a doctor! He's got to be sick. He's never said that before!"

"Well, I mean it, Kitty. I wouldn't have chucked in a good job if I didn't think so." Alden's face shadowed slightly.

"Wait," said Pulaski, "here comes the kicker."

"A free and open society," he said. "It's the ideal toward which we aim, isn't it? Even if we don't always manage it."

"Hey, mister," said Pulaski. "I think we do pretty damn well." She looked around the room. "And you know what? I think these folks are doing pretty damn well too."

Parmak raised his glass and clinked it against Pulaski's. "I'll drink to that," he said.

Lang and Alden raised their glasses. "To the ideal," said Lang. "Elusive, and perhaps ultimately unattainable. But always worth the effort."

Later, when Pulaski returned to her suite, she replicated a glass of wine, kicked off her shoes, and slumped back into the deep orange sofa. She picked up her padd and found that Efheny had sent over a more detailed version of her schedule—timed down to the minute and beautifully color-coordinated. The next day began with a series of interviews for the 'casts, and then there were meetings, tours, a public lecture . . . a busy few days leading up to the medal ceremony itself.

Pulaski put the padd down with a sigh. She'd worry about it all in the morning. She turned on the viewscreen, but all she could find was rolling news. She didn't want to explode with rage just before bedtime so, instead, she went back to the padd and, hunting around the university's library, found Lang's works. She downloaded the shortest and began to read.

"*For Cardassia!*" it began, unpromisingly, but soon Pulaski found that she was impressed with Lang's clear and unfussy prose, and her clarity of thought. It only took a page or two before she was deeply absorbed in Lang's analysis of a famous Cardassian novel, and her diagnosis of the ills of her own society. Pulaski checked the date of writing—years ago, back when the Obsidian Order vetted every publication, attempting to control every thought of the Union's unlucky citizens. And Lang had dared to write and publish this. "Damn," muttered Pulaski, with frank admiration for her courage. "Goddamn."

There was a tap on the door. Pulaski looked up and, checking the chrono, was surprised to see how late it was. Probably Efheny, come to go through some minute detail of the day and make sure that Pulaski was comfortable—which she would be, if people would leave her alone for five minutes. She rubbed tired eyes and yawned.

The tap came again, rather more insistently. "Come in!" Pulaski called. The door opened, and Peter Alden came in, carrying a bottle. Pulaski peered at the contents suspiciously.

"What the hell is that?"

"*Kanar*," he said.

"Dammit, Peter, it's *blue*."

"It's incredible," he said, plunking himself down on a chair. "You've got to try some."

She shook her head. "I've drunk enough tonight. I'm going to bed—"

"Come on, Kitty," he said. "Don't tarnish your reputation."

"Reputation?"

"Head for hard liquor."

"Ah. That reputation." She accepted a glass and sniffed carefully at the thick weird liquid. Floral. Surprisingly pleasant. She knocked it back. "Sheesh!"

"Yep," he said, smiling. The doctor waved her glass at him, and he poured her another.

"You were quiet tonight," she said. "One might even say you lurked."

"I was interested in hearing Lang."

"I'm not surprised. She's impressive. Certainly more impressive than Therok."

"Oh yes?" He looked at her with interest.

"Well, he's a type, isn't he? The type that gets senior appointments."

Alden looked around the room, as if not entirely interested in the subject. "He seems to have done a good job. Can't have been easy keeping U of U going in the bad old days of the Order. He certainly gave Lang space to say whatever she wanted."

"I guess that was all at her own risk. Let her

speak; keep his distance. Therok had everything to gain by association and nothing to lose. He'll have kept himself alive by being something to everyone." She pondered that. "I'd like to know how he made it through the end of the Dominion War."

"The Fire," said Alden. "That's what they call it here. The Fire."

"Damn," she said, shaking her head in wonder. "This place . . . But Therok—powerful friends, I guess."

"Probably," said Alden. "Hey, what about Lang? I know you were impressed, but I found her rather closed."

"Well, if she's hoping to succeed Therok, she's probably being wise. One wrong word right now might put the kibosh on the promotion."

"Yes, yes, I understand that," Alden said. "Still . . ."

Pulaski shrugged. "Maybe there's more to this appointment than meets the eye."

"It is Cardassia," Alden agreed. "There's always subtext."

They drank for a while companionably. "I wish I'd gotten more from the castellan," Pulaski complained at last. "You know, Peter, if I was a more thin-skinned woman—"

Alden snorted.

"Watch your step, mister," Pulaski said. "But if I was more thin-skinned, I might have been insulted by the way the castellan spoke to me."

Alden put his hand upon his chest theatrically. " 'Don't you know who I *am*?' "

"Lay off," she said. "Efheny keeps telling me that I'm a very honored guest. Yet the castellan treated me like . . . Well. Like an annoyance."

"Can't imagine that has ever happened to you before."

"Not on first meeting. Second meeting, yes, but not on first meeting. Well, not more than a couple of times."

"Perhaps he's read your file." Alden laughed. "Why 'perhaps'? Of course he's read your file. He probably created your file."

"It's more than that."

"Well, trying to make the conversation about Julian Bashir didn't endear you, dear Kitty." Alden shook his head. "It really wasn't the time or the place."

"I only want to *see* him!" Pulaski exclaimed. "What's so unreasonable about that? He was a colleague—and not just in Starfleet! A fellow doctor. We worked together. I put my career at risk for him—"

"There are ways and means, Kitty. Cornering the castellan at a public reception in your honor probably isn't the best way of going about getting what you want."

Pulaski threw her hands up. "What else am I supposed to do? I put the request into his office weeks before coming here. He's here all alone, Peter!"

"I bet he's getting some of the best medical care in the quadrant."

"You know what I mean. Not among his own people. Among strangers."

Alden stared down into his glass. "Perhaps the Federation isn't the best place for him."

Pulaski shot him a sharp look. "What do you mean by that?"

Alden's face was shadowed, and Pulaski was reminded, suddenly, of his prior career. "Come on, Peter. What do you mean?"

Alden shifted in his seat. "I'm not entirely fond of someone who sells out their government."

"If you mean the Andorian affair, mister, you'd do well to remember that I sold out our government too."

Alden sparkled a smile at her. "And I am, of course, ludicrously fond of you, Kitty."

"Don't try and change the subject."

Alden stood up. "It's late. Let's leave it. I agree that Julian Bashir did incredible things. I spoke out of turn." He stretched. "Indeed, he was a veritable superhero."

Pulaski leaned forward to continue the argument, but Alden was already halfway to the door. "Good night." He stopped. "Hey, what's on your agenda tomorrow?"

"What isn't on my agenda? I'm doing some interviews first. Want to tag along?"

"Interviews?"

"Some early morning program."

He smiled wickedly. "Kitty," he said, "I wouldn't miss that for the world."

Usually in the evenings, Garak and Parmak worked in companionable silence for an hour or two and then finished the day with *kotra*, conversation, and *kanar*. Even at his busiest, Garak tried to honor this commitment. Recently, however, the games of *kotra* had become more sporadic, and Garak's conversation had a tendency to lapse. This evening, the silence was strained. At length, Garak, who had been plodding resentfully through the day's intelligence briefing, put down his padd.

"Come on," Garak said. "Spit it out."

Parmak looked up. "Spit what out?"

"You're angry with me. Tell me why and then we can get back to being friends."

Parmak put his book down. It was the collection of enigma tales by Sayak, Garak noticed, with some bitterness. He hadn't yet had a chance to do more than flick through it. Parmak didn't even like enigma tales.

"I'm not angry," said Parmak. "I'm confused."

Garak gave him a winning smile. "I thought my inscrutability was one of my most appealing features."

It didn't work. Parmak was still unhappy. "You know what I mean. Pulaski—"

"Oh, *Pulaski*." Garak picked up his padd again. "She was exactly what I had been led to expect. Do you know what Picard said about her?"

"I don't think I want to know."

"I wouldn't have believed a man like that had such words within his arsenal. The universe is full of surprises. But—Pulaski. How *marvelous* she is. She is going to make a *magnificent* speech, and the visit will be a *tremendous* success. The medal is indeed a *great* honor but *hugely* deserved for her *remarkable* contribution."

That was a précis of what he'd said at a press conference a few days ago. There was a brief and icy pause. After a moment or two, Parmak said, "If I didn't know better, I would say that you were trying to handle me."

Hearing the hurt in the other man's voice, Garak looked guiltily down at his padd. That was exactly what he had been trying to do. "I'm sorry," he said, genuinely. "I have no problem with Pulaski, although I suppose I find her rather brusque." He held up the padd. "I should get on with this."

"Yesterday, I couldn't make you read," Parmak said. "Tonight you're engrossed."

"If I could only tell you the contents of this file you'd know why." Garak held his hands up in mock horror. "Such scandals as you could not believe possible—"

"Stop *handling* me, Elim!"

Garak bit his lip. "I'm sorry."

"Is there a problem with her seeing Bashir?"

Garak stared down at the padd. Silence, then, "I really do need to read this."

Parmak persisted. "She was a colleague of his. Risked her own career and reputation to save the Andorians. I know you're concerned about reprisals, but he must have trusted her."

Garak gave a quiet tut and started the current section again.

"You're never going to get over this, are you? You're not even going to start."

Garak stared at the padd, and then gave up, setting the briefing aside. He looked directly at the other man. "What can I say, Kelas? I remember Julian Bashir when I first saw him on Deep Space 9." He smiled in fond memory. "You would've laughed! He was hopelessly out of his depth. So young. So awkward. Always said the wrong thing. But so full of hope. And some of that . . . some of that transferred itself to me. I would not have survived my exile without Julian Bashir. I mean that. I would've died without Julian Bashir."

"I know how much he helped you," Parmak said.

"It was more than being an attentive doctor."

"I know that too."

And Garak knew, too, that on some level, that hurt. He struggled to explain further. "It was everything he represented. His capacity to see good—even in me—his capacity to strive, to seek to find and not to yield . . ." He could hear his voice catching. *I am delivering a eulogy*, he thought, *for a man who is not yet dead*. Abruptly, he got up from his chair and walked over to the window. Outside, the lights of the capital shone against the night sky, but tonight they seemed hazy. Was the dust coming in already? Garak wiped a hand across his eyes. After a moment, he became aware that Parmak was standing beside him.

"It's a beautiful night," said Parmak. "I know you miss the house in Coranum, but I like it here. I love this view."

Garak closed his eyes. "I can't bear to see it," he said softly. "To see him. All that intelligence, that quality, extinguished . . ." He shuddered. "And for what? A spy game, of all things! Of all the stupid, ridiculous things he could have done! After all I said, 'Don't play the game, Julian, the game *eats* you.'" He shook his head. "He should have stuck to the holodeck. Tuxedos and champagne. There are too many spies in this world already. Too many spies, and all of them wasting their time and squandering their lives."

"You couldn't command him, Elim. And I don't think he could have done anything different and remained himself. Remained the man that you loved."

And that, Garak thought, was the bitter truth. He made a move to go back to his chair and the intelligence briefing, but Parmak's hand was on his shoulder, holding him there. Garak didn't resist but he did turn to look out of the window. He wished he could see his garden. He would feel better, he thought, to be in his garden.

"What do you see?" said Parmak, eventually.

"Are you planning a new career for me as tour guide?"

Parmak smiled. "Just tell me what you see."

"I see what I always see. The river. The Assembly building. The lamps around Alon Ghemor's stone garden." Funny how the eye drifted there. "Damar's memorial."

"Don't be morbid," said Parmak. "Look for life."

"I see the tenements down in Torr. Skimmers passing through. There goes a tram. Busy. Lit up."

"I can almost smell the *gelat* brewing," said Parmak with a smile.

"The university campus. There's a black spot, to one side, where the land is still ruined. But you told me not to be morbid."

"Look at the lights," said Parmak. "Who could they be?"

"Students. Working, maybe. Living, loving, laughing, hoping. I hope . . ."

"You were wasted in the Obsidian Order."

Garak carried on staring at the city. "I see . . . shadows of the past, of course. They're part of us, aren't they? It will be a long time before we can banish them completely. But you're right, as ever. I see lights too. I see how far we've come. Ten years ago this was a wasteland. And now . . ."

"Look on your works, Elim Garak, and hope," Parmak said softly. "Julian Bashir saved your life, you say. Saved your life for you to come back here. Which means that none of this would exist without him. An incredible tribute, don't you think?"

Perhaps, Garak thought. He was grateful to Kelas

for this attempt to help him. But what use were tributes to Julian Bashir? He sat each day upstairs, looking out at this very view, but Garak knew he couldn't see it. He couldn't see anything. Nothing that had made the man was there any longer. Garak thought he would swap the whole Union if it would restore Bashir. But it wouldn't. No grand gesture, no great sacrifice, could restore that vital spark. All that one could do was hope, and Garak feared that that was little more than self-delusion.

But that was not Parmak's fault. Garak turned his back to the window. He reached out and rested his hand, lightly, upon his friend's shoulder. "More than I ever imagined possible."

He smiled, too brightly. Parmak frowned. Garak went back to his seat and picked up the padd. The last thing he had seen was his father's house; his house now. "*Do your chores, Elim,*" he murmured to himself, in a passable impression of the old monster. "*I told you to do your chores.*" Garak often alluded to the words of others, but this reference, he suspected, would bypass even Kelas, who surely knew him better than anyone else alive. Garak still kept a few secrets, which was, perhaps, good.

My dear Doctor—

Let us leave the official residence behind. It is very grand, in its own, way, but these buildings tend to be similar whatever the civilization. A complex of rooms, mostly for official purposes, and therefore no matter how grand the furnishings, no matter how they have been designed to impress the visitor, they are, in effect, glorified offices. Even my private quarters, despite my efforts, have a rather impersonal air, as if my presence there is temporary—a kind of exile, one might say, from my real life. Sometimes I feel about these rooms much as I did my quarters on Deep Space 9. And yet the time that I spent there, in your company, and the company of the others, has done more to define me than any other chapter in my life. I wonder if this chapter currently unfolding will count for as much. I hope so.

I do wonder what will come next. Will the epic of my life repeat itself? Will I be proven guilty, yet again?

Yes, let us leave the confines of this building and go outside. Right now, it is spring in the capital, and therefore the city is at its loveliest. We do have four seasons here, contrary to popular belief, but two—summer and winter—are very long and very harsh in their own inimitable ways. Spring and autumn are shorter, and all the more welcome for it, soft seasons of color and pleasure. But they do not last long enough, and what comes next is hard. Autumn's kindliness becomes winter's cruelty, and the fresh spring becomes polluted summer. Throughout our history we punished our land, Doctor, as we did each other, driven by hunger to farm with great violence. The land, like much else, did not thrive in our hands, and we created wastelands. Now the land punishes us in turn. The summer brings not only baking heat, but high winds, and with the wind the dust clouds roll into the city. We struggle to breathe, and we put on masks. We all carry our masks. We are never far from them.

Yet even as we suffer these bad summers, those of us who have lived through all those long years since the Fire know that they are not as cruel as they once were. With your help—the help of Starfleet and the Federation—we have been busy. We have been clever. The lands beyond the capital are reestablishing themselves, and we hope that one day there will be a summer free from the chastening dust, when the whole city will look up at the sun and a bright blue sky without taint and be glad. Peoples change (as the poet does not quite say), and smile.

Perhaps you might change too one day, Julian. Perhaps one day you might smile.

Garak
[unsent]

Three

Antok was yawning and doodling through yet another committee meeting, when her mind soon wandered back to the previous evening with her family. Her sketches were of candles, she realized, and she felt warmth—happiness—suffuse her whole body. The coziness of their home and the beauty of the little ceremony, lighting the candles and sharing the sweet cakes and thanking the Prophets. How blessed she was, how grateful. How different life was these days; how different life was for her two children, and how much promise the future held for them. Antok had been born in the dying days of the old Cardassia, when the people had been crushed under the double tyranny of the Central Command and the Obsidian Order. Just as she reached the age of emergence, she had seen these two powers collapse, and she had come to U of U as a student during the first civilian administration, that cruelly short time when it seemed that democracy might take root in Cardassia. She had found the courage then to explore her Bajoran roots, albeit still passing as fully Cardassian, but studying the history of those Bajorans who had come to Cardassia Prime. And then Dukat seized power, the Dominion arrived, and everything changed.

The university changed within weeks. Directives came down stating what could and could not be studied. Some teachers complained and were promptly suspended. The shelves in the library thinned once again. Outlandish topics such as hers were sidelined, with the grants and prizes going to more traditional accounts of great guls and battles won. Antok had been discouraged by this turn of events, leaving her studies before she was pushed out. She worked for a while in a *geleta* house and then at a restaurant in Barvonok, waiting on the businessmen who were making a fortune from the trading opportunities that had opened up with the Dominion worlds, and from the war. She doubted many of them had lived to enjoy their wealth, but the change of career had saved her life. She had not been on campus when the Jem'Hadar arrived there to conduct their massacre. She had been asleep in her basement flat after a long shift, staying hidden down there while the building above her was destroyed and the city all around was flattened. She dug her way out, in the end, emerging hungry and frightened after three days to find that the world had ended.

A dark time had followed, for her and all the others who had somehow survived the Fire; years of hunger and labor and fear, and then . . . Then one morning you found that you were sitting in a bright new purpose-built building, doing work that you loved, and that the city outside was no longer rubble and ruin, but thriving and renewing. And last night you and your beautiful family had spent the evening eating Bajoran food and praying Bajoran prayers and laughing and loving, and you were all so happy that the worst of your troubles was a lengthy and somewhat tedious meeting. Antok drew another candle and silently thanked the Prophets.

The meeting ended with a decision to postpone the decision until the next meeting, and Antok gathered up her files to hurry off to the archive. Her colleague Nevek, who had been sitting watching her doodle, said, "You're full of sunshine. Wild night last night?"

Antok smiled. "You know me. Family girl at heart."

Nevek smiled back. "One day you'll do something to shock us all."

Antok dashed off across the campus as soon as she could get decently away, and returned to her desk at the archive. She wondered again why she simply didn't say what she and her family had been doing last night. Nevek was nice, a mother of four; she talked about what they did all the time. Like most Cardassians, she did not follow any religion, but there were the solstice festivals, and the fireworks on Liberation Day, and all the small holidays throughout the year when Cardassians remembered their history and commemorated both their many dead and their lucky escapes. Nevek, she knew, wouldn't give two hoots that Antok had been lighting candles to thank the Prophets for the gift of the Emissary. In fact, given that Nevek was a sociologist, she would probably try to snag an invitation to their next celebration, and not just for the free food. Did anyone care, on the new Cardassia, that Elima Antok and her children had Bajoran genes? Would they really mind, seeing her family pray to the Bajoran gods? Antok thought not, but still some small part of her felt that discretion was needed. Old habits die hard. Perhaps when the boys were older; they were so small, too small to be exposed to the potential hostility of others, and she did not think she had the right to make that decision on their behalf. It could wait. Perhaps it would be their children who would be able to celebrate openly.

Antok opened her padd to see what the morning held. The U of U archive had a small team of techies dedicated to trying to salvage data from the devastation caused by the Fire. With few survivors, and little surviving infrastructure, the process was like an archaeological project, Antok thought, digging through the rubble and trying to pull out something, making guesses from very small, limited finds. After more than a decade, such finds weren't all that frequent, but earlier in the week one of the team had been in touch to say that he'd found something he thought might be of interest to her. He still had some work to do on making the files accessible, but he thought they should be ready for her to examine today.

He was as good as his word. A little data packet squirted onto her comm—no, not that little, as it turned out; really quite substantial . . . Antok rubbed her hands in anticipation. There might well be some good pickings here. She murmured thanks to the Prophets again: this find was pretty miraculous, given how much of the city had been destroyed by the Jem'Hadar and how little tangible remained.

Antok opened the first file. Her expert eye immediately recognized the seal of the Administrative Committee of the Office of the Academy—the main decision-making body of the old U of U. The files were marked confidential, but that didn't set Antok's pulse racing. The old U of U had marked everything confidential, even when they were discussing something as banal as whether or not to install new showers in the gymnasium, or whether the anthem should be sung at the end of classes as well as at the start, or what texts were to be removed or readmitted to the libraries. The old Cardassia could always find a reason to be secretive. The new U of U, like all of Cardassia's new institutions, made so much information available that the more cynical sometimes suggested they were trying to bury bad news.

The files were encrypted, but Antok knew most of the keys that would decrypt prewar U of U data. These files, however, proved to be unusually stubborn.

Corrupted data? Or a key she hadn't yet found? That in itself would be valuable, even if the files themselves turned out to be about nothing more than how to make some sweaty undergraduates less sweaty. Antok had a bundle of documents on file that were, so far as she could make out, gibberish, but might become intelligible with a new key. And her techie colleagues loved a good puzzle.

She played and played, but the data remained impervious to her charms. After an hour or so, she was running out of options, but not out of curiosity. She stood up, stretched, and went to get a cup of red leaf tea in the staff room: the bookish person's alternative to going and standing under a hot shower and Antok's preferred method of breaking a block. The archivists were there, on a break, and handing out *ikri* buns, and there were a couple of other colleagues from her department. A little later, fueled by tea and office gossip, she came back to her desk. As she sat down again, inspiration struck. She remembered some long-forgotten passwords, and gave them a go.

The third one did the trick. The characters on the screen began to unscramble before her eyes. The first words she saw were:

PROJECT ENIGMA.

She wriggled excitedly in her seat and leaned in over the comm. How mysterious! What could it be? In general, Cardassians liked giving long and impressive names to things (as "Administrative Committee of the Office of the Academy" demonstrated), and so the brevity of this piqued her interest. Burying bad news? Or simply not important?

Pages were unscrambling faster than she could read them, but Antok had been trained to read quickly and for comprehension. She was soon deeply immersed. After about twenty minutes of reading, she stood up, closed the comm, and went outside, where she stood gulping in deep breaths of fresh air.

Project Enigma, it transpired, had been a hush-hush project arising from conversations between the medical school and the government Office for Bajoran Racial Equity. It dated back to the last few years of the Occupation. The project, so far as Antok had been able to make out, had set out to identify children of Cardassian-Bajoran liaisons and bring them to Cardassia Prime. For what purpose, Antok had not yet been able to identify, but the involvement of the medical school was filling her with foreboding.

Do I want to know what is in this file, she wondered, thinking of her boys. She had read so much about the horrors of the Occupation; she knew already the depths that had been plumbed, and she was afraid to find out more, particularly when it struck so close to home. Her father, herself, her boys . . . Did she want to know?

Antok took another deep breath. The fact was, she *had* to know. It was her job. It was her responsibility. But more than that—it was her history. She needed to know. She had to know. She went back inside, sat down again at her desk, and went to work.

*   *   *

Pulaski stayed awake reading Lang until well into
the night. She was so impressed that she even located
a copy of the novel that Lang had been dissecting,
The Never-Ending Sacrifice by Ulan Corac, but a
few pages demonstrated that while Lang's analysis
of its content had been witheringly accurate, she
had skimped on eviscerating Corac's style, which
was deadly. Long sentences, contorted for effect; ex-
tensive digressions; and an overwhelming sense that
the story wasn't going anywhere but back again and
again over the same ground. Pulaski wasn't a great
reader of novels at the best of times, but at least this
one did the trick and sent her to sleep.

She was fresh and alert when her alarm woke her,
and found that she was excited about the day ahead.
When she had received this invitation, her acceptance had been out of duty rather than enthusiasm.
Her impression of Cardassia Prime, like many people
in the Federation, even so long after the war, was
of a dusty brown world where people lived a grim,
subsistence-level life. True, the world was still harsh,
and the land reclamation projects were still in their
infancy, but Pulaski was finding Cardassia fascinat-
ing. How often did you get to see firsthand a civilization rebuild itself? So far, all signs were that the
Cardassians had met the challenge admirably. Sure,
there were bound to be problems—Pulaski was a
seasoned enough traveler to know that—and she bet
there were still pockets of poverty here in this city

and across the Union. But the Cardassians were getting there.

The skimmer passed through the campus and out toward the city circular. Chief among these signs of growth and change was the liveliness and variety of the news. It was everywhere, she saw: the big public screens in the main squares, the tabletop tickertapes, the constant updates on personal comms and padds. Pulaski could live without all this—as long as there wasn't a major war happening, she could happily stay uninformed, but she understood how, for the Cardassian people, this new freedom and vibrancy of the press must still be a novelty. Certainly it added color and flavor to everyday life, and Pulaski was more than happy to provide some content.

"Wool-gathering, Kitty?" said Alden.

"Enjoying the sights," she said. "I don't think I'll see anywhere like this place again."

The first item on Pulaski's intricately detailed schedule for the day was an interview with one of the major news 'casters. Efheny had explained that the interviewer, Edek Mayrat, was one of the most respected journalists on Prime. His two daily 'casts— morning and evening—were watched by millions across the Union. Efheny clearly thought that the interview was a great coup, and he had gone to some effort to secure it. Pulaski wasn't bothered either way, but if it did something for Efheny's resume, she was happy to oblige. But with even only a vague interest in the whole process, she had to admit she was impressed

with the studio building when she arrived—another
of these fine buildings that filled the city skyline—
and the facilities were certainly state-of-the-art. She
was introduced to the producer of the show, a female
named Ista Nemeny, who quickly set her at her ease,
ran her through the process, and introduced her to
Mayrat.

Mayrat was a focused and intelligent male of
middle age, whose direct style she liked immediately.
"Welcome to Cardassia, Doctor Pulaski. Thanks for
coming here today."

"A pleasure. Happy to try something new."

He eyed her thoughtfully. "You don't do much
'casting?"

She shook her head. She wasn't, generally, let in
front of journalists, not without a minder, and not
unless her superiors were either bored and in need
of a busy afternoon or desperate. The problem was
her tendency to tell the truth as she saw it. Someone
had offered her "media training" once. They hadn't
offered again.

"Uh-uh," she said, shaking her head. "Not my
world at all."

Mayrat smiled at her. "I promise not to be difficult."

"Me too," she said. Out of the corner of her eye,
she saw Nemeny signal that they were going live, so
she took a sip of water and waited to begin.

There was some brash music, and on the monitor in
front of her, Pulaski saw some garish graphics resolve

into the 'cast's logo, with the word *Today* emblazoned across it. Mayrat did some spiel to the holo-camera, then made a fine introduction that emphasized Pulaski's eminence. They'd done their research: he knew about her work in genomic therapy, and he didn't just talk about the work she'd done with Bashir, although naturally this was mentioned. His introduction finished, he got right to it.

"Doctor Pulaski, how do you like Cardassia?"

"I like it very much. No, really. Everyone's making a fuss of me. What's not to like?"

Mayrat laughed. Perhaps this was the moment he saw that Pulaski wasn't going to be his usual guest, holding back and equivocating. "Nothing you haven't liked?"

"It's pretty hot, obviously, but then, I'm a very ordinary mammal with very ordinary warm blood. I don't think there's anything anyone can do there. I'm drinking plenty of fluids, keeping my hat on, and staying out of the midday heat. That's great advice, by the way, for any of your listeners who also happen to be warm-blooded."

"Tell me some of the things that have struck you about Cardassia Prime," said Mayrat.

"How little devastation remains from the war," Pulaski said promptly. "Sure, there are places here and there where there's clearly still some rebuilding left to be done. That blight on the campus is a tragedy, for one thing. But the most striking thing, when you come in to land, is how complete the city looks.

Also, things work. Your infrastructure's great. I'm dying to get a ride on the trams."

"We have the Federation to thank in part for the infrastructure, I guess," said Mayrat.

"That's very courteous of you, and maybe that's fair if we're talking about bringing the stuff here, and replicating more stuff, but we've been gone a few years now, haven't we? If things are running well now, it's not just a question of being well designed. It's about the will to keep it running well."

"Sounds like we might be able to persuade you to stay."

Pulaski shook her head. "Nuh-uh. No chance. Too much fish juice in the sauces."

"Anything else you like?"

"I like the hound-racing. Those beasts are beautiful. Poetry in motion. I'd like to get to ride one before I leave."

Mayrat smiled. "I imagine half the teams on the circuit are contacting your aide right now to be the first in line."

They talked for a while about the purpose of her visit, her work on the Andorian genome project, and her impressions of the university. He also asked, politely, about her current work, and she spoke warmly of the *Athene Donald* and the projects and plans for that ship. She hoped her colleagues would hear this and be pleased at what she'd had to say. (She didn't have to worry on that score. Katherine Pulaski's colleagues never missed any of her broadcasts. One of the other pools that ran on board the ship concerned how long it would take her to cause a diplomatic incident. Her best friend on the *Athene Donald*, the Trill Director of Research, Maurita Tanj, was about to clean up.)

"I understand you're giving a speech at U of U later in the week," Mayrat said. "Could you give us some idea of the topic?"

"Well, I don't want to give away all my secrets, and this is heavy-duty stuff for a morning show, but without spoiling either my speech or your viewers' breakfasts, I'm going to be discussing ethics in the practice of medicine and in medical research. What our responsibilities are, not just to patients, but to society as a whole."

"A topic bound to interest many," he said. "I don't know if you're aware, Doctor, but we are, as ever, in the midst of a debate over our past at the moment. You may have seen something on this very channel."

Pulaski, dimly sensing that perhaps the conversation might be moving onto trickier ground, briefly regretted all the time spent watching the hound-racing. "I've not heard, no."

"To sum up a very long and complex situation," he explained, "a report has just been published by a senior assemblyperson into war crimes on Bajor."

About damn time, thought Pulaski, but even she guessed that probably wasn't the best thing to say on a live broadcast to the whole nation. "And what has this report concluded?"

"It's advised that there should be further and

more specific investigations leading, if necessary, to prosecutions."

He paused. There was some dead air. Eventually, Pulaski said, "Is there something you want me to say?"

"Well, it's what everyone's talking about. The Federation is a good friend and our closest ally. We'd like to hear your take on it."

"You should talk to our ambassador," she said.

"I will. But you're here speaking about ethics. You must have an opinion—"

"An *opinion*? What—you mean, do I think war crimes should be prosecuted? That's something of a leading question, isn't it? On the lines of 'so when did you stop beating your wife'?"

Mayrat looked confused.

"I mean," Pulaski went on, "what do you expect me to say? That war crimes shouldn't be prosecuted? Of course they should, to the fullest extent of the law."

"So, as a representative of Starfleet, you would say that—"

Pulaski gave a short laugh. "I doubt Starfleet wants to claim me as their representative within the Cardassian Union. Like I say, we have a great ambassador who surely knows more about this than I do. But speaking as a private citizen—speaking as a doctor—of course I think war crimes on Bajor should be investigated. People should be prosecuted, and if they're found guilty, they should be imprisoned—

you don't have the death penalty anymore, do you? No? Good. Then investigate these crimes, prosecute where there's evidence, and imprison the guilty."

Mayrat, she saw, was deeply interested. Why? She was only speaking common sense. "So you don't see any exceptions to this—"

"Look, I'm not an expert," Pulaski said. "I'm telling you how it seems to me. There's a lot of talk about Cardassia coming to terms with its past, and that's clearly important work that needs to be done. But really, this has nothing to do with Cardassia. This is about the people who suffered at the hands of mass murderers and torturers—"

She saw Mayrat's alarm at this.

"All right," she said, "*alleged* mass murderers and torturers. But the focus needs to be on the victims. These people deserve their hearing. They deserve justice, they deserve restitution. Dammit, they deserve closure."

There was a slight pause. Mayrat seemed to be pondering his next question. "Do you think that anybody should be immune from prosecution?"

"Why?" said Pulaski.

Mayrat blinked at her. "That's a very good question."

"Come back to me when you have an answer," said Pulaski. She was vaguely aware, out of the corner of her eye, of Ista Nemeny shaking with silent laughter.

"I'll try to think of one," said Mayrat with a smile.

"One last question, Doctor Pulaski. Who's your choice for chief academician?"

"My choice for chief academician? I can give you a tip for the 10:52 hound-race at Orlehny, if you like?"

"I'd love that."

"Riddle Runner's in great form."

"Thanks. And chief academician?"

"I met Natima Lang last night," said Pulaski. "I think she'd be great."

"I think everyone in the Union would agree," Mayrat said with a smile. "Well, almost everyone." And with that, the interview wound up. Nemeny came over and thanked her profusely. She was looking extremely cheerful. Not so Peter Alden, who, when Pulaski joined him, had his head in his hands.

"Are you okay?" Pulaski said.

"Oh, I'm great," Alden said. "I've just lost a bet."

"A bet?" She frowned. "Hey, where's Efheny?"

"He's trying to alter your schedule."

"Don't tell me a racing team has been in touch."

"Yes, several in fact, but right now that poor lad is trying to fit in a short meeting with the Federation ambassador for you before the end of today."

"The Federation *ambassador*?"

"Yes, the Federation ambassador." Alden shook his head. "What were you *thinking*?"

She looked at him in bewilderment. "What? What have I done now?"

"What have you *done*?" He looked up at the heavens. "Kitty, you're unbelievable!"

"Was it the racing tip? Was that too flippant?"

"It wasn't the bloody racing tip!" Alden put his hand to his brow. "You can't visit somewhere, then go around saying you think their head of state should be imprisoned!"

"When did I say that? I didn't say that!"

Alden lowered his voice. "He's ex–Obsidian Order. Everyone knows that."

"I know that. What are you saying? If he's guilty of a crime, he should be punished. It's not rocket science, is it?

"No," said Alden. "Neither is it diplomacy."

"I'm a doctor," said Pulaski with a shrug, "not a diplomat."

"We know, Kitty," said Alden. "We know."

Arati Mhevet, the chief of the city constabulary in the Cardassian capital, had first met Elim Garak a few years ago. This was under circumstances that both, should they ever come to write their memoirs, would describe as "difficult," and then would pass over without offering any more detail. Mhevet, at the time a senior investigator, had found herself in possession of evidence relating to the murder of the Federation president Nan Bacco. Garak was the Union's ambassador to the Federation; he announced his candidacy not long after the terrifying events of those few days, when he was riding high on a popularity bounce received after an attempt on his life. The whole affair had brought about a swift change at the top in many Cardassian institutions. The head of the Intelligence Bureau had resigned publically over failing to prevent an attempt on Garak's life; in actuality because he had taken sides in the forthcoming election for the castellanship. The castellan at the time, Rakena Garan, who misguidedly attempted to conceal the information that Bacco's assassin was a Cardassian, had been left in an untenable position. Her decision not to run again had left the way clear for Elim Garak to sail safely into the position, defeating a rather nasty demagogue on the way. And Arati Mhevet had taken charge of the city constabulary, one of the most important policing jobs in the Union.

She and the castellan had a professional relationship, naturally, but Mhevet knew that Garak saw himself as her mentor, and she welcomed his interest. Not that they drew attention to any of this: it was vital that the police were apolitical. They didn't talk shop . . . They talked . . . Well, they talked abstractly. Mostly they talked about what Garak was reading, now Mhevet came to think of it, and, by implication, they talked about what it meant to do their respective jobs ethically. For swiftness of action, decisiveness, and sheer bloody nerve, Mhevet knew she could get more from watching Garak for a morning than from years spent working alongside other people. She had brought much of this to her new role, although she did not have Garak's addiction to risk, and was more cautious. But there was more that tied them together.

Mhevet and Garak shared a vision of their world, a common understanding of how it worked—one might even call it a belief in a certain kind of . . . *Order*. They both understood that left unwatched, Cardassia corrupted—not by conscious will, but because that was the way their world drifted. They both shared a burning desire to never let this corruption happen again. They watched for it and, most of all, they watched each other for it. Garak, Mhevet suspected, took as much from their quiet relationship as she did. They tried to meet, if only for a little while, once a week. The castellan kept a supply of coffee in store for her—she'd gotten addicted to the stuff working alongside Starfleet personnel during the reconstruction period.

"Filthy muck," he said, whenever he saw her drinking it. "Of all the Federation habits to pick up. You might at least have acquired a taste for wine."

She had, over the past week, been diligently reading reviews of an anthology of new enigma tales that she suspected might pop up in conversation with him (she had no intention of reading the actual book). In between all the briefings, policy documents, and everything else, Garak somehow managed to keep up with his reading. However, they'd not yet had a chance to speak. Right now the castellan was involved in a delicate conversation over the comm with Assemblyperson Chenet, one of the chief authors of the war crimes report that was currently the lead story on all the 'casts. Mhevet had a great

deal of respect for Chenet, who represented a province that had once contained Lakarian City, before
the Jem'Hadar destroyed it. Regions such as his were
often less likely to be persuaded of the need to make
reparation for past, when such obvious harm had
been done to them. But Chenet had been steadfast in
his belief that whatever their suffering, Cardassians
could not ignore the harm they had caused others.
Given he had also managed to pull more Federation
resources into his province than any other member of
the Assembly, he had a great deal of capital with his
electors to be able to get away with this.

Chenet was also, Mhevet noticed, not trying to
browbeat the castellan. Wise move.

"I do sympathize with your dilemma," Chenet said.
*"I'm not here to tell you your job. I'm sure your sources
can tell you much more about public opinion than I can.
But I'm concerned by the delay in you making a public
statement. You really can't put this off much longer."*

"There's a press conference scheduled for the end
of the week."

Chenet looked unhappy. *"That's several days. Do
you think that's a good idea?"*

"I'd like the public to get the impression that I've
thought about this carefully."

*"They might also think you're vacillating, which
could undermine the report. Worse than that—I've
heard some people muttering that the military has gotten to you."*

Mhevet's eye ridges shot up. She glanced at Garak.

She didn't need to see what he thought of that. "The military," said Garak softly, "wouldn't dare."

Perhaps not, thought Mhevet, but she'd bet her stash of coffee beans that they'd tried.

"I think they might try, Castellan, if they haven't already." Chenet smiled. *"I suspect you'd give them short shrift."*

Garak blinked once, very slowly. Yes, Mhevet thought, they'd tried, and like the blunt instrument that they were, they'd made a mess of it. Garak, she guessed, had run rings around them and then sent them packing.

Chenet sighed. *"You're an old hand at this game, and I doubt I need to tell you that what matters most is perception. We've done exceptional work on this report. If we're going to push this through, we need to be brisk and forceful. The will for this is there, I'm sure, but we don't want to give the opposition time and space to marshal their argument. This could be caught up in litigation for a generation. And that serves nobody."*

"You're right, of course." Garak started tapping at his comm. "I'll clear some space. I want a little time to think more carefully about what I'm going to say, but it will be said by midday of the day after tomorrow. Is that soon enough for you?"

"Of course. I hope you know how much I appreciate the care you're bringing to this."

"You don't know what I'm going to say yet," Garak pointed out.

Chenet smiled. *"I think I do."*

Garak frowned, as if to say, *Don't take anything for granted*, but there was no real threat behind it. "Good-bye," he said. "Give my regards to Carnis. And my assurances. This report will not suffer death by litigation."

The communication ended. The seal of the Office of the Castellan—green, white, and purple—flashed up on the screen. Garak tapped a button, and the rolling news came up. He kept one eye on this and one on Mhevet, sitting opposite.

"Nobody's expecting that you're going to say anything other than that you're giving full support to the report's recommendations," Mhevet said. "That is what you're going to say, isn't it?"

Garak shrugged.

"Who came to see you?" Mhevet mentally ran through some names. "Renel, I bet."

"Good guess."

"Well, he's been the loudest voice raised in defense of the military."

"And, I daresay, one of the most articulate." Garak pondered this. "They do make some good points, you know. Not least the hypocrisy of my position. How can I support prosecutions, given what I have—"

Mhevet lifted a warning hand. "Careful. Remember you're talking to the police."

"—what I may or may not have done in the past."

Mhevet rubbed at a jagged fingernail. "Better."

"Careless talk costs lives."

"I appreciate you're worried, but you're not being

asked to prosecute yourself, are you?" Mhevet said. "You're not even being asked to investigate yourself. You're being asked to open investigations into a series of specific people, at specific times, in specific places, and see whether prosecutions should be brought."

"With a view to setting a precedent for similar investigations in the future," Garak pointed out.

"Well, who knows what might turn up?" Mhevet said. "Who knows even whether there are decent records?"

"The Bajorans have done good work in this respect since their liberation. Almost as if they were hoping this day might come. Not that I mind record keeping per se," Garak said. "My colleagues and I also kept good records. Most of those, however, no longer exist."

"But it's what those records might contain that worries you."

"Everything worries me . . ." Garak murmured. His attention was more than half on the rolling news now, Mhevet saw. She got up from her seat and came around to his side of desk, in time to see the last part of Katherine Pulaski's interview on Mayrat's *Today* show. When she heard the part that implied that the castellan should be prosecuted for war crimes, she knew they would not be discussing enigma tales today. "Oh dear," she said. "That's not exactly helpful."

Garak turned on his comm. "Akret," he said, with commendable restraint.

"I have the Federation ambassador's aide on the line, sir, and it looks like she'll be free later this morning. We can delay the start of the meeting with the representatives from the education forum for a little while."

"I should go," said Mhevet. "I know how much you look forward to speaking to ambassadors."

Garak fell back in his seat. "Will *someone* preserve me from these meddlesome Federation doctors?"

The official residence of the Federation ambassador to the Cardassian Union was high up in the hills of Coranum. The buildings, just after the Dominion War, had been constructed as part of the Headquarters Allied Reconstruction Forces, and had, until recently, housed some of the Starfleet personnel tasked to assist the Cardassian people with the postwar rebuilding. When the HARF mission had ended, nearly three years ago, many of the buildings had been taken down, and the land turned to other purposes, but some were refitted for the use of the embassy. The view was great. Pulaski only wished she could enjoy it more. She was very conscious of Efheny, sitting beside her in a pleasant but bland waiting room, sighing over the turmoil into which she had thrown his meticulous schedule. She felt bad about causing him trouble.

Eventually the doors to the ambassador's office opened, and a smart young Trill aide led Pulaski into a rather funereal room. The new ambassador from the Federation to the Cardassian Union, T'Rena, had re-created a little part of Vulcan here in the Cardassian capital. She rose from her desk as Pulaski entered, greeted her with formality, and then gestured to her to sit down. Pulaski sat and waited while T'Rena studied her thoughtfully.

"I must say," T'Rena said at last, "that in fifteen years in the Federation diplomatic corps, I have never seen a single interview cause so much furor and delight."

Vulcans, thought Pulaski. *You never knew if you were being praised, patronized, or both.*

"I'm not sure what to make of that," she said frankly. "So I'll just say 'thank you.'"

"Certainly the 'casts are abuzz with your intervention. The Cardassian people enjoy current affairs as much as their hound-racing. Do you know that you have been a great hit with the Cardassian people?"

"That's good, isn't it?" Pulaski said.

"Not entirely. Speaking from my perspective, and reading between the lines of the rather frosty communication I received from the castellan's office, I have to say that it's something of a pity that you familiarized yourself only with the intricacies of the hound-racing."

So the castellan hadn't liked hearing the truth? That was his own damn problem. "Even if I was up to speed with every damn story happening right now across the whole damn Union, I would've said the same thing," said Pulaski. "War crimes should be prosecuted and their perpetrators punished. I don't think I'm saying anything too outré here. I bet the Cardassian people agree with me."

"Many do," conceded T'Rena. "Although there is some considerable opposition from parts of the military."

"I bet," Pulaski muttered.

"And may I remind you as a Starfleet officer you are bound by the Prime Directive, which forbids involvement in the affairs of other civilizations?"

"Rubbish," said Pulaski firmly. "These crimes were committed on Bajor. Bajor is a member of the Federation. We're already involved."

T'Rena barely raised an eyebrow. Pulaski had the distinct impression that the ambassador didn't particularly disagree with anything she was saying. But diplomacy was a tricky business, or so diplomats liked to tell her. Well, someone had to eat all those canapés and live in all those grand official houses. "Perhaps," said T'Rena, "keep your upcoming speech away from current affairs." Dryly, she added, "Feel free to discuss the hounds in as much detail as you like."

Fair enough, thought Pulaski. She didn't *want* to cause these damn diplomatic incidents. They just seemed to *happen*. "I'll say sorry, if you like," Pulaski offered. "I'll say sorry to whoever you like. Particularly the castellan. If that would help."

Did she see a faint blanching of the other woman's impassive face? "I will deal with the castellan," T'Rena said. "There's something else over which I'd like you to exercise some discretion."

"Fire," said Pulaski.

"The post of chief academician."

Pulaski looked at her in amazement. "What? Don't tell me I said something wrong there? Surely Lang is a given?"

"One would imagine so," said T'Rena. "And yet it's quite clear that the castellan doesn't want her."

"Doesn't want *Lang*? Why ever not? She's surely the most experienced, most capable, and most respected senior academic at the U of U?"

T'Rena lifted up her hands. "And yet here we are."

Pulaski thought for a while. "Are you sure you've got this right? I know sometimes Cardassians don't always say what they're thinking. All the damn subtext, all the time."

"I am quite sure. When the castellan says to me, 'I have a younger candidate in mind,' as he did at your reception last night, I am inclined to take him at face value."

Pulaski snorted. "Age, huh? Ain't that always the way? She's older, she's a woman—"

T'Rena shook her head. "I don't think it's anything to do with that. But he has a clear preference."

"Who's the lucky boy? I'm guessing it's a he?"

"As it happens, yes."

Pulaski gave a hard laugh. "Color me unsurprised."

"He's a surgeon. More to your liking, I would have thought. His name is Vetrek. I spoke to him at the reception last night. He's talented, clever . . . is what I think one could call likeable."

"I surely think the world could do with more medics in charge," said Pulaski. "But why not Lang?"

T'Rena leaned back in her chair. "The castellan does not make his thinking clear to me in all things," she said, "but I can offer some conjecture. Vetrek is part of a generation that did not hold power during the last days of the Occupation or during the last days of the war. This generation has grown to prominence entirely in the postwar era—by which I mean, under the push for democracy. Many of them already hold significant posts—the current head of the city constabulary, for example, is really quite a young woman. Part of this is because there were so few people left that many were promoted early. And it's clear to me that the castellan is keen to see them advance further."

"Oh, I see," said Pulaski. "Time to nudge the old guys toward retirement."

"I believe that's the message the castellan hopes to send. That the balance of power between the generations is beginning to shift." There was the faintest glimmer of a smile. "But as yet to nothing more significant than the administration of a university."

"I guess they've got to start somewhere. Seems a shame for Lang, though. Can't say I approve, to be honest. We older women have a lot to give, don't you think?"

T'Rena inclined her head.

"So much intrigue over a university appointment of all things!" Pulaski said with a laugh. "Could the stakes be any lower?"

T'Rena looked up sharply. "Here, I think, lies your misunderstanding. The University of the Union holds a special place in the hearts of the people of this city." She glanced down at a padd on her desk. "I've seen your itinerary. You have a visit to the campus massacre memorial scheduled for later in the week. I'll send you our briefing about that. You'll find it instructive. Lang is important. To many Cardassians, she's a rare uncorrupted figure from their history. They hold her very dear. If Garak doesn't want her to become chief academician, for whatever purpose, then I imagine he wants to tread carefully. It would assist me greatly, Doctor, if you were scrupulous about following the Prime Directive. The Federation has no official interest in who is appointed, and, as a new ambassador, I would prefer not to offend my hosts so early on."

Pulaski understood. If T'Rena—or anyone from the Federation—was seen to take sides on this, the ambassador stood to lose negotiating power with the castellan, power she might need for more important battles. Pulaski shook her head. Damn diplomacy. It *stank*. "Still not fair to Lang, is it?"

T'Rena pondered this. "On the surface, no. But, as you say, this is Cardassia, and there will be subtext here." Her brow furrowed. "I would like to be able to work out what that is, mind you."

"I *am* sorry about all this," Pulaski said. "I'll run the acceptance speech for the medal past your office too, if that would help."

"That," said T'Rena, "would certainly set my mind at rest."

My dear Doctor—

So at last we have escaped the residence, and, if we can only slip away from my security detail for a little while, we will find ourselves walking through the streets of Tarlak. Here, under the old dispensation, stood the government buildings from which our great Union was administrated. And, because we are creatures of habit, and because we did not wish to detach ourselves entirely from our past, we have built many of these places again; but, because we do not wish to smother ourselves entirely with our past, we have retooled them. Here you will find the Assembly Hall, where the old Council Chamber stood. The Detapa Council, in our so-called glory days, did nothing more than rubber-stamp the decisions of the military, but our Assembly forms policy, debates policy, and legislates. You will find the offices of our new Intelligence Bureau here; the Obsidian Order was, of course, more dispersed, inhabiting dark corners, and operating primarily through the fear it instilled in the hearts of our citizens. The old city shaped the contours of the new, but has not directed its operations.

When I was serving as our ambassador to the Federation, I took the time to visit as much of your beautiful world as I could, Doctor. As you know, I made my home in Paris, but I saw many of your cities, particularly in that blood-soaked continent of Europe. In London, I wished the stones could talk, as each one seemed to weigh heavy with history. In Rome, I glimpsed the origins of your dark and violent past, in the laws that made some people citizens and other people slaves. And in Berlin, I saw a city that had redeemed itself. I walked through a district that had at one point been the administrative center of a vile regime, and which had been laid low at the end of a great and bitter war.

I loved Paris, Doctor, but I knew Berlin. I pass through a city like that every day.

Before we leave, let me show you a place that matters to me greatly. Here before the Assembly is a little stone garden. As you know, Doctor, water has always been scarce here, and our gardens could easily be poor things, sad plants struggling for life. In our stone gardens, however, we turned this scarcity into a virtue, making the rock itself a source of beauty and variety, their natural geological patterns coaxed into formal and abstract mosaics. And, here and there, the fragile flowers, clinging on. This garden was built to remember Alon Ghemor. He was my friend from boyhood and, later, my Castellan, and he died. He died. So many have died.

And I live to grieve another day.

Garak
[unsent]

Four

Throughout the long day, Elima Antok worked, bringing all her careful and methodical skill to the task at hand and, slowly, under her patient and forensic glare, Project Enigma began to surrender its secrets.

Antok knew from her own family history that the story of the Bajoran-Cardassian children was a great stain on the Union's history, and that there were few happy endings to be found. Some of these children—a very few, she would say, and she was the expert—might have been products of love, but even then the disparity in power between the Cardassian soldiers and the Bajoran women they had taken to their beds made it hard to see the liaisons as consensual. Take her own grandmother, for example—brought to Cardassia Prime by her lover, but kept secluded on a distant country estate, passed off as a housekeeper, and rarely seeing her son. Had it been worth it to buy that child's safety? From where Antok was sitting, alive and free and in no danger, yes, it had been worth it, because that was the reason she was alive. But what had that poor woman's life been like? Antok grieved to think about that. Had there been family back on Bajor? A husband? Other children? She had been unable to find out much about her grandmother's life on Bajor. Despite the Bajorans' best efforts, the Cardassians had not cared enough to document their subjects' lives in detail. Perhaps it was a blessing in disguise.

Antok's grandmother had been one of the lucky ones; her son had thrived. They had been unusual. More common was the story of the orphans abandoned on Bajor, the products of rape, most likely, whose mothers had died or did not want them, and had left them as double outcasts—unwanted reminders of a cruel past. Antok had worked with several charities on Bajor that helped such children. All were adults now—those who had made it—and life had eased considerably since Bajor's admission to the Federation. Many had left Bajor, where they were still not readily accepted, and had moved to other worlds. Some had found homes, and happiness, but almost all of them still carried scars. None had come to Cardassia.

And now there was Project Enigma, and learning its secrets only brought her more grief. There had been twelve children involved, of varying ages, taken from Bajor to Cardassia Prime. This Antok had learned early on—but what she had not yet been able to establish was why. So she read on, through file after file detailing their ages, their health, their attainment levels. The documentation had been meticulous but unrevealing. And then she found the medical files, and she began to understand.

They were wanted, these children, and they were wanted because they looked Cardassian—as her own father had. Family had been everything in the old Cardassia, raised to a moral imperative, and powerful families lost status if, for whatever reason, they could not or did not produce large families. Adoption within families was a time-honored way around this; adoption outside of the family sometimes happened, but rarely, because it was the bloodlines that counted. Why these children? What did they have to offer?

Antok read on through the medical files. That fear of exposure that her own grandfather had risked—that his son's children might look Bajoran—was exactly what Enigma had been set up to address. The twelve children—half male, half female, mostly toddlers and babies—had been treated with experimental gene therapy to remove the Bajoran part of them. For three of the children, this had not been a happy experience. Their health was already poor, even before the therapy. One had died; two had been left infertile and therefore useless for the purpose for which they were being retooled. She saw records of their removal to a state orphanage—but those, in the old Cardassia, did not have a good reputation. Orphans were considered superfluous, a drain upon family resources. Children from these institutions usually progressed straight to some of the worst work details in the Union. She doubted that they had lived very long. Still, Antok took note of their names, and swore to them that she would move mountains to discover their fates, and, if need be, say the right words over them, the right prayers.

That left nine other children. On these the treatment had worked, apparently—Antok drew the line at calling it a "success"—and, as a result, the children had been adopted, all by well-to-do families. Presumably, therefore, they had gone on to live as Cardassians, and given the kinds of families they had joined, they had most likely enjoyed the best of what the old Cardassia had to offer. No grubbing around dirty fields in remote provinces for them, or hoping that the water ration would not run out before the next one arrived, or rifling through garbage for scraps. There would have been good food, good schools, and the promise of busy, fulfilling lives. Much better lives than they would ever have lived as mixed-species children on Bajor. Antok could hear the justifications for the project running through her head already. If they had survived the Fire, these children were no doubt living as Cardassians now, with no idea of what had been done to them—for Cardassia.

At this point, Antok had to stop for a while. She left her desk, but she could not bring herself to sit with colleagues in the staff room and trade gossip. Instead she went for a walk and tried to clear her head. This was the downside of her chosen field of study, she thought as she sat by the lake and watched the waterfowl. You thought you had come to the end of the horrors of the Occupation, and then something else was revealed to you, some new depravity that sickened you to the core. Under different circumstances, her father could have been one of those children—taken from his mother, forced through treatment (and who knew if and how that had hurt), and then handed out like a prize. He had spoken to her about his past, their heritage, once and once only, just before the age of emergence.

"I know that your grandfather hoped that I would become Cardassian," he said. "But I never forgot her, you know. I never forgot where I came from. Don't forget, Elima. Don't forget the other part of you. Keep it alive, somehow, even if you have to keep it silent."

The afternoon was settling in. Antok went back to her desk, promising herself she would read to the end of the files today. She almost regretted this decision by the time she was done. With the medical files read, she moved on to some of the official documentation related to the project.

Over the course of its life, the medics behind Project Enigma (and Antok had made a note of their names too, in order to see whether they had survived the Fire) had come three times to the Administrative Committee of the Office of the Academy to ask for funding. The committee members were all familiar names from her research into the university. Most of them were long dead; some had died well before the Fire, and a few during. On the third agreement for an extension to funding, a new committee member had joined, and her name was tragically familiar.

Doctor Natima Lang.

At first, Antok thought she had made a mistake. But there it was: plain as day. She checked the dates against what she knew of Lang's career; yes, this was around the time that Lang had taken up several senior appointments at U of U, including acting as a member of this committee. At this point Antok stopped reading, because she couldn't bear to read any more. Her heart was broken. She packed up her files, left the archive, and tried not to cry.

It was Mikor's turn to pick up the children, so she went back to her office for a little while, and wondered what she should do. Her first thought had been sorrow that Lang, of all people, had agreed to this horror, but the more she reflected upon what she had learned, the more she saw the ramifications. This material was explosive; if true, it could destroy the career of one of the most respected public figures in the Union. Antok felt queasy. She, like everyone else, had deeply admired Natima Lang. As a girl, before Lang had defected, she'd harbored ambitions of studying with the professor. She, like many others, had run considerable risk to get her hands on Lang's writing and read what the clearest and most trenchant critic of Central Command had to say. There wasn't an academic of her generation who didn't mention Lang as an inspiration and a model for intellectual fearlessness and personal courage. Antok was not naïve, and she knew that in the old days many people had made accommodations with the authorities in order to survive. She had no doubt that Lang must have done the same. But to give consent to a project like this . . .

Again, Antok had to work to quell her nausea. She shouldn't be shocked, not really, she thought. In the old Cardassia, everyone had been guilty of something, like in the enigma tales that Lang had so recently spoken about so eloquently and so learnedly. But some part of Antok, some idealistic part of her, had hoped that this was not the case for everyone who had lived through the old days. Who could have believed it of Natima Lang?

She took a swig of tea. It settled her stomach, a little, and helped clear her mind. She had decisions to make. She was a historian, and judging the truth or otherwise of historical documents was her trade, and she intended to study them in more detail to be sure. Perhaps these files had been corrupted in some way; perhaps the page with the names had come from another set of files, been detached and then somehow attached to these . . .

In her heart, Antok knew she was clutching at straws. She had obligations, not just to history, but to the living. Lang was poised to become the chief academician. If she took this appointment, and these files came into the public domain, as they surely must eventually, it would harm the U of U. And what about the victims of this? Those children taken from Bajor, experimented on, and sent to live with Cardassians. Surely they deserved the chance to know the truth about their past? Perhaps there were mothers, back on Bajor, who wanted to know what had happened to their children.

Antok sighed. There were many difficult issues at stake here, and not all could be her responsibility. There was only one course of action. If a crime had been committed—and it was a crime to subject children to experimental treatment without consent—then it needed to be investigated. She had to go to the police. They could look at the files, decide whether there was anything that needed to be investigated, and proceed accordingly.

Decision made, Antok felt much better. She sent a message to Mikor to say that she was running late. She copied the files onto a data rod and switched off the lights. She locked her office door and headed down the corridor. There were a few students hanging around the common room (she waved back politely when they said "hi"), but otherwise the building was empty. She walked out onto the campus and went off to the skimmer park. She had just opened the door to her little skimmer and was about to get in when she felt someone put their hand on her arm.

"Don't turn around," a voice whispered in her ear. "No, don't move! Listen. I know what you've found.

Enigma. I know what's in there. And you'd better keep quiet, Doctor Antok. Because I know where you live, and I know where those two little boys go to school. So leave it. Forget you ever saw it. Because I'm watching. And I'll know."

The hand moved away. Antok, too shocked to move at first, leaned against the top of the skimmer for a moment or two. By the time she had gathered her wits and turned around, there was nobody to be seen. *The boys*, she panicked, diving into the skimmer and locking the door. She called Mikor. "Everything okay?"

"*Sure. Kicking a ball around the courtyard. Evrek agitating for* ikri *buns—any chance you can get some?*"

"Of course," she said.

"*You going to be much longer?*"

She took a deep breath. "On my way."

Antok decided that, after all, she would sleep on it.

Katherine Pulaski would be the first to admit that she had many flaws. She knew she was brash, abrasive, and that she rubbed people the wrong way. She knew that there were three ex-husbands roaming the quadrant who would tell anyone willing to listen what a goddamn pain in the ass their ex-wife was. She knew that ambassadors quailed, captains blanched, and admirals swore when her name came up. She didn't deny any of this. But she knew other things about herself too. She knew she was a brilliant scientist, an inspired researcher, a staunch mentor, and—unlike many of her colleagues—a gifted lecturer. No mumbling with her head buried in her padd. When Katherine Pulaski walked up to the lectern, people paid attention. It wasn't just that the content was good—although that was more than half the battle when talking to other scientists, who tended to be swayed by facts rather than performance. Pulaski had struggled through too many deadly lectures in her time. She believed in what she did, and she thought you should believe in it too, and she went out with all phasers blazing to convince you.

It helped that the Cardassians seemed to have taken her to their collective bosom. But leaving that aside, Pulaski knew within minutes that this was one of the best lectures she had given in her entire career. All of it came together: speaker, audience, and subject matter.

"I'm here as a doctor," she said. "I'm here to talk about the nature of the task we perform as doctors. A human poet—and I know how people just *love* poetry—said, 'Physician, heal thyself.' So let's talk about that. How do we practice medicine, and how do we conduct medical research, so that we do no harm? What are our responsibilities, not just to our patients, but to society as a whole? How do we keep ourselves whole, and healed?"

They loved it. They loved it all. They loved her style, frankness, and sense of humor. Pulaski wasn't complaining. She was used to being admired, she was used to being obeyed. She wasn't used to being loved.

When she finished, there was a long question and answer session, where she behaved herself and managed not to be drawn into anything related to war crimes or university appointments. "Give me a break," she said to one questioner who tried to push her for answers. "Or, rather—give the Federation ambassador a break. She's only been here a few weeks. I've caused enough diplomatic trouble today to keep her busy for the next few months. I'm here to talk about science. I'm here to talk about the risks in science."

"But you've argued yourself science can't be divorced from the political," someone called out from the back of the auditorium.

"Of course it can't," said Pulaski. "But do no harm! Just try to do no damn harm! Let the politicians clear up the mess they make. That's why they're paid the big bucks."

She realized, hearing the applause, that she'd been a hit. She found her fondness for the good people of Cardassia increasing significantly by the second. The reception that followed the speech, the kind of lavish and cheerful affair in which academics across the species specialize, only endeared the Cardassian people to her further. What's not to like about having folks come up to you, sing your praises to your face, and tell you that was the best keynote they'd ever heard? People pressed drinks into her hand. Others asked for her racing tips. *I am a mascot*, she realized, somewhat drunkenly. *I am a good luck charm*.

She felt a tap on her arm and turned to find herself face-to-face with a Cardassian male, average height, rather intense eyes. "Hi," she said. "How can I help?"

"I was looking for . . ." He had a slight stammer. "For Peter Alden."

"Peter?" Typical Alden, stealing her thunder. "What do you want with Peter?"

"I guess, well, I guess that you could say I'm in the same field. I read his . . . his last paper. I was very interested."

Pulaski looked around the room. She saw Alden tucked away in a corner with Efheny and pointed over to him. "There he is. He'll be pleased you've read his stuff. So you should—it's good stuff. Great stuff. He should have done it sooner, rather than muck about with that spy nonsense. Do you want me to introduce you?"

"No need," said the Cardassian. He went off across the room but she lost track of him as another figure lumbered into view. It was Therok, smiling at her, and waving a glass about.

"Doctor Pulaski! A triumphant speech! Triumphant!" He grabbed another glass from a tray being carried past and pressed it on her. "*And* you managed to stay on message! Your ambassador must be very relieved."

"I certainly hope so." She glanced around and lowered her voice. "But go on, you can tell me."

"I'll tell you anything, dear lady."

"Then tell me who you want as your successor."

"Speaking confidentially," he said, leaning in, and Pulaski thought, *You're drunker even than I am.* "Speaking confidentially, I don't care." He burst out laughing. "Doctor, I'm heading off into retirement. I've given the best years of my life to the U of U. I saw it through its worst days under the old regime. I saw it through what we thought was its demise. I rebuilt it. Whoever takes over—they can do what they like. I'm done."

Dimly, Pulaski became aware of Alden hovering at her elbow. Most unlike him: he usually had no qualms about inveigling himself into a conversation. "Peter! Come and join us. You remember Peter Alden, don't you, Therok? My colleague from the *Athene Donald.*"

Therok gave Alden a bland smile. "Nice to meet you," he said. Pulaski watched his eyes drift elsewhere. *Ouch*, she thought.

Alden smiled and offered his palm to Therok. "We met the other night, but it's nice to meet you properly."

"So it is, so it is," said Therok, but he had long since decided he didn't need to waste time on this individual. "Excuse me," he said. "Old colleague I must catch . . ." He wandered off across the room, glass still in hand.

"Huh," said Pulaski.

"Well," said Alden, "he is a busy man."

"Pleased with himself too."

"He has reason to be," Alden said, and took a sip from his glass.

"Hmm. Well."

"You have something against him, Kitty?"

"Just defending your honor, Peter."

"Bless you, Kitty, but I think my honor can take care of itself. What's your problem?"

"I just think," said Pulaski, "that if you can't be bothered with the little people, you're probably not so great yourself. That's all."

"I'm flattered to learn that I'm little people," Alden said dryly. "But Therok doesn't need to justify himself. He's done enough for a lifetime. Rebuilding the university after the war. Keeping its reputation intact."

Pulaski gave him a sharp look. "What do you mean by that?"

"Well, you said it yourself. It's easy for research to get corrupted. Imagine what it must be like under a dictatorship," Alden said. "There must be a lot of pressure for it to become all about weapons of war."

"I guess we're guilty of that in the Federation too," Pulaski said.

"Maybe. But my point is if there are any scandals attached to U of U, Therok has avoided them."

Pulaski watched the big man charm his way across the room. "Or he knows how to bury bodies."

"Yes, the bodies," murmured Alden. "This is Cardassia, after all."

"Did you meet the guy I sent over to you?" Pulaski asked.

Alden gave her a puzzled look. "Which guy?"

"Someone who'd read your paper. Wanted to talk to you."

Alden shrugged. "He didn't find me. Must have decided I wasn't worth it." He smiled fondly at Pulaski. "Little people, remember, Kitty? We can't all be big shots."

"I know," she said. "But it's a shame not to meet your only fan."

Antok went to bed, but did not sleep. She read for a while, and turned off the light, and then shifted restlessly on her side of the bed. She lay with her eyes open, listening to Mikor's breathing become slower and steadier as he fell into sleep. She twisted and turned. At length she got up. She checked on the boys, both deeply sleeping, and then went into the small living room, curling up on the sofa and trying to think what was the best thing to do. She heard movement out in the corridor and for a moment was shot through with terror. But it was only Mikor, crumpled and sleepy and tousled.

"Hey," he said. "What's the matter?"

She thought about saying it was nothing, but she had never lied to him. She had trusted him early on with her family secret, and he had not minded, and had become her mate.

"I learned something today, something horrible. I don't know what to do."

He came and sat beside her and picked up her hand, holding it between his and stroking the scales very gently. "Is it something to do with the war crimes report?" he said.

She shook her head. "No. Tangentially. Perhaps."

He nodded. He could put two and two together. He was a smart man. Mikor knew she was working in the archives. He knew that the material she read sometimes concerned people who were still alive. "Mikor," she said, "somebody threatened me today. Somebody threatened the boys." She felt his hand tighten around hers, and then she felt him force himself to relax and begin stroking her hand again. "Someone came up to me in the skimmer park. I didn't see his face. He told me to leave the files alone. He said he knew where we lived, and he knew about the boys."

"All right," Mikor said after a short pause. "Here's what we're going to do. We're going to have a nightcap, and then we're going back to bed. In the morning, I'll take the boys out for the day, up into the country. And you will go and see the police."

"Are you sure about this?"

"Of course I am. Threats about your work? Threats against our children? This isn't the world we've struggled so hard to build! You know it isn't! And I won't have anyone getting away with this. We'll tell the police, and we'll get them to sort it out."

They had their nightcap, as he'd said they would, and then they curled up together, and at last she slept, with his arms around her and their breathing in unison. When she woke, he and the boys were already gone, but he'd left a note.

Let me know what they say. I love you. Be brave. This is not the world we want.

And he was right, as ever, so she dressed and went to constabulary headquarters. She gave her name, and her place of work, and said she wanted to report a threat against her. The officer went off into a back room for a moment and then came out again.

"Could you come this way, please, Doctor Antok?"

She followed him through into a meeting room, where he asked to her wait. After a little while, he came back with a pot of red-leaf tea.

"Will I be waiting long?" she said.

He smiled brightly. "Hope not."

She sat and waited. The room was comfortable enough, but rather sparse when it came to distractions. A small, oval screen on the wall gently burbled out news, but after a while she turned the volume down. She drank some tea. She waited. A message arrived on her personal comm from Mikor, with a picture of the boys in a roadside eatery, stuffing their faces with something sweet and sticky. She wasn't sure whether she was supposed to take a picture of herself in this room, but she risked one anyway, pulling a face to make the situation comical. Then she waited, and she drank some more tea, and waited some more.

After about an hour, the shadow of a figure passed outside the door and halted. Antok heard voices, but couldn't make out what they were saying. Then the door slid open, and a tall woman came in. She wasn't wearing a uniform, but she did wear a small badge on her lapel with the insignia of the constabulary. Antok started to stand up, and the woman gestured that there was no need.

"Sorry to have kept you waiting," she said. "I was across town. Has anyone gotten you something to drink?"

Antok tapped the pot of tea in front of her. It was still warm.

"Great." The woman sat opposite, putting a cup down on the table in front of her.

"Do you want some more?" said Antok politely, gesturing at the teapot. The woman was about her age, Antok thought, perhaps a little older, although she had an air of authority about her that Antok could never pull off. She wondered who exactly this was. An investigator of some sort?

"No need. Coffee." She gave a wry smile. "Mild addiction. Thanks, Starfleet."

Antok smiled. Yes, they were about the same age. They had spent their formative years working alongside Starfleet and Federation personnel, and picked up a taste for their food and drink. Antok still liked the occasional curry. "I didn't catch your name."

"I didn't give it—sorry. I'm Arati Mhevet. I'm the chief of the city constabulary."

Antok stared at the woman in alarm. The chief of the city constabulary was the most senior member of the police in the whole capital. Why was she here? "What is going on?"

Mhevet raised her hands to placate her. "It's okay. You're not in any trouble—"

"I sincerely hope not!"

"What I mean is—we don't usually bring in the big guns for every visitor. The truth is, I'm keeping an eye on anything related to U of U. There's a big decision ahead, and I think we all want to make sure that there are no surprises coming."

Antok took a breath, but she was still pretty alarmed. She'd come in to speak to someone about Enigma, yes. She hadn't told anyone yet, and they'd brought out the police chief? "If you don't want any surprises, you're going to be disappointed."

"Okay," said Mhevet, "let's take this from the beginning. I understand you've been threatened, yes? Where's your family right now?"

Antok explained what her husband had done. Mhevet listened. "All right, I understand why you did that, although it's put them somewhat at a distance. I'm going to send someone out to look after them. Can you tell me why you've attracted this attention, Doctor Antok? Do you think it's connected to your work for the war crimes report?"

Of course, that would be why Mhevet was here. "I'm afraid not," Antok said. "I'm afraid it's more complicated than that . . ." Slowly, reluctantly, she took Mhevet through what she had discovered.

When she'd finished Mhevet sat back in her chair. "Okay," she said. "Right."

"I told you it was complicated."

"And a pretty unpleasant surprise."

Antok covered her face with her hands. To discover that Natima Lang, of all people, was implicated in the most unsavory kind of crime arising from the Occupation? Unpleasant hardly covered it.

"I read your book," Mhevet said unexpectedly. "Incredible work. I wish I could persuade more historians to come over to the constabulary." She looked wistful. "The U of U is turning out some pretty impressive researchers. You'd make great investigators."

"What I need to know," said Antok faintly, "is that I've made the right decision bringing these files to you."

"You've made absolutely the right decision," said Mhevet.

"And I want to understand what happens next."

"Well that," said Mhevet, "is a very good question, and one that I can't entirely answer. Not least because the law on this will soon be in flux, not to mention the jurisdiction under which any crime might be prosecuted. Will it be Cardassian law? Bajoran? Federation? Was the crime transplanting these children from Bajor, or scrubbing their genes, or giving them false identities? I don't think we know yet."

"It was all of these things," said Antok hotly, "*all* of them were crimes."

"Yes, they were," said Mhevet softly. "And we'll be investigating all of them, and if Lang has committed a crime, then she'll be prosecuted."

"She's a very high-profile public figure."

"I know the castellan still hasn't commented on the Carnis report, and I wouldn't presume to know his mind, but I imagine that nobody will be immune from prosecution. Even public figures. *Especially* public figures." Mhevet's personal comm chimed. She read the message and stood. "I'm sorry, Doctor Antok, I have to go and deal with this. Please—don't worry. We take this very seriously. And we take the threat against you and your family very seriously. If you can wait a while longer, I'll send someone to talk to you about how we can protect you. They can take you to your family."

She went off in a hurry. Antok waited, but nobody came for a while. She felt deeply uneasy about the interview she'd just had. It was not that she'd been disbelieved: quite the contrary. Mhevet had listened carefully to every word. And that, perhaps, was what left her uneasy. Antok lived and breathed her research, but she didn't think other people would. Why so much attention to this? Why the chief of the constabulary? Was it simply as Mhevet said, that Lang was so feted? Why did she feel something else was going on? Why did she get the feeling that she was being watched as much for what she might do as for her own protection?

She got up and left, slipping through the busy entrance hall and out onto the street. She didn't want to be watched or protected, she wanted to be left in peace. She wished she had never found those files. She considered her next move, saw a street vendor on the corner, and decided on lunch. As she started to walk along the street, she thought she saw someone move behind her. She turned around, quickly, and saw nobody—or, rather, saw only the usual city crush. *This is silly*, she told herself firmly. *This is isn't the old Cardassia* . . . She bought some *canka* nuts and flatbread from the vendor and sat on a low wall nearby, eating quickly. When she was finished, Antok pulled out her comm and contacted Mikor, saying that she would join them.

But first there was someone she wanted to see. She sent another message to an old university friend, now working for one of the 'casts.

"Lunch?"

There was a pause, then the reply, *"It would have to be second lunch."*

"I'm up for that."

They made quick arrangements, and then Antok jumped on a public skimmer heading out toward Barvonok. She studied all the other people in her carriage carefully, but everyone who got on at the same time as her got off earlier. Soon she and her friend Pa'Kan were eating Federation-style noodles in a trendy café near Pa'Kan's place of work.

"Are you going to tell me what's in these files?" said Pa'Kan, rolling the data rod around in her fingers.

"I'd rather not."

"Okay," said Pa'Kan. "Then why do you want me involved?"

"Backup," said Antok.

Pa'Kan stopped eating with her chopsticks half-way up to her mouth. "Elima, what's going on?"

The good thing about the café was that it had private booths. The bad thing about the café was that you couldn't be sure who was listening. "There might be a story here, but I don't want it breaking yet."

Pa'Kan nodded her understanding. She was in the position of not having to generate news for the ever-hungry 'casts. She was there to work on long-term stories. All the newscasters were obliged by law to devote a certain amount of the resources to careful, long-form journalism. The Cardassians were serious these days about the fourth estate.

"Okay," said Pa'Kan. "But why backup?"

Quickly, Antok outlined her meeting with Mhevet. "I was left uneasy," she said. "I knew she was interested, but I knew she wanted me to leave it entirely in her hands."

"Might be a good idea."

"I'm going away for a couple of days," said Antok. "Taking the kids up to the lake."

"Going off the sensors?"

"Mm. But I'm worried—" Suddenly she grasped her friend's hand. "If I disappear," she said, "if I don't make regular contact—do something. I don't know what, you'll know best what to do, but do something."

At first, Pa'Kan looked as if she was going to laugh. Then she saw how deadly serious Antok was. "Of course, Elima. But really—we're past all that now, aren't we?"

"I don't know," said Antok. "I thought we were. But perhaps I was wrong. Perhaps we've all been wrong."

They pressed palms and parted. The day was wearing on. Antok left to get her skimmer. She had a long journey ahead.

I'm drunk, thought Pulaski, not unhappily, as she entered her suite. She called out for the lights and fumbled to close the door behind her. *Kanar*, she thought, was devilish; exactly the kind of potion you'd expect Cardassians to concoct. Sophisticated on the palate and vicious on the skull. Two nights in a row. Pulaski wondered how quickly the stuff became toxic for humans. She searched the room until she found a glass, and then she drank half a liter of water. That was a start, but what she really needed now was to be outside, taking a gulp of night air to send any potential hangover packing. She filled the glass again, pulled open the sliding doors that led onto the balcony, and went outside.

She drank some more water, then put the glass down by her feet and rested her arms on the rail, looking out. The night was warm, but not unpleasantly so; in fact there was a gentle breeze that, she learned, was the first harbinger of the summer dust clouds that would soon roll over the city, making the air thick and all but unbreathable. But tonight some of spring's freshness remained, and she caught the scent of herbs on the breeze, sharp and pungent. She felt better outside, less claustrophobic. She liked the sounds of a city at night, liked the lights and the sleeping power, and she was starting to be able to pick out landmarks. Coranum was on her left, up on the hills; the bright lights and bold architecture of the Barvonok business district were straight ahead; and, looking down to the right into the bowl of the river and beyond, she saw the Torr district, densely lit and populated, with the shimmer of the trams as they rattled through.

She put her elbows on the wall and looked out, contemplating this city, thinking about how much she liked it and how surprised she was by that. She found herself humming some of the music that had been playing that evening, and then she laughed. Cardassia Prime, of all places! Who would've guessed that she would take to it this way? She closed her eyes, and yawned. So perhaps it was the *kanar*, or the lack of sleep, or her reverie, or a combination of all three. Whatever it was, she didn't hear anyone come up behind her, and she was unaware she was in trouble until she felt a hand go over her mouth and nose, and caught the queasy, unmistakable whiff of a sedative. *Hell*, she thought, as she blacked out, more annoyed at her own carelessness than anything else.

Pulaski woke with a start. The pale pink of early morning was painting the ceiling above. She lifted her arms, and was slightly surprised to find that she had free movement; for some reason, she had assumed there would be restraints. Slowly, carefully, she sat up, swung to sit on the edge of the bed, and looked around.

She was not in her suite on the campus. She was in what seemed to be the bedroom of a fairly ordinary apartment block, albeit very sparsely decorated. A rental, perhaps? Pulaski had no idea. She had no idea where she was, how she'd gotten here, who'd brought her here, and what the hell was going on. The only thing she was sure about was that she had by some miracle dodged the hangover. "Count your blessings, Kate," she muttered.

She walked across to the window and looked out. Up high, maybe the fourth or fifth floor. Other buildings of a similar height were across the way, obscuring any view of the city that might give her a clue to where she was. She looked down at herself. Dress uniform still on, if rather disheveled, and combadge gone, obviously. Comm on the table disconnected. She went over to the door, and, to her surprise, it opened at her approach. She poked her head out, carefully, but there was nobody there. She tiptoed out. She was at one end of a straight, bland corridor, without pictures or decoration, and with a couple of shut doors on either side. She inched her way forward. The first door she passed opened with a gentle *whoosh*, and she winced, waiting for someone to come dashing out. Nobody came. She peered into another plain bedroom and caught her breath. Someone was lying on the bed.

Her captor? Not a very accomplished one, Pulaski thought, leaving doors unlocked and falling asleep on the job. She slipped quietly into the room and approached the bed softly. The figure remained still, curled up in the middle of the bed. As Pulaski got closer, the figure suddenly sat up. She was a Cardassian female, fairly young, clearly very frightened, and holding her palms out. "Keep back!"

"Okay," said Pulaski.

"Who are you?" the Cardassian said. "What's going on? Why am I here?"

"Hey, you're stealing my lines!"

The young woman stared at her. "You're human."

"You're very observant."

"Are you Katherine Pulaski?"

Pulaski stared at her. "I know I have a reputation, but that's ridiculous."

"You're human, and you're wearing a Starfleet dress uniform. There aren't that many Starfleet officers here in the capital these days. Three years ago, yes. Not now. And you were all over the 'casts."

"Huh," said Pulaski. "Don't mention that to our ambassador, if you ever meet her." She looked around the room. "Do you mind if I sit down?"

The woman moved over to let her sit.

"You're right," she said. "I'm Katherine Pulaski. And I'm pretty fed up."

"You and me both," said the woman. "Actually, strike that. I'm not fed up. I'm terrified."

"Prisoner too, huh? Kidnapped?"

The woman nodded.

"And I'm guessing we *are* prisoners," said Pulaski. "I won't insult your intelligence by assuming you haven't tried the doors and the comm and banging on the floors and ceiling and whatever the hell else came to mind?"

"Banged *hard*," said the woman ruefully. "I don't think there's anyone above or below. I think it must be one of those new blocks that are going up everywhere."

"Let's hope people are keen to snap them up and the morning brings a steady stream of visitors," said Pulaski. She glanced at the woman and saw how anxious she looked. "Hey, don't worry. Someone will come looking for us soon. You know, you've got the advantage. How about you tell me your name?"

The young woman lifted her palm in greeting. "I'm Elima Antok. And I hope someone is going to come looking for us soon. Because I really am terrified." She lowered her voice. "I think someone powerful is trying to kill me."

My dear Doctor—

We are heading north now, and a little east. We are leaving behind the public buildings, and coming to the place where people make their homes. This district is called Paldar, and, once upon a time, if you had come this way, you would have been impressed by the leafy streets and the tall townhouses. It was a fine district, civilized, inhabited by what you would probably call in your culture the professional classes—civil servants, academics, and the army of administrators who kept our Union going. Doctors too. Kelas had his home here, once upon a time, but that is long gone. If ever he harbored a desire to return here, he has never mentioned it.

It was such a pleasant place to live, Paldar, and exactly where one would want to bring up a large family. We tended to large families. In fact, as I know from a recent report on the birth rate, we are tending that way again—good news for the Union, as a baby boom always heralds growth and social dynamism, in its infancy at least. These days, our birth rate speaks of our new confidence, our sense that we have a future. In the past, we had many children because we did not think they would all survive. Not in Paldar, of course, which was, after all, such a civilized place, but the old pressure to reproduce remained. Mind you, in the dying days of the old civilian regime, before the Dominion arrived, I believe you could see lines in the streets for water even here.

But until then, this was a comfortable place, with its tall and roomy homes, the shady walks beneath the tall ithian trees, the small shops and pleasant cafes. I would sometimes walk this way as a young man, and look through the windows into other people's lives, and watch the families together, and wonder what that must be like.

There is sadness walking around the place now. The houses are all gone, of course, and so are the families. I gather that when the Jem'Hadar arrived in Paldar on their death march, many of the people here didn't realize what was happening. They didn't realize that it applied to them. Death was for soldiers, or Bajorans, or the poor. They died in great numbers here. Of all the districts of my city, I think this is the most changed. Some came back, despite their losses, and I have seen a few of the old houses carefully restored, with window boxes, and their iron railings, and their fine mosaic work around the doors and windows. One day, I think, this district will thrive again, and fill with families. But it will take a while. And it can never be what it once was.

Garak
[unsent]

Five

The painting was half one thing, half another, but the sum transcended its parts. It was an abstract incorporating floral designs from two worlds, and it rewarded close study. Garak had studied it closely almost every day for some years now. His eye naturally fell on the Edosian orchids, which had, after all, been put there for him, and also for Cardassia there were *meya* lilies, and *mekla*, and long elegant *ithian* leaves, and a scarlet dash of *perek* flowers for the dead. The Bajoran flora he knew less well, but there were lilies for Kira, and basil, and *moba* leaves. He had spent time on Bajor, of course; all Cardassians of his generation and profession had, but he was ashamed at how little he still understood the symbolism. True, their ancient culture was complex, but he should have learned more, even as a conqueror. The artist would have educated him, had she only had the chance. Her painting was the work of someone on the verge of a major flowering, and its creator, half-Cardassian and half-Bajoran herself, had epitomized the best of all possible worlds. She had died pointlessly, but Garak was making it his life's work to ensure that she was not forgotten.

Very gently, he touched the signature, a swiftly done and confident *Z*. "Deep breaths, Elim," he murmured to himself. "Deep breaths." Slowly, and with infinite care, he lifted the painting down from its hangings and carried it over to the packing case. He felt a strange sense of foreboding as he did so. The painting always hung in his place of work, wherever that was. It had hung for a while at the back of the tailor's shop, and then it had traveled with him all the way to Earth. Now it was here, facing him when he sat at his desk in the official residence of the castellan of the Cardassian Union. He carried it with him wherever he went because it kept him conscious of what was at stake. It was there to remind him not to falter, to ensure he did his best—for her, for all Cardassia. Removing it left him anxious. But Garak was not a superstitious man—he was a realist, with many pressing tasks at hand, and he had no time or patience for fancies. The painting was going on loan to an exhibition for a few weeks, where it would hang and be greatly admired, and would make Ziyal's brief and brilliant career better known. And when that was done, it would come back to him. Somehow, in the meantime, he would endeavor not to return to his old murderous ways.

Still, he would not trust anyone else to the task of putting the painting away, so he packed it lovingly and closed the lid of the case, making sure it was secure and sealed. Then he called for it to be taken away. Akret, coming to retrieve it, took the rare liberty of touching him gently on the shoulder. Once Garak was alone again, he lifted the vase of *perek* flowers that always stood before the painting over to his desk, and, with a sigh, he sat back down. One of the scarlet petals was detaching, and he removed it gently and placed it upon his palm. *Perek* for the dead, he thought; the flowers formed the central part of the rite for the dead. He always had them here for her, fresh and real, because he would not replicate them when he had sat by her body on DS9. There had not been *perek* for so very many.

He laid the petal reverently down upon the desk and then picked up a padd, scanning once again the notes his advisors had prepared. An unnecessary ritual—almost, one might say, superstitious: he was on top of his brief, as he always was, but it filled a few moments before proceedings began. He checked the time. Not long. He did some more breathing. He was starting to feel calmer when the comm on the desktop chimed. A private channel, direct to him, bypassing even Akret, known only to a very few, and this caller in particular had never abused the privilege.

"Arati," he said gently, seeing her worried expression, as one might to a beloved child. "Are you quite well? Whatever is the matter?"

"Sorry, boss. I know the press conference is coming. I've just come out of an interview with Elima Antok."

Garak placed the name immediately: he had, after all, been reading some of her work very recently. "The historian? The one who gave evidence to the war crimes committee?"

"That's the one."

Garak, cursed with a fertile imagination, ran through a hundred nightmare scenarios. Was she retracting evidence? Had something emerged to make her change her mind? "What did she want? Is this a problem for the report?"

"Your team can tell you that—I don't know. She's found something in the archive. Something from before the war. If it's true, it's bad news for Natima Lang."

Garak's eyes narrowed. "Oh yes?"

Quickly, Mhevet brought him up to speed on Antok's find. Children, thought Garak; it always had to be children.

"Poor Natima," said Garak, when Mhevet finished, and said nothing more.

"Is that all?"

"What do you want me to say?"

Mhevet rubbed an eye ridge. *"I'm not sure. I thought you might have some idea whether or not it was true—"*

"How would I know either way?"

"Weren't there . . . well, wasn't there a file on her?"

An Order file, she meant. "I should imagine there were numerous files on her," Garak said calmly. He knew this for a fact. He'd devoured Lang's files voraciously, almost as voraciously as he'd consumed her collected works. "She was not," he lied, "a special area of study."

Mhevet was studying him thoughtfully. From the corner of his eye, Garak saw a dash of scarlet petal, like a wound opening beside him. He collected himself. "Arati, I'm not sure what you need me to say. I'm not responsible for Natima Lang's actions before the war. If she made some hard decisions and compromised some dear-held principles, then I am sympathetic, but we are none of us without fault, and we lived in difficult times." He shifted in his seat. Some had contributed more than others to making the times difficult. He checked the time on the chrono. The press conference really was *very* soon . . . "What's worrying you?"

"It's convenient, isn't it, that this has come up now, just as Therok is retiring and Lang's in the running for the job?"

"I see what you're suggesting. That it's less convenience than contrivance."

"Well, yes—"

"If the accusations are baseless, then an investigation will find that."

"But perhaps not in time to save her reputation."

"You'll be amazed," said Garak, "at how far you can get with a bad reputation."

Mhevet pondered him thoughtfully. *"Antok was threatened."*

"That must be deeply unpleasant," said Garak. "I

understand she has young children. Have you offered her protection?"

"Yes, but—"

Garak took a deep breath. "Arati, I have a press conference starting very soon."

"I know, boss. But—"

"But what?"

"Castellan, I have to ask—do you know anything about this?"

Garak stared at her. After a moment or two, she flinched, but she didn't look away. "I'm not going to dignify that with an answer."

Anger, hot and red, flashed in her eyes. *"That is below you, and unjust to me—"*

"Let me be clear what you're asking," he said. "Are you asking whether I have planted files implicating Natima Lang in experiments on children for some reason—perhaps to prevent her becoming chief academician? Or are you asking whether I have had someone knock on the door of a prominent young intellectual in the middle of the night in order to give her the fright of her life? Neither would reflect terribly well on me, would they?"

"It wasn't a knock on the door in the middle of the night—"

"There we are then. I really do have no idea. If I did have anything to do with this, by the way, and had decided to conceal that from you, do you think I would tell you the truth?"

Mhevet, he saw, was furious, and just about reining it back. *"I hope you'd feel you did not have to conceal anything from me."*

"I would suggest that you continue in that hope."

"That," she said, *"is a master class in equivocation."*

The door opened. Akret poked her head around, and, with a fierce expression on her face, jabbed her finger at the chrono on the wall. "I have to go," Garak said. He took another deep breath and controlled his breathing and his rising anger. "Look, Arati, I'm sorry if you think I'm equivocating. I'll tell you one thing, though—the last thing I want is for this whole business to blow up in my face. I trust you to do what you think is best."

She still didn't look happy. She would have to come to terms with that. *"Okay, boss,"* she said, and cut the comm.

Garak gathered his wits and picked up his padd, a helpful prop that gave him something to do with his hands rather than gnaw his nails. On a whim, he grabbed the *perek* petal and tucked it into his pocket. Outside his office, a few of his advisors were flapping about, but his expression, which he imagined to be thunderous, was enough to suppress them. One could tell the truth as much as one liked, he thought, but if nobody believed you anyway, you might as well go back to lying.

He strode down the corridor and out into the glare of the press room. As he walked up to the podium, there was a huge buzz of chatter and a rising whirl of noise as holo-recorders kicked into action.

He took a moment to quell his rising anxiety—and his nausea—and he placed his padd on the podium and gripped its sides. He waited until the walls no longer seemed to be looming. He could control that. Sometimes he thought he could control anything, if he put his mind to it. If he did his chores. He cleared his throat and abandoned the speech his advisors had so carefully prepared for him. He did this a lot. They hated it, and most of all they hated that he invariably gave a much better speech. He knew he was shaving years off their lives. But Garak wasn't getting any younger, and he still had a great deal that he wanted to do, and there were more and more days when he just didn't have the time or the inclination to do anything other than speak his mind.

"You've all read the report," he said to the waiting journalists. "Assemblyperson Carnis and her team have done exceptional work. I commend their professionalism, their meticulousness, and their steadfastness in the face of what must at times have been deeply distressing material. They never lost sight of their goal, which was justice for those who have suffered. I will tell you now that I accept the contents of this report, and I accept their recommendations to the full—"

The room went crazy with questions and noise. Garak lifted his hand for silence. He looked straight down into the holo-recorders, and he imagined he was speaking to all the shades who haunted his days and his nights: the ones who were guilty, the ones

who were innocent, and the ones who were somewhere in between. "Nobody will be immune from
prosecution," said the castellan of the Cardassian
Union, a man whose hands were drenched in blood.
"*Nobody.*"

"Elima Antok, huh?" Pulaski wrinkled her brow, trying to place the name. She was sure she'd seen this
young woman somewhere before. She snapped her
fingers when she remembered: a documentary she'd
watched on her first day, on one of Cardassia's eight
separate dedicated history channels. "I know! The
expert on Bajor!"

Antok looked rather pleased. Typical academic,
Pulaski thought with a smile. Not even kidnapping
could spoil the pleasure of recognition. "Cardassian-
Bajoran relations, more specifically," Antok said,
"with an emphasis on social history."

"Huh?" said Pulaski.

"Interspecies relationships. That kind of thing."

"Oh, I see. Touchy subjects."

Antok sighed deeply and looked around. "Apparently so."

Pulaski cocked her head. "You think your research
is the reason that you're here?"

"It must be," said Antok. "It has to be . . ."

"So what's going on? Is someone trying to make
you pull back from your findings? Someone trying to
avoid being prosecuted?"

Antok shook her head. "No, I think it's something

else. Earlier in the week I found some files dating back to before the war. Dating back to the Occupation. They were from a university committee—"

Pulaski was startled. Never in her wildest dreams could she imagine university committee minutes being so explosive that someone would kidnap over them. "Really?"

"No, really," Antok insisted. "From the medical school."

"Ah," said Pulaski. "Let me guess. Children."

Antok shuddered. "How did you guess?"

"Oh, it's always children," said Pulaski. Not for the first time she wondered why people bothered having kids. They always led to trouble. "Children and the medical school. And you're an expert on Cardassian-Bajoran relations. Let me guess—these were Bajoran kids. What the *hell* were they doing to them?"

"They were children born on Bajor, to Bajoran mothers and Cardassian fathers," Antok explained. "They were forcibly relocated to Cardassia and subjected to gene therapy to remove their Bajoran nucleotides."

"Jeez," said Pulaski, pulling back in revulsion. "Do no harm, folks," she muttered. "Do no goddamn harm. How many lived?"

Antok didn't reply. She put her head in her hands. Pulaski put her arm around the young woman's shoulder. "Horrible thing to find," she said. "Are you okay, Elima? Shall I get you some water?"

"I'm okay," Antok said quietly. "But I should explain—I'm quarter Bajoran."

"No wonder this has hit so hard. Dammit! Why do people *do* these things?"

They sat for a while until Antok was back under control. She glanced at Pulaski and gave an embarrassed laugh. "I've never told that to anyone. Well, my mate knows, of course, but not anyone else. I don't generally go around broadcasting it. None of my friends know; none of my colleagues."

"It's because I'm Federation," said Pulaski. "Nobody gives a hoot whether you're half one thing and half another and half something else. Infinite diversity. Where I come from, it all just adds to the general gaiety of life."

"I miss the Federation," said Antok wistfully. "I loved having you here. All your people—they were so young, so friendly. They laughed a lot, like there was something to laugh about, like they could see that the future was going to be okay. After a while it sort of rubbed off on you. You started to believe them when they said everything would be okay. And one day it was."

"Yeah, well, we've gotten ourselves into plenty of our own messes, you know," Pulaski said. "So you found these files, and the next thing you knew you were here. Why do you think that was? Is the castellan involved or something?"

It was a cheap shot, but Antok, to her amazement, took it seriously. "Oh, no! Not the castellan! It's worse than that—no, really. The files were about funding. Approval was given by a committee—almost all dead now. One survivor." Antok rubbed her brow. "Natima Lang."

Pulaski nearly fell off the bed. "Well, *shit!*"

"Yes," said Antok. "That's what I thought."

Pulaski stood up and walked across the room. The window here gave a better view over the city than hers had, but she just stood and stared and tried to think of something to say that would encapsulate her shock and dismay. After some considerable thought, she came up with, "*Shit!*"

"Quite," said Antok.

"I met Lang the other day," Pulaski said. "She was impressive. It seems damned unlucky that these files turn up just as she's in the running for a prestigious post."

"I agree it's not consistent with Lang's past," Antok said. She sighed and came to join Pulaski by the window. "But that's what things were like before the war, wasn't it? I know we joke that everyone was guilty of something, like we were all living in some kind of enigma tale, but in reality there were plenty of innocent people. Those kids were half Cardassian, and they never hurt anyone. But the other side of that is that sometimes people had to make some hard choices. Maybe signing off on this project saved lives that we know nothing about. Lang ran an underground railroad that saved many of her students, got them out of Cardassian space before the Order could get hold of them. Maybe letting someone get on with this research meant they turned a blind eye to someone escaping the Order." Antok shuddered. "Still, I could never have put my name to that. I could never have given that authorization."

"What I mean," said Pulaski, "is that it could be faked."

Antok frowned. "Faked?"

"Think about it," said Pulaski. "You can't believe Lang could do such a thing. I can't believe Lang could do such a thing. So let's take Occam's razor to the whole business and assume that she *didn't* do such a thing. Perhaps someone wants to ruin her reputation. By someone here," she added, "I mean the castellan."

Antok looked at her in astonishment. "The *castellan*?"

"He doesn't want her to take over after Therok, you know."

"He's wrong," said Antok. "Lang is the obvious person—the best person." Her face went sad. "She *was* the best person."

"Not according to Garak." Pulaski wondered dimly whether the ambassador had meant her to be discreet with the information. She decided not to worry about that.

"But to destroy her reputation to remove her from the running?" Antok shook her head. "That's completely over-the-top."

Pulaski sucked her teeth. "How much do you

know about your head of state? I mean, *really* know? Do you know what kind of man he is?"

Antok looked out of the window. "Everyone knows about the castellan."

"Well, knows what?" Pulaski pressed.

"We know that he was a voice for the Cardassian people within the Federation during Dukat's reign. We know that he and Damar led the resistance against the Dominion. We know that he was a vital voice at that time for our interests within Starfleet. We know that before that he fought with the Federation against the Dominion, and that after the war he stopped the military seizing power. We know he was our ambassador to the Federation at a time when our reputation was nothing in the quadrant. We know he's one of the chief architects of our regeneration— not just the buildings, but something else, something just as important. He's taught us self-respect, the ability to look at each other and not feel dread or shame, but to feel proud again, because we've worked so hard after losing so much—"

"Yeah, yeah," said Pulaski. "And the weather's better too since he came to power, and everyone's favorite hound always wins. You know that isn't the whole story."

"Garak," said Antok stubbornly, "has done remarkable things."

Pulaski lost her patience. "For pity's sake, he was in the Obsidian Order!"

"Well, I know that!" said Antok. "We all know that!"

Pulaski was incredulous. "Don't you *care*?"

"Care? Of course I care! The Order blighted people's lives! They were completely out of control!"

"Then how on earth," Pulaski said in exasperation, "do you all accept this man as your head of state? He was right in the middle of it all!"

"It's complicated," said Antok.

"You bet!"

"Look," said Antok, "it's quite obvious the castellan isn't the man he once was. People change."

"They don't change that much."

"Enough has changed—his view of the world, maybe; the way he operates, certainly. Do you think we're stupid, Doctor? Do you think that we're ever going to let a swaggering bully like Dukat near power again? You tell me that you can't believe that Natima Lang would have anything to do with a project like Enigma. And I tell you that I can't believe that Castellan Garak would destroy an innocent woman for no real purpose. Once upon a time, perhaps." She gave Pulaski a steely look. "Remember that my specialism is the prewar period. I probably know more about Cardassian behavior on Bajor than anyone else in the Union. I have no illusions. But the castellan would not do that."

Pulaski snorted. "Well, you're more trusting than I am."

"Not Castellan Garak. He might campaign for his preferred choice, but if Lang got the post, he'd accept that."

Pulaski shook her head but left it alone. Garak

was a serious player, she could see, and he liked to get his own way. He'd surely done a lot worse in his time than smear an innocent woman. "Hey," she said. "I don't want to quarrel with you. You're my best friend right now."

Antok smiled. "I guess you're my best friend right now too."

"Bad luck," said Pulaski with a grin. "So, what are we going to do next? Will anyone be looking for you?"

"Mikor is expecting me to join him and the boys in the country. He'll start to get worried soon. And I saw a friend of mine just before I got knocked out. I said that I was worried that something might happen to me, and I asked her to get help if I, well, disappeared . . ."

"Commendable paranoia," said Pulaski. "But it won't do us any harm to try to get away under own steam, will it? Cause some trouble for our common enemy? Confound his politics, frustrate his knavish tricks." She looked out of the window. "Do you have any idea where we are?"

Antok looked around. "It's hard to guess, I can't see much. But these buildings look like one of the new developments out on the western edge of Paldar."

Pulaski tried to remember the map of the city she'd looked at. "Not so central, huh?"

"Not really."

"So how would we get back to the center of the city?"

Antok didn't get a chance to speak. The door behind them opened.

Pulaski swung around to see a Cardassian male standing in the doorway. Antok shrunk back, and Pulaski put herself between her and their captor. "Are you the bastard that's brought us here?"

"Doctor Pulaski," he said.

"That's me. What do you want?"

He stared at her. "Why are you here, Doctor?"

"Huh?" she said. "You're the one who brought me here—"

He took a step or two forward, out of the shadows, and she recognized him right away as the Cardassian who had spoken to her at the reception, the one who had asked her to direct him to Alden. She also saw that he was carrying a phaser. "Sonny," she said, "if you wanted to go out for a drink after the party, all you had to do was ask."

"Stop it," he said. His gray hand on the phaser was quivering slightly. This was a person under stress. She moved, very slowly, farther in front of Antok.

"All right," she said, in gentler tones. "I'm trying to understand what you want."

"I want to know why you're here on Cardassia Prime."

"Son," she said, "I think you're expecting an answer I can't give. It's all completely straight-forward. I'm here to make a few friends and to get a medal. I don't think that's the answer you want, but it's the truth."

His hand shook more. "I don't believe you—"

"It's true," she said. "Nothing more, nothing less. If you think I'm here for some deep dark reason, you're mistaken. I know you're in a fix right now, but we need to think about how we can all get ourselves out of this. Yes? Work together? Do you understand me?"

She heard the soft chime of a personal comm. He looked down, fumbling in his pocket, and read whatever message had arrived. Pulaski saw his face change, to something ugly and angry and not entirely balanced. *Hell*, she thought. *He's going to lose it.*

The doctor knew that what she was about to do was a risk, but watching his face, she genuinely believed she had to take that risk or face far worse consequences. He was armed, and he was dangerous. So she made her move. She sped across the room and grabbed at the arm that was holding the phaser. It unbalanced him, and for a moment she thought she had him. But his reactions were superb—training, she wondered, or just living on the streets? He twisted around, and was soon back in control. She felt the snub nose of the phaser up against her, and then he fired. As she went down, stunned, she saw him grab Antok, pull her screaming from the room, but she could do nothing. Her limbs were numb and dead. A minute later, everything went black.

Natima Lang was looking forward to a long break. She was taking the next term as writing time, in her country home in the Perok district. Second homes were surprisingly common on Cardassia Prime, and not always the prerogative of the very wealthy. The cities had suffered great destruction when the Jem'Hadar had gone on the march, but distant country houses, often standing empty, had tended to survive, and ultimately somebody had to inherit. Natima Lang had inherited from an old friend, a woman who had once been head of state. Meya Rejal had been part of the dissident movement and had later formed the first civilian government of the Cardassian Union. Her rule—and her life—had ended when Dukat seized power. Dukat had briefly installed one of his lackeys in the house, but after the war, and the Fire, after the first terrible years of privation and despair, the wheels of justice had slowly begun to turn, and Natima Lang found, to her amazement, that she was a beneficiary of Rejal's will. The house—and what was left of its once considerable library—were now all hers.

And there she was going, in a few days' time. The last of her lectures was now delivered, and she had only a single tutorial left to give, and she was going through her usual end-of-term ritual of clearing through old files. She was performing the task with more thoroughness than usual. She knew that her life was on the verge of a great change, although she was not sure yet what form that change would take.

Lang was not a vain woman, nor was she the

kind to believe that she was entitled to a position, no matter how qualified she was. She did not assume that the post of chief academician was hers by right. But she knew that many people believed that she was the right person for the job, and she thought so too. Her years of battling for the university's independence while they were at the mercy of Central Command; her defense of students that had saved the life of some of them; her tireless work on committee after committee, helping the U of U rebuild since the end of the war: all of this, now, was surely about to earn its reward. Pausing for a moment in sifting through her recent correspondence, Lang looked out of the window across the campus. The lawn before the building was busy: groups of students dotted here and there, working together to prepare for exams. Lang smiled. So much industry; so much hope. It was a privilege, she knew, to be part of forming the aspirations of so many young people. It was a great responsibility too: helping to furnish the minds of people that would go on to produce policy, work for the Assembly, go into the newscasts, and create the art and literature that would challenge the politicians and policymakers that their peers would become. She smiled looking out on them. She loved this place. More than anything in the world, she wanted to lead it. She had a vision for the university, as a place at the heart of a civil and democratic society. They were close, so close, but she knew she could do more . . .

And yet the castellan thought that Tret Vetrek was better suited. Lang sat back in her chair, considering this. What, she wondered, had she done to earn the castellan's disapproval? He had read her books, she knew, and he admired them—he had told her that at a reception a year or two ago—so she had been surprised, and more than a little wounded, to discover via the grapevine that she was not his first choice to be Therok's successor. They had met all that time ago, on Deep Space 9 . . . She pondered that meeting, but was embarrassed to realize that she hadn't paid much attention to the lowly tailor. Had she offended him then? Had she slighted him? Quark hadn't thought much of him, but Lang had not always taken Quark's opinion on face value. Yet there it was. The castellan did not want her to be chief academician, and the fact was that the castellan's opinion carried considerable weight on Cardassia these days. While he had not come out and openly stated a preference, he had allowed it to become known where his preference lay, and that might well be enough to swing the vote of the governing body against her. Vetrek was an energetic and clever man, progressive, and Lang knew he would do good things at U of U. But that would be poor consolation.

And if she did not win this prize? What then? She looked through a set of notes from earlier in the year. Retirement, she thought, surprising herself with this sudden decision. One more year, perhaps two, then leave the university to that upcoming generation.

Perhaps she would travel. She had seen very little of the Federation, and she thought she would like to see more. She would like to see a mature democracy, see how it worked and what the dangers might be, maybe of complacency and forgetfulness. Yes, she thought, consigning the files to oblivion. She would start with Bajor, and she would work deeper into the Federation and she would write another book . . .

There was a tap at the door, and her new aide, Servek, put her head around. Lang tensed up. She didn't much like Servek, who had come from Therok's office at the start of this term. The move had made sense once Therok announced his retirement: Lang guessed that passing on his staff to her was meant to be a nod and a wink that she was his chosen successor. But the truth was that she would rather Servek had gone somewhere else. The woman was constantly saying things like, "I'm a very open person." Lang found her secretive. If this had been prewar Cardassia, Lang would have assumed that Servek was from the Obsidian Order. She was old enough to have been an adult before the Order collapsed, Lang knew, so perhaps there was some truth to that. Not an Order operative, but one of those all-too-many citizens who was happy to be an informer. Perhaps she had never quite lost habits acquired then. Still, Lang was stuck with her, and so she forced a smile to her face.

Servek looked quickly—surreptitiously, Lang thought—around the room. "Clear-out going well, Professor?"

"Very nicely, thank you. Can I help?"

"That was really what I came in to ask you."

"I think this is something that needs my personal attention. But thank you."

She turned back to her computer. Servek hung around the door.

Lang, forcing another smile, looked up. "Was there something else?"

Servek, she saw, had a pained expression on her face. "I don't know how to put this, Professor . . ."

Lang leaned back wearily in her chair. "Please don't feel constrained around me."

"Well, I *am* a very frank person," Servek said. "It breaks my heart to say this, but I feel like you don't trust me, Professor."

I don't, thought Lang. Still, she thought she'd done a better job of concealing it.

"I worked with the chief academician for many years, you know. Before the war too. I'm very discreet . . ."

She went on in this vein for a while. Lang listened with an attentive expression on her face. The problem these days, she thought, was that people didn't have enough genuine problems to worry about. Not that she would wish the bad times back, but some people really found grievances in the most trivial of things.

"I hear what you're saying," said Lang, almost, but not quite, embarrassed by the shameless manipulation of such a statement. "It's a pity we've not quite managed to find a way to work together yet. I must admit that I'm not used to having assistance." This was not quite true. The department in which Lang worked had a press officer dedicated to handling her public appearances, and Lang got along with her just fine. She saw Servek's face: she was thinking the same thing. "What I mean is, I'm used to handling my administration myself."

"That's a significant burden, Professor. I can *help*."

"I have very well-established practices."

Servek looked down at the ground and gave a pained sigh.

Help, thought Lang. *I've been pinned down by a passive-aggressive colleague.* "Perhaps you could look at some of the correspondence from the start of the year," she said, keying in some codes to give Servek access. "See if there's anything that needs to be followed up."

Servek smiled and left. Lang rolled her eyes and carried on with her work. She was starting to think that Therok had simply wanted to get rid of Servek. Lang made her first executive decision. If she *did* become chief academician, Servek was not coming with her.

Elim Garak and the Federation diplomatic corps had been in an amicable war of veiled insults for the best part of a decade. Actually, thought Garak—that was not entirely fair. He had been unfailingly polite in all his dealings with the Federation diplomatic corps. They, meanwhile, seemed to do things specifically designed to offend him. For example, when Garak had taken up the post of the Union's ambassador to the Federation, he had been given a splendid residence in Paris, the City of Light. Garak adored Paris. He thought it was the most beautiful place he had ever seen, not least because of the thriving fashion houses. But he loved it too because its architecture was not blandly Federation-standard as was the case in so many other cities he had visited on Earth (he shuddered to remember the horrors perpetrated in Cambridge).

Garak's official residence in Paris had been a grand old town house. Naturally, he had researched its history, and thus he had discovered—as his hosts no doubt intended—that it had, at one point in its history, been the residence of a representative of a government so brutal, so vicious, that their name had become a byword for horror in human history. Garak had considered being offended, and then decided to take it as flattering that he was considered worthy of such a carefully calculated insult. When Garak returned to Cardassia and became castellan, the Federation diplomatic service had risen to the challenge once again, and sent him a Bajoran as their ambassador. When she was recalled, he did not think they could surpass this. But they had. With the exquisite cruelty that they had shown to him on so many occasions, they had sent him a Vulcan.

Garak, at his best, could charm even Bajorans. (Not Kira Nerys. Charm had not been key to winning over Kira. Killing other Cardassians had been necessary to prove himself to Kira.) But Garak had never, to his certain knowledge, managed to charm a Vulcan. They were, he thought, entirely without charm. Cardassians, for all their faults, could be passionate. The trick had been to divert these passions away from things like murder, conquest, and national pride, and toward healthier pursuits like democracy, lifelong education, the news, and hound-racing. But Vulcans, now. Vulcans were a trial.

Ambassador T'Rena lifted her cup of red leaf tea and gently breathed in the vapor. "An unusual combination of flavors and scents."

"Wait till you taste it," said Garak. The problem was, he knew, that Vulcans tempted Garak into flippancy. And really one could not be flippant about war crimes. Particularly not when one represented the perpetrators.

T'Rena tasted the tea. "Not unpleasant."

"Mostly harmless," said Garak.

She looked up at him calmly. "I beg your pardon?"

"It's a quotation from a human classic," said Garak. Rather a flippant one. He tried to get a grip on himself.

T'Rena studied him until he felt rather like a specimen splayed out and awaiting dissection. "Of course," she said. "You have made a special study of human literature."

She made him sound like a professor. The truth was that there had been many long, lonely hours to fill on Deep Space 9, and Garak had wanted things to talk about with Bashir. Still, he thought, should he ever find himself in need of a new job, he could probably write novel reviews for a living. He pondered that possible future. He discovered he was rather taken with it.

T'Rena took another sip of tea and nodded. They would get by, he supposed, if she liked red leaf tea. He wondered what *kanar* would do to her.

"We welcome the news that you are accepting the report in full," she said. "I do not believe I am speaking out of turn when I say that the Bajoran people also welcome this news."

"I've spoken privately to the chief minister," said Garak. "There was some discussion of a ceremony of reconciliation. There are complications, of course, surrounding inviting a Cardassian leader on a state visit to Bajor. Many people think it's too soon. Many people think that I am not the right head of state."

"There's a long road ahead, Castellan," she said. "And while symbolic meetings certainly have their place, I believe the Federation is interested in the legal ramifications of this policy." She studied him thoughtfully. "In my preparation for this role, I spoke to many victims of the Occupation. They all spoke of the desire for justice, and their need to see their tormentors punished—"

"I share that desire," Garak said softly.

"Many also told me that they did not trust Cardassian justice." She picked up her cup again and drank. "They have experienced it. They do not want anyone prosecuted under Cardassian law. They want extraditions to Bajor."

Garak bit his lip. Carnis, in her report, had anticipated this, but had dodged making any recommendation. Sensible woman. Pursuing war criminals was one thing. Trying them under Cardassian law was another thing. Extraditing them to face trial on Bajor—which now, of course, meant to face trial in the Federation—was yet another. *Why,* Garak thought peevishly, *is doing the right thing always so complicated?* His eyes drifted over to the wall, to the space where Ziyal's painting customarily hung. He reached into his pocket and found the *perek* petal there, soft and soothing to the touch. T'Rena, he saw, was observing him carefully. "An issue for another day," she said.

He got the impression that she was being kind to him, which left him rather off guard. He was not used to people being kind to him. He was rather touched. He was also not entirely prepared for her next question, which she asked when his cup was up to his lips.

"Are you concerned that you might face trial?"

Garak, with significant self-restraint, did not spit out his tea. Instead he swirled the liquid around in his mouth, swallowed, and then looked up at her. "Commendably direct, Ambassador." The chime on his desktop comm sounded. "Saved by the bell," he said. "Do you mind if I take this?"

She nodded, almost imperceptibly. As a rule,

and as a matter of courtesy, he didn't generally take calls when speaking to the representatives of foreign powers, particularly of allies. But he also didn't want to carry on the conversation. As he read the message from Mhevet, however, he began to think that he might have been better off ignoring it and facing that gentle, passionless interrogation instead.

"Ambassador," he said, "I have some most concerning news."

One delicate eyebrow was sharply raised. She would know that he would have chosen his words carefully and she would parse them correctly: "most concerning" being some considerable distance from "very bad." She would know that war, at least, was not imminent, but that life was perhaps in danger. "The young man assigned to Doctor Pulaski went to her suite this morning, but it seems that she cannot be found."

T'Rena went still. "Was there any sign of force?"

"None that we can see—but there are traces that a transporter was used, twice, during the night."

T'Rena nodded.

"Let me assure you that everything is being done to find her," Garak said. "This is obviously not acceptable, and my best people are on it." He closed his eyes and pressed his fingertips against them.

"Castellan, is there something else the matter?" T'Rena said.

"There's nothing else," he lied. She did not need to know Mhevet's other piece of news: that they had lost track of Elima Antok. He would prefer not to look like things were spinning out of control. To lose one doctor could be regarded as a misfortune; to lose two looked like carelessness. Losing three was nothing short of a tragedy.

"Nothing at all."

My dear Doctor—

Now we come to the heart of the empire. We have come to the hills of Coranum. Here the powers of the Union once lived in their mansions, as your Greek gods once sat upon Mount Olympus, and the Union was their playground. Money begets money, and power begets power, and by the end, the people who lived in Coranum might as well have been living on the moon, like the Autarch of Tzenketh, who, you may or may not know, really does live on a moon, high above his subjects, who gaze up adoringly at him while he looks back down and presumably thinks what a bunch of gullible idiots they all are.

Ab-Tzenketh is a very silly place. I'll tell you more about it one day.

Coranum. I suppose they were happy here, the rich, al-though my father lived here, and I can't say that he was exactly happy. Self-satisfied, often, but never happy. He, like most of the people running Cardassia by the end, was completely detached from reality. But then, it has been my observation that the very rich and powerful do not have to bother much with reality. They are entirely cushioned from it and the conse-quences of their actions. For that reason, at least, I am glad that my father died in prison. I doubt he reflected much upon his actions in his last days—you could tell me more about that, I suppose—because reflection was not in his nature. But if for one brief moment he understood even a little of what he had done, grasped how many lives he had blighted . . .

I am fooling myself, of course. You might remember that almost the last thing he said to me was to issue orders about whom I should kill next for him. Then he tried to bribe me with a memory, and then he died.

For reasons that one of your Starfleet counselors would not find difficult to guess, I have made my home here. It is not a mansion, by any stretch of the imagination, although it is built, in part, from the ruin of one. I came home to nothing. I brought back with me only what I had acquired on the station, and I had lived lightly there, hoping that I would suddenly be called home. Even after the Obsidian Order fell, and I knew that it would take nothing short of a miracle for me to return, I had lost the habit of acquisition. I brought some books back with me, some clothes, some pictures, and many memories. It was a start. Most of what I own now I have pulled from the wreckage. I live among the flotsam and jetsam of my species.

My home is five small rooms built from some of the larger pieces of stone that I found, and a pile of building material supplied by the Federation when they were here. I will be the first to admit that it has a ramshackle air. But I am comfortable here. The rooms are comfortable. The chairs are comfortable. The kitchen is comfortable. I was mad to leave.

My real pride is, of course, my garden. I have worked hard here. Parmak helps, although he has a tendency to kill plants on touch—worrying in a doctor. He can't do too much damage. The plants are hardy, the flowers have their own agenda, and not even Parmak can kill dry stone monuments. At night, when the air is clear and there is no dust, you can *sit outside in the lamplight, among the cool stones and the sweet herbs, and you see the whole city below, and you are content.*

Come and visit one day. You will like the view from the hill.

Garak
[unsent]

Six

Pulaski woke and groaned. She was lying on the floor and she felt sick. She rolled over, groaned again, and grasped out for the side of the bed. She felt for her combadge. Nothing there. She opened her eyes and slowly, with her legs wobbling beneath her, pulled herself up from the floor and came to rest sitting on the edge of the bed. She gave another groan.

"I am too damn old for this damn nonsense," she grumbled to the room at large.

The empty room. There was no sign of Antok and no sign of their captor. Pulaski rubbed first one leg, then the other, trying to shake off the last of the numbness. The effects of being stunned were, she thought, considerably less pleasant than a hangover. The treatment was much the same, however. She needed to drink plenty of water.

As soon as she had the queasy feeling under control, she hauled herself up and hobbled over to the bedroom door. It opened at her approach. Whoever this guy was, if he wanted to be a success in the kidnapping business, he needed to start thinking about locking doors. She poked her head out of the door.

"Hey," Pulaski called out, looking up and down the corridor. "I'm awake. I'm not going to try anything funny. I *can't* try anything funny, not after you stunned me. But I need a drink of water, okay?"

No reply. She left the bedroom and inched her way down the corridor, partly through incapacity, partly because she didn't want any passing Cardassian kidnappers jumping her. Again. She tried the doors, one by one. The bedroom where she had initially woken was empty. There was a small bathroom on the right-hand side of the corridor, also empty, and the door at the end of the corridor opened into an empty L-shaped living space. She poked her head in and called out, "Hey! Elima? Are you there? What's going on?"

Nothing. She went into the room. Nobody. She found the kitchen area, equipped with basic equipment, and tried the tap. Water came sputtering out. She ran it until it was cool (a Cardassian would have looked on in horror at this profligacy), filled a glass, and sat down with a bump on the nearby couch. This could be a nice apartment, she thought, looking around. A young professional couple would probably be very happy here before their family arrived. Space would be tight after that. Yes, it would be great for them. However, Pulaski was eager to be free of the place. She gulped the water down, feeling better as she did so, and pondered her situation.

The first thing that puzzled her was how her captor had a Starfleet phaser, but a little thought soon resolved that. Starfleet had been here for years leading the reconstruction effort and, even with the best intentions, equipment, even weapons—particularly weapons—had a way of walking off. It was not ideal, but it happened. There were safeguards, but there were also ways to work around this. Presumably this phaser had been stolen and left behind when Starfleet removed all its forces and equipment from Cardassian space. So no clues there, other than that her kidnapper knew how to lay his hands on a stolen weapon. Well, he hadn't struck her as a particularly upstanding and law-abiding individual.

Her next question was why she of all people had been snatched. Her captor, before resorting to violence (all right, before she'd taken a pop at him), had said something about wanting to know why she was on Cardassia. Well, she'd been pretty clear about that, or so she thought: she was here for a speech, to accept a medal, and to generally press the flesh with some politicians and academics, and create goodwill (and ideally not create any more diplomatic incidents). There wasn't anything complicated about this, just as there wasn't really anything complicated about Kitty Pulaski, but for some reason this Cardassian had gotten the idea she was up to something. Antok was sure that she had been taken because of what she'd learned about Lang. But why Pulaski? People didn't generally tell Pulaski secrets, particularly not state secrets. She'd only go blurting them out to the nearest passing journalist. No, if this Cardassian thought she was here for some nefarious purpose, he'd picked the wrong person.

"Should be talking to Peter," she muttered, and laughed. But her humor was gallows humor: what worried her was that she wouldn't be able to persuade her captor otherwise. That could get nasty, if she didn't get a move on.

She stretched her legs out, thumping each one in turn to get the circulation going.

"Come on, Kitty," she told herself, "time to get moving."

Pulaski stood up and walked gingerly over to the big windows that took up the whole of one wall. She looked out across the city. Antok had said she thought they were on the far side of Paldar, a district to the north and west of the capital, but she might as well have said they were in Brigadoon for all the good it did Pulaski. She peered out at the other buildings. They looked deserted. Did anyone even live here? Did the trams run out here? How could she contact someone to arrange her rescue? She drank some more water. Again and again she came back to the question: Why the hell was she here? Who was her captor? Who was he working for? Pulaski pondered this. She knew she had put her foot in it during her interview with Mayrat: Could it be connected to that? Had she said something to anger supporters of the military? How did this all square with Elima Antok and what the historian had told Pulaski about Natima Lang?

Pulaski had publically supported Lang, and the next thing she knew she was kidnapped and held with a woman who had discovered files that could discredit Lang. That couldn't be a coincidence, could it? Did someone think that Pulaski had been sent here with instructions to ensure Lang succeeded Therok? But the figure lurking behind the campaign against Lang was none other than . . .

Pulaski leaned her head against the reinforced plastic of the window.

. . . the castellan.

Pulaski knew that people could change. Yes, yes, people were amazing, they had revelations all the time that transformed them. They got religion, took up sports, or created performance poetry, or got a lover, and all of a sudden it was like they were twenty years younger. But did people really change? Could they? *Would* they, if they were in power and intent on securing a particular outcome? Would Elim Garak, former operative of the Obsidian Order, hesitate for even a couple of minutes to put a young historian and a grumpy doctor (Pulaski balked at "old") out of action for a while in order to get a desired outcome? Pulaski was very afraid that he would not. The castellan was easily the most powerful man on Prime. He'd been part of the Obsidian Order, one of the most effective surveillance organizations in the quadrant. He'd been in power for three years now—long enough to reestablish the Order's networks and their working methods. Who would stop him? He was,

by all accounts, almost universally admired. Even
Antok, a quarter-Bajoran, with more reason than
most to loathe the Order, had made a pretty good
apology for him. But he wasn't a good man, was he?
Bad men did good things all the time, most often to
distract from the worse things they were doing. And
kidnapping didn't rate highly in Pulaski's book.

All of this made the doctor feel pretty precarious.
It also made her keener to get the hell out of this
empty apartment. "Empty?" she muttered, looking
around. "Downright creepy." She hated the quiet,
the sense of abandonment, and, most of all, she was
deeply afraid—not for herself, she was game for anything, but for Elima Antok. Sure, Antok had grown
up on Cardassia during its toughest times, but their
captor was twitchy. That meant he would probably
make split-second and not entirely rational decisions.
For Antok's sake, Pulaski needed to get out of here as
quickly as possible and get help.

She finished the water and headed for the exit.
Extraordinarily, it opened. She went out of the apartment onto the landing and looked around carefully.
Nobody to be seen. No alarms going off. The whole
situation was baffling. Why go to all the trouble of
capturing her, she wondered, and then leave the way
open for her to escape? Had her captor hit some difficulty and been delayed? Was the stun supposed to
last longer? Whatever the case, those were his problems, and, on balance, Pulaski was happy to leave
him to them. She wondered if she was meant to get

away, but dismissed the idea as too complicated even for Cardassians.

"Don't assume cleverness when a cock-up is the more likely explanation," she muttered, and walked along the landing. She decided to avoid the elevator, in case she met her captor coming back, and took the steps down instead. She slipped out through an emergency exit and stood outside. The air felt markedly grittier this morning, and she coughed a little at first, but that soon settled. She'd have to get a mask for the rest of the trip. Efheny would get it. She looked around the empty estate. No one about. No one to ask for directions. She had no idea which way to go, but downhill seemed better than uphill, so off she went.

It was a strange district, she thought as she walked through. A series of squat, brand-new apartment blocks, only some of which seemed to be inhabited, and then not completely. A few private skimmers stood around here and there. Perhaps one day there would be plenty of families here. She'd heard that the birth rate was soaring. So perhaps it would become busy, vibrant, lived-in—one day. Right now it was sparse and even rather bleak. You couldn't help thinking about the families that might have lived here, the children that might have been playing outside, if only the Jem'Hadar hadn't had their way on Cardassia Prime.

"Get a grip, Kitty," she told herself. "You're getting morbid."

She had plenty of her own problems right now; she needed to focus. She walked along the road and saw a skimmer heading toward her. Could it be him, her captor? She looked around, but there wasn't anywhere to hide, and she was pretty conspicuous—a human wearing the most crumpled Starfleet dress uniform this side of graduation—so she just strode on. The skimmer went past and didn't even slow down.

At length the road came out onto what she guessed must be part of the main circular going around the city. She wasn't too keen on walking along here, given how quickly the traffic was speeding past, but there was a narrow access pathway for pedestrians, and, besides, there was nowhere else to go. She walked on. She guessed from the position of the sun that it was past the morning rush hour; the traffic wasn't heavy, but it was steady, coming past her at speed. After about a quarter of an hour, she reached another access road, and there she saw a small building, built from gray Federation plasticrete and, from the boxes displayed outside, clearly a shop of some kind. She went down toward it and strode inside. The proprietor, a middle-aged male with greasy hair and a scar along one cheek, took one look at her—human, in disheveled Starfleet dress uniform—and pointed to the public comm in the corner.

"I don't have any money," Pulaski said.

"You lot never do."

"But I do need to use the comm."

"Don't worry," he said. "Your need looks greater than mine. Besides, I always liked Starfleet. Taught me how to play soccer."

He threw a keycard over to her, which she caught ("Thanks!") and stuck into the comm. "Hey," she said, when Alden's face appeared on screen. "It's me."

"Kitty?" Alden sounded beside himself with relief. *"Where the bloody hell are you?"*

"No idea." She called over to the proprietor, who shouted back their location. "Exit 49, just northeast of Paldar. Mean anything to you?"

"It'll mean something to somebody—"

"Don't bring anyone! Come yourself!"

"Kitty, what the hell is going on?"

"I'll tell you when I see you. Bring some painkillers, will you? I've got the mother of all headaches coming on."

She cut the comm. She handed the keycard back to the proprietor. He took a good look at her and handed over a bottle of water, which she accepted gratefully. She went outside to wait, sipping steadily at the water. Yes, the air quality was definitely worse. A few more days of this and you'd struggle outside. After about five minutes, she heard the throb of engines overhead. She looked up. Two air skimmers were heading this way. They came closer. The proprietor came out. "Hey," he said, "I don't want to interfere, but are you on the run by any chance?"

"What?"

"Those are police skimmers."

She looked up, and suddenly she had a very bad feeling. She looked around.

"If you're thinking of running for it, you should probably try that way," the proprietor said, pointing off behind the shop. "The other way is open countryside. At least that way you might get into Paldar and under cover."

"Thanks. Hey, this won't get you into trouble, will it?"

He shrugged. "I told you, I like Starfleet officers. Doctors in particular. I'll be fine." He looked up. "Don't rate your chances much, though."

"I'll take them," said Pulaski, and ran. Because one thing she knew for sure—she didn't want to end up in the hands of the Cardassian police. Not with Elim Garak calling the shots.

Once upon a time in the Cardassian capital, the Torr sector had been its most densely populated area, housing the service grades that kept the city running. Tucked alongside the bend and the curve of the old, slow dirty river, with narrow dead-end streets of crowded tenements, rickety walkways, tiny eateries, and busy *geleta* houses, it had been fertile ground for the Jem'Hadar death squads. They had killed and killed and killed, and then dragged all the buildings down upon the dead. Clearing Torr—as Elim Garak could tell you, as Arati Mhevet could tell you—had been one of the lowest, most desperate, and most grievous episodes of the aftermath. Those memories, no matter how hard one tried to push them away, surfaced at the oddest moments. Nobody who had dug, with sticks and bare hands, through the rubble of Torr in the hope, dashed over and over, of finding life, or who helped carry out the bodies and stack them high, would forget that time. Nobody who had experienced their stench would forget the great funeral pyres, darkening the sky with ash that seemed never to clear, clogging dry mouths with the reek and residue. But things can change. Cardassia had changed. More than ten years after the Fire, Torr was a shadow of the vibrant, grimy place it had once been, but in recent years, as the page turned slowly on the past, some of its old spirit had begun to return.

As any xenosociologist can tell you, social class is not a monolithic construct but is complicated in multiple and intersecting ways, and the two main districts of Torr, although united in their lack of financial and social capital, had quite distinct cultures. North Torr, rubbing up against the factories and silos of the Munda'ar sector, had been home to the laborers who drudged on the assembly lines and distribution centers. Sometimes this life was not enough and their children looked to make their fortunes elsewhere, worlds that the military had conquered. Northerners had, in times gone by, been proud of their long tradition of sending their sons to be the foot soldiers of the Union. Since the war they had taken less easily to the new open culture than others of their species, longing for the security and pride of the past. But they had, after some gentle persuasion, taken somewhat to Elim Garak, grudgingly admitting that for all his inexplicable fondness for Federation things, he wasn't the kind of man to let humans get the better of him. There was something undeniably Cardassian about Garak that drew the northerners to him. They did not believe that he would forget them or their sacrifices—and they were right. Garak knew that their resentments, if exploited by the unscrupulous, would mean the end of his democratic project. For this reason alone, Garak would not forget the people of North Torr. Besides, he had sympathy for them. He too had drudged long years for the old Cardassia, sacrificed again and again the better part of him, and like the northerners that had brought him nothing but sorrow.

But Garak's heart lay elsewhere. At the center of the district was a bustling open market, and passing through this, either by foot or across the narrow walkways covered in graffiti, or going by tram down the narrow streets, one quickly came to East Torr. There was little money here either, but the eastern part of Torr had a very different flavor from the north side. Here, migrants from client worlds had often found a home, and more so since the end of the war, when many of these worlds had been left derelict, and they brought with them their own distinctive foods and fashions. Students too were drawn to eastern Torr—both from U of U and from the old technical schools—looking for cheap rent and ease of access to their classes across the walkways onto the campus. One could even sometimes find the odd scion of an old wealthy family, slumming it among the service grades, sharing an apartment that had been bought by their parents, renting out the remaining space to other students, the rich extracting more money from the poor in time-honored fashion. East Torr had a buzz about it: it was here, in the days before Dukat seized power, that the civilian freedom movement had found fertile ground. It was here where troops had, once upon a time, opened fire upon a peaceful march of protestors who were asking for free elections. The pride of the easterners was no less than that of the northerners, but for different reasons. This was where the exiles drifted, those who lived beyond the families and institutions of the old Cardassia, those whose entire existence was precarious. Even as castellan, Garak felt precarious. He had been convinced at an early age of his own conditionality; he had never entirely shaken off the sense that he was, ultimately, disposable.

He loved to come here. He loved its variety, its liveliness, the sense he had that if he ever hit rock bottom again, he could find a space here, crawl into it, and make a home. And he loved its vibrancy. East Torr was where many of the most exciting artistic initiatives of the Union often started, in the attics of tenements and the spaces behind *geleta* houses, in murals on the end of blocks and the dry walls of parched and tiny stone gardens, and its current residents had revived this tradition.

This was what brought Castellan Elim Garak to East Torr late this spring morning, to an exhibition of art exploring the shared themes in Cardassian and Bajoran visual art. The gallery had opened the previous year, with support from the People's Artistic Fund, a new program of which the castellan was a trustee. He was directly involved in choosing which projects to finance. This particular project, proposed by a group calling themselves the Friends of Bajor, had immediately attracted his attention, and the centerpiece of this exhibition was a painting loaned by the castellan, a painting by a promising young artist whose career had been cut short before it had started: Tora Ziyal.

Garak had come today intent on enjoying himself, putting aside his current worries, and although there were necessarily many formalities related to declaring the exhibition open, and much small talk to be endured, he *was* enjoying himself. In part, this was because the pieces displayed had been chosen with great sensitivity and, given the small space, demonstrated an impressive variety of skill in numerous media: paint, ceramics, fabrics, and holo. He was particularly drawn to a tapestry banner using threads spun from both Cardassian and Bajoran natural fibers, combining bold Cardassian colors with more pastel Bajoran shades. It depicted the liberation of both capital cities, with ordinary people up front and center. He was considering asking whether this piece could be displayed in his official residence, and he had already quietly contacted Akret to get her to run background checks on the artist before he gave her his official endorsement.

But the artwork was not the only reason Garak was enjoying himself. He was also greatly amused by his hosts. The Friends of Bajor turned out to be a deadly earnest group, serious and high-minded. One or two of them even sported Bajoran earrings: Garak assumed that there was some mixed heritage here that legitimized this choice; otherwise it struck him as a massive lapse in taste. Of course, it was hardly the kind of question one could easily *ask*, although he had, by more subtle means of interrogation, established the backgrounds of some of the artists present. He was in the midst of listening to an achingly young ceramic artist dressed in flowing Bajoran robes explain how her work explored themes of spirituality across both cultures and how she hoped to spend some time next year at a Bajoran monastery, when, from the corner of his eye, he became aware of someone trying to catch his attention. He glanced over, saw Arati Mhevet, and his heart sank.

"Please excuse me," he murmured. "I must speak to a colleague briefly."

He extricated himself and went over to join her.

"This had better be good," he said.

"It's not," she said. "Antok's files on Enigma have gotten into the public domain."

Garak didn't move a muscle and kept a bland

smile on his face as Mhevet handed him a padd. Quickly he digested the contents of her brief. Yes, the files were out there, and the 'casts were rapidly picking up the story. Natima Lang, he thought, was about to find out how good her press person was. "Thank you," Garak said, handing the padd back.

Mhevet tucked the padd under her arm. "Is that all?"

"What else would you like me to say? We have yet to ascertain whether or not any of this is true. If false, we can dismiss this as an attempt to discredit the professor and investigate who is responsible. If true, Natima will have to answer questions about the case. For me to say anything would be inappropriate."

She gave him a look that was full of doubt. Did she really think that he was responsible? "Any news on Pulaski?"

"Were you expecting any?" she said.

"I'd assumed," he said coolly, "that the constabulary would be exerting all of its powers to find her."

"We are. It's almost as if there are forces ensuring she will not be found."

"*If* there are," said Garak, "I'm sure you'll discover them."

"No sign of Antok either," said Mhevet. "Since you ask."

"I'd assumed not," said Garak. "Otherwise you would have mentioned it."

"I wish that . . ." Mhevet began, and then stopped.

"Go on," he said.

She looked around the room. There were a few people looking at them with interest. "No, it's okay. I'm sorry to have disturbed your morning. There was no need. I just . . . I didn't want you to be blindsided by this. I'll contact you via comm if I hear anything more. I just thought you'd want to know."

She turned to leave, and he reached out with his hand, barring her. "I did want to know," he said. "Thank you, Arati. Please don't worry. We'll get to the bottom of all this." He smiled. "Why not stay for a while? Come and look at the art. I think you'd like it."

Mhevet had grown up in East Torr, he knew, and she had been born in the north. She was part of this place; whereas for all his fancies, he would always be grafted here. "I'd love to," she said, "but I've got to get back to work. Enjoy the show."

He nodded, and she left, with a smile, but he had seen the doubt in her eyes. He watched her go, regretfully, and turned back to his hosts.

Lang was deep in preparation for her final meeting before she went away, reading the draft of a promising student's thesis on the history of the enigma tale. All studies such as these in the new Cardassia were, by necessity, also archaeological tasks. The literature of an entire culture had, in its physical form, gone up in flames when the Jem'Hadar had set out on its task of not only exterminating the Cardassian species, but destroying all evidence of its existence: architecture, art, literature, and music. Much of the work conducted by Lang's students these days involved tracking down lost texts: chasing leads on client worlds where small holdings sometimes revealed tiny but lovingly kept libraries; begging copies from other powers; chasing down the files of dissidents, who had kept their own secret archives during the glory days of the Obsidian Order. Lang's own texts had been purged from most public and private archives long before the Dominion occupation, when she had defected. She frequently counted her blessings on this score: her own writings had survived as a result of her taking them with her. But many of the sources she had used were no longer in existence in any form. Such cruelty, she thought; the Founders had acted with such cruelty when they had given their orders. Every single working day Lang grieved for something that was lost, and she knew that her colleagues studying in other art forms experienced the same sorrow. Whole schools of art were no longer in existence. Whole musical forms had been silenced. Some dances would forever go undanced.

The student whose work she was reading had tracked this process of literary archaeology with great sensitivity. The thesis was much more than a piece of scholarship: it was a personal exploration of loss. Reta Ghemeny's mother had been a writer—she had written enigma tales, in fact, very popular ones that had sold well. She had been murdered by the Jem'Hadar in the capital on the last day of the war, although the little girl, Reta, who had been evacuated to the countryside and was staying with a grandfather, had survived. Ghemeny's thesis discussed the process of trying to locate her mother's work after the Fire, reading much of it for the first time, analyzing the stories within the broader tradition of the enigma tale, and of getting to know her mother through her writing, and coming to terms with her death and the loss of her world. It was a superb piece of work that had on several occasions brought tears to Lang's eyes. All the loss, all the pain, all the years spent sifting through burned fragments of what had once been their great and subtle civilization—Ghemeny captured all of this. In the description of searching for her mother's work—hunting out tiny libraries on distant client worlds, begging for favors from the archives of other powers, sifting through the rubble of the Central Archive here in the capital—Reta somehow found a story of hope, of renewal, of the possibility of connection with the past. Sometimes, something was found.

There was a tap on the door. Lang, irritated, looked up. She liked to be totally immersed when reading student work, particularly at this advanced level; some of her best ideas arose from responding to her students. But now her concentration had been disturbed. "Come in," she said, leaning back in her chair.

It was, of course, Servek, peering around the door with an expression of apology on her face that came close to simpering. Steadily and politely, Lang said, "How can I help?"

"I am *so* sorry, Professor," Servek said, "but there's something on the 'casts that I think you should probably see."

Lang looked down at the padd. She was almost done with Reta's thesis—barely a dozen pages left. "I'll look when I've finished this," she said.

"Really, Professor," said Servek apologetically, "I think you should look now." She came into the room and, taking what Lang thought was quite the liberty, turned on the small oval viewscreen on the far wall.

"Servek—"

"Please, Professor. You must."

Lang, trying to conceal her frustration, stood up and went over to the screen. Servek had put on one of the newscasts. To Lang's amazement, she saw her own face on there, and she realized that her own career was being dissected. She moved closer, her attention now completely riveted. Slowly, and with the help of the tickertape, she began to piece together the story of the day.

"Oh my stars," she whispered. "*Children . . .*"

"Professor, I'm so sorry."

Lang turned to Servek. "I don't understand—"

"Some files have gotten into the public domain. From before the end of the Occupation. And . . ." Servek looked pained. "Your name is on them."

"But there were children involved," said Lang. "Children."

There was a pause. Lang turned back to the viewscreen.

"Professor," Servek said at last, "you should go away for a while."

Lang, barely able to drag her attention away from what she was seeing, turned to Servek. "I beg your pardon?"

"Go away for a while. Until all this blows over."

"I am going away."

"I mean today."

"That's impossible—I have a tutorial tomorrow—"

"Your student won't mind—"

"Reta's very close to submission—"

"You can speak to her—"

"This is her thesis I'm talking about! Her license to teach and research."

Servek stared back at her, and, not for the first time, Lang wondered whether this woman actually understood what a university did.

"I'm sure it's very important to her, Professor," she said, "but you have to think of the university's reputation—"

"The *university's* reputation?"

The comm on Lang's desk began to buzz furiously. Lang, striding back to her desk to answer, found that Servek was ahead of her, switching the console to offer a general message. "Servek," said Lang, her voice stern, "what do you think you're doing?"

"That'll be the press office," said Servek. "They'll want to speak to you."

"I have no problem with that—"

"Professor, listen to me! Go away. I'll tell the press office you're aware of what's happening, that you have nothing to say, and that you've decided to start your vacation early. I'll contact this student too. She'll understand." Catching Lang's expression, Servek hurried on. "She can come out and see you at the house, can't she? Out in the country. I bet she'd like that. You can talk through her essay—"

"Her *thesis*. Her doctoral thesis."

"Okay, yes. You can still talk it through, but not here. Professor—the best thing for you right now is not to be around."

"But there's nothing to this," Lang said. "It's a mistake. I should go out and deny it." She made a move to the door, but again Servek was there.

"Professor, that doesn't matter. They're not interested in whether or not it's true. They're interested in filling their 'casts. Don't fall into that trap. Go away and let the press office handle it." She coaxed Lang back to her chair. "Finish your reading. I'll go and change your ticket. You can be on your way by the end of the day. Trust me, Professor—this is the best thing to do."

Lang looked down at her student's draft. Servek was already back at the door. "Servek," she called out, "you don't believe I had anything to do with this, do you?"

The other woman's split second of hesitation told Lang everything she needed to know. "Of course not, Professor. Of course not."

Garak left the gallery as soon as he decently could, and with considerable private disappointment. He had been looking forward to the event, and, perhaps inevitably, the whole thing had been thrown completely off the rails by Mhevet's appearance. He tutted to himself. She could easily have let him know that the story was about to break via his private comm, and she should have known better than to come to this event in person. It drew attention to their relationship that they really shouldn't allow. He wondered whether he had made a mistake allowing her such access to him. It could easily be misconstrued. But she had been so impressive during the events surrounding Bacco's death, so solid, and she had so clearly understood the nature of her tasks in the new Cardassia. He sighed. He often thought that it was a mistake letting people in, but the simple fact was that he couldn't do this job alone. Not and remain sane. Not and remain on the right side of the law. Garak had isolated himself before, and he knew where that led. Into the echo chamber of his own mind, where he was always able to find a justification for the most terrible actions. No, he could not run that risk, not now, and certainly not in this role, when the power he held was so great and the stakes were so high. The truth was, he needed Mhevet. He needed her scrutiny, and he needed her to ask him the difficult questions that she was asking. He was angry at her seeming lack of trust, but this was what he had asked her to do. To watch him and to tell him when she was afraid.

The air quality was markedly worse today. The dust had always had a tendency to linger in Torr, down in the bowl of the river, with the buildings cramped so close together. Garak stood on the steps of the gallery, flanked by bodyguards, waiting for the official skimmer to arrive. He coughed and rubbed his eyes. "Sorry for the delay, sir," one of the bodyguards said. "I should've remembered the masks."

"That's all right. It's come a little earlier this year, I think."

"This skimmer should be here," the guard said darkly, looking up at the high tenements, as if every window or doorway might contain an assassin or two. Garak smiled to himself. His personal comm chimed, and he lifted it out to see a message from Parmak. *Sorry it's been spoiled*, it said. Garak had a pang of guilt. He had a feeling that he had not been treating Parmak well in recent weeks, and he needed some time with the other man to make amends. They needed to talk about . . .

About Bashir. As if Garak could put any of that into words, other than what he so often found himself saying.

I'm sorry, Kelas. Please—forgive me.

The big skimmer pulled up, smoothly and quietly.

Garak took a step forward, but before he could reach its sanctuary, there were some yells and cries, and he looked around to see a whole flock of journalists coming his way. He thought about making a quick dive into the skimmer, but there was no way to achieve that and maintain his usual urbane dignity, and the thought of how it would play on the 'casts held him back. He would hear what they had to say about Lang, offer some bland pleasantries, and then go on his way. "Gentlemen, ladies," he said as they screeched to a halt in front of him, "how *nice* to see your familiar faces! How *gratified* I am at the attention you pay to my schedule!"

"Castellan, do you have any opinion about this breaking news?"

A little warning bell chimed in Garak's head, and he remembered one of his first lessons: don't surrender information. He gave his best smile and played for time. "Well, Letek," he said to the journalist asking the question, "I have a vast number of opinions, on a wide range of topics. You should come to dinner one evening. I should warn you that you'll probably be sick of the sound of my voice long before dessert arrives."

"Castellan, you must have something to say about the legate's decision?"

Garak smiled back blandly. That warning bell, he thought; he had been absolutely right to pay attention. Not for the first time, Garak thanked his lucky stars for his intuition. He had absolutely no idea what the journalist was talking about and absolutely no intention of revealing this fact. So, he must keep them busy until one of his advisors managed to brief him. It was a good job, he thought, as he surreptitiously slid his comm into the palm of his hand, that he liked to talk, so very, *very* much.

"Ah," Garak said, "the legate." (*Which* damn legate?) "I have often found myself pondering the ways of the Cardassian military, and particularly its senior echelons, who I think we can all agree are a *marvelous* if occasionally *opaque* group—" He could see the journalists getting restless. This was soon going to look exactly like what it was: playing for time. The comm, mercifully, vibrated in his hand, and, faking a slight cough—plausible given the air quality—Garak was able to check the message and learn, to his considerable dismay, that the three officers who had visited him—Legate Renel, Gul Telek, and Gul Feris—had made a public statement earlier that morning announcing their immediate resignations of their commissions. Garak coughed again. Time to put a stop to this sideshow, get in the skimmer, and be properly briefed. "But the answer to your question, Letek, is—no, I have nothing to say about the legate's decision. I would suggest that you talk to him. Without the demands of his position, he no doubt has a great deal of time on his hands." He moved toward the skimmer. "A pleasure as always."

He sat down inside, and the door slid closed after him with a quiet *whoosh*. He let his head fall back on the seat. He wasn't entirely sure he'd gotten away with that. His private comm buzzed again. Parmak again. *Really, really sorry it's been spoiled.* Garak glumly turned to the console built into the seat. One of his advisors was on the line, ready with a briefing, and he also found a 'cast showing Renel's announcement. It was even worse than he'd realized: not just the trio had resigned, but three more guls and another legate had joined them.

"*We strongly oppose this attempt to smear the reputation of the military,*" Renel said. "*We are looking into legal remedies, for example, statutes of limitations, whether these were crimes under Cardassian law at the time, whether individuals can be legally tried for crimes that took place somewhere that is now under a different jurisdiction . . .*"

Garak snorted. The reputation of the military indeed. He started to feel slightly better. Even as he spoke, Renel was tacitly admitting the military's guilt. He was looking for technicalities, rather than arguing innocence.

One of the journalists at the press conference said, "*I've heard reports that the Federation might seek extraditions.*"

Garak would have preferred to have kept that quiet. "Vulcans," he muttered, and turned to the messages coming in from his advisors. By the end of the ride back to his office, they had a well-worded and entirely bland statement on the resignations to give out to the press. Garak went to his desk. Akret had a pot of ettaberry tea ready, a welcome balm for itching eyes and a sore throat, and a promise that lunch was on its way.

She watched him anxiously as he drank the tea. "Will this make trouble for you, sir?"

"Oh, I should think so," said Garak.

She gave him a sympathetic smile and left. He noticed that she had arranged for a vase full of spring flowers, bright and cheerful, to be put on the desk. He reached into his pocket and drew out the *perek* petal. Its color was fading, and it was beginning to shred.

The door opened again, and Akret put her head in. She looked like she'd been surprised. That wasn't a good sign. He shoved the petal back into his pocket.

"Akret? Whatever is the matter?"

"Castellan," she said, "I have—"

She stopped suddenly as someone pushed past. Garak's faint hope for lunch was quickly disappointed. The human male, Pulaski's friend, dark-haired and pale-skinned, came striding in, with Ambassador T'Rena behind him. Garak fumbled around for a name. Alden, that was it, Peter Alden. Pulaski's silent sidekick. Not so silent now.

"Where is she, you Order bastard?" he yelled. "What have you done with Katherine Pulaski?"

My dear Doctor—

We have come down from the heights, but we are entering an area that seems no less rarefied to me. I confess, Doctor, that I am rather in awe of the university. Such places have always been closed to me—my own education was rather narrowly focused and intent on producing some quite specific learning outcomes—and whenever I come to this place I feel slightly at a disadvantage. My defense is not particularly subtle, but it seems to do the trick: I wear my best clothes and I smile enigmatically, and that seems to persuade even these fine minds that I am a brilliant and sophisticated man. It was the same when I was young—all these clever young people, most of them from those rich or comfortable homes in Coranum and Paldar, all widely read, and able. They made me feel gauche and stupid.

Perhaps I do not strike you as the kind of person to feel tongue-tied, but it's true. And, of course, this all worked in the Order's favor. I was not alone in my feelings, and so it was easy to get our operatives to sneer at those young people filling their days with study and ask what contribution they made. We never struggled to find people willing to go undercover to the university, although we never had much success. I blame Natima Lang.

Does it give me some satisfaction, then, to have had a hand in the rebuilding of the university? I will not deny it. But it has not been motivated out of scorn or spite. What the university suffered at the hands of the Jem'Hadar was particularly grievous and now, when I think of that lost world, I regret those young lives that we made so difficult, and I can only applaud the courage they showed in trying to learn in the face of best efforts to keep them ignorant. Lang was committed to an idea of an institution as much as I was, I think, but she certainly chose a better one.

Still, I do feel like an intruder upon its turf, even as I desire the way of life it offers. In some alternate timeline, where we all of us live our best lives, I am sitting quietly in a room somewhere, reading.

Garak
[unsent]

Seven

The castellan of the Cardassian Union considered his best response to this gambit. Anger would suggest he was out of control, and, besides, his throat still felt raw from the morning outside and shouting wouldn't help. So he leaned back comfortably in his chair and visibly relaxed. Meanwhile, his heart pounded in his chest, and he tried to ignore the fact that the walls seemed to be bending inward slightly.

"Well," he said, "that would be a bold opening move in any conversation, never mind with the head of state of a friendly power." Garak dismissed Alden and turned his attention to T'Rena. The ambassador, he thought, did not look entirely comfortable. There, perhaps, was the way to turn this to his advantage. "A pleasure to see you, Ambassador, as it is always a pleasure to see friends from the Federation. I hope your journey here was not too unpleasant. The air quality is markedly worse today, I believe, and it can be uncomfortable for people not familiar with the experience. Would you care for some ettaberry tea? It's very soothing."

T'Rena moved forward at a stately pace, taking her time, trying to impose herself upon proceedings. "Thank you. That would be most pleasant."

Garak nodded to Akret, still hovering, and she left, closing the door behind her. Garak stood up, his hand drifting into his pocket to touch the *perek* petal as he did. He gestured to T'Rena to follow him away from his desk and toward the seats near the window. He took his preferred chair, the one that put his face in shadow, and T'Rena made herself comfortable on the couch. She did not seem perturbed to find herself looking into the light. She was very focused on him. Alden, meanwhile, was still standing by Garak's desk and quivering with rage. Garak knew how he felt. The walls were only just beginning to retreat.

"Doctor Alden," Garak said. "Would you care to join us, or would you prefer to stand?"

Slowly, Alden walked over. Garak kept his eyes on him and Alden, to his credit, didn't blink. Garak had to applaud both his nerve and his training. He had read Alden's file, of course, as soon as he had seen the man's name on the list of visitors. The Obsidian Order had gone for the kind of person that was good at disassociation, but Starfleet Intelligence seemed to like a different type: clever and introverted, rather cool and self-contained. Bashir had become like this; no, Bashir had always been like this, from the start, hadn't he? Despite all the gaucheness, he had been concealing the not so small matter of his genetic enhancements. Alden reminded Garak strongly of Bashir; his accent made the resemblance stronger. It was distressing and disturbing, particularly given Alden's palpable anger. Garak had to make a conscious effort to push thoughts of the doctor away.

As Akret poured the tea, Garak smiled pleasantly at T'Rena and Alden in turn, reviewing what he knew from Alden's file. He had gone undercover on Ab-Tzenketh. Resigned from Starfleet Intelligence after a near breakdown not long after a tense mission involving the Tzenkethi in which he had been implicated in planting a bomb on a base. Alden's link to the bomb had not been proven, and there was a strong possibility that the Tzenkethi had done it themselves. Garak recognized the trick, and thought Alden was most likely guilty. The man was highly strung and had, as the years went by, developed a tendency to lose self-control. Garak sympathized. Ab-Tzenketh had nearly driven him mad too: all that bowing and scraping, not to mention nearly being buried alive. At least he hadn't been in deep cover. Ab-Tzenketh was the most claustrophobic and airless society Garak had ever visited. Deep cover there would have finished him off.

Garak sipped his tea. So Alden had a tendency to go off the rails. That could come in useful.

"The tea is very pleasant," said T'Rena.

"Yes, it is," said Garak.

"I can see how it will be of great assistance when the dust arrives in earnest."

"I'd advise a mask too," said Garak. He looked at Alden. "Cover the mouth."

There was a short pause. Alden picked up his teacup. His hands, Garak saw, were a little shaky.

"My apologies for this interruption," said T'Rena.

Garak inclined his head. "I am of course at your disposal. But my schedule is rather tight."

"We'll go as soon as we have answers," said Alden. "Where is she?"

"I'm afraid that you have me at a disadvantage," purred Garak. "Where is who?"

"Katherine Pulaski, of course!"

"I have no idea," Garak said. "The city constabulary are investigating Pulaski's disappearance. They have no information as yet—"

"You're not fooling us, you know!"

T'Rena held up her hand. "Please, Doctor Alden!"

"Drink some tea," Garak advised him. "You'll find it very soothing." Certainly Garak was enjoying its more pacifying effects right now. There were pieces missing from this *kotra* board, he thought; he couldn't see everything, and he wasn't sure he knew yet who all the players were. Was this some kind of bluff? Was T'Rena trying to trick him into admitting some culpability in Pulaski's disappearance? If she was, she had sorely overplayed their hand and made a tragic mistake bringing along Alden. The man looked frantic. Garak did not like this, he did not like it at all. What did Alden know that was making him so anxious? Was it simply concern over Pulaski's where-abouts? They were good friends, by all accounts, despite the surface sniping. But that wouldn't explain these physical symptoms of distress, surely? This was a man who believed that things were out of control. Surely it wasn't fear of Garak? Garak was the first to admit that he could have some fairly unpleasant effects on people, but he hadn't, so far as he knew, done anything to Alden to earn this response.

There is something going on here that I don't know anything about, Garak thought. He didn't like that. He never liked that. And he was getting sick of all these accusatory stares. They were wearying.

"Now," Garak said, "let me see if I've got this straight. You have come here because you believe that I know the whereabouts of Doctor Pulaski."

"And Elima Antok," said Alden.

"Elima Antok," said Garak. "I see. May I ask to what purpose I would spirit away an honored guest visiting from our closest ally, not to mention an esteemed academic with a significant public profile whose evidence is key to a report upon which I have recently staked significant political capital? I'm curi-ous, you see, to understand my own reasoning—or my reasoning as *you* understand it."

"I've no idea what passes through your mind," Alden said. "It's something to do with Natima Lang, I bet. These files that have mysteriously turned up, just when she's about to become chief academician—"

"Let me assure you," Garak said quietly, "that I am in no way served by seeing Professor Lang's reputation in ruins."

"As for Katherine—you couldn't have shown your dislike more clearly. From the first second you met her you took against her—"

"In fact, my reaction to Doctor Pulaski was framed by her decision to wade in with her opinions about the report. I know that for some members of Starfleet, the Prime Directive has become less of a rule and more of a guideline, but there are ways to deport yourself when visiting an allied power. Doctor Pulaski fell rather short of this." He saw Alden open his mouth, probably to tell Garak that he deserved it, and he turned to T'Rena. "Ambassador, don't you agree?"

T'Rena inclined her head. "I asked Doctor Pulaski to be a little more circumspect in her pronouncements in future," she said. "But I am deeply concerned about her disappearance—"

Garak, however, had turned back to Alden. He'd achieved his first goal, of detaching him from T'Rena. Now he could finish this off. "Even your ambassador agrees that I should approach Doctor Pulaski with caution."

"You brushed her off at your first meeting! You won't let her see Julian Bashir!"

Garak slowly drained his tea and placed the cup down upon the saucer. He was by now the angriest he had been in some years, and he needed a moment to compose himself. He stood up. "This meeting is over." He turned to T'Rena, now standing, and addressed her directly. "We're at the very early stages of our relationship, Ambassador, and you represent our closest ally and a civilization to which Cardassia owes a great deal. I'm going to overlook this incident. I don't know why you were persuaded to do this, and I'm prepared to assume you, at least, were acting in good faith. But I trust nothing like this will ever happen again."

He saw her shoot a quick glance at Alden, and her lips tighten. Yes, she was annoyed, in her passionless Vulcan way. Not as much as Garak, but this was certainly not how she had intended this meeting to play out. "I do have many questions about Doctor Pulaski's disappearance, Castellan—"

"As do I," said Garak. "And while I wait for those questions to be answered by the high-ranking officers whom I've asked to investigate, I do not throw around baseless accusations. Particularly accusations that imply that I am spearheading a resurgence of the Obsidian Order—"

"That's not what I meant," said Alden quickly.

"No?" Garak felt his chest tightening. He breathed in deeply. "What *did* you mean, exactly? You know I was in the Obsidian Order; I know I was in the Obsidian Order. The Cardassian people know it; Starfleet, your ambassador, and your president know it. But the Order is dead—long dead and buried. I am the castellan of the Cardassian Union, and when a burned-out junior intelligence officer barges into my office and accuses me of kidnapping, he had better be presenting better evidence than supposition, history, and prejudice. Do you have any such evidence, Doctor Alden?"

There was a short silence.

"No, sir," said Alden. "I'm sorry. I shouldn't have mentioned the Order."

Garak felt himself become calmer or, perhaps, cooler. "No," he said. "You shouldn't." He turned back to T'Rena. "I'm going to pretend this didn't happen," he said. "I suggest you do the same. As for your *associate*—" He nodded at Alden. "You should probably get him examined. I'm sure there are plenty of counselors available to him. He should take advantage of their services at the earliest opportunity."

He knew he could have stopped there, but something pushed him onward. Later, Garak would understand that it was because he was still angry, that all his effort for all of these years was not enough to persuade people that he was not a liar. Still, he regretted what he did next.

Slowly, he approached Alden.

"It's hard, isn't it," Garak said, in a very soft voice, "when the nerve goes. When you start to second-guess every move that you make. When the anger becomes so all-consuming that you feel you might well burn alive. When things don't turn out as planned, and you know in your heart that it's because you are at fault and are making bad decisions." He studied

Alden with gentle cruelty. "I'm sorry you took such harm on Ab-Tzenketh. I'm sorry the Tzenkethi did this to you. They're a cruel people, aren't they?" He held up one hand and squeezed it shut, like a vise. "They can press the life out of you."

"Ah," said Alden, and he seemed to double over slightly.

"Castellan," said T'Rena firmly, waiting until he turned to face her. "You've made your point."

Garak turned away. He walked across the room to a little alcove in the wall where a painting usually hung. He heard the door open, and T'Rena said, "I'll contact you with any news, Castellan. I know you'll reciprocate."

He turned, and nodded, and watched her leave. Alden followed, but, as he left, he made the mistake of turning back to look at the castellan. Garak gave him his full, bright blue stare. Alden blinked, shivered, and left. *You've been played by a master player*, Garak thought. *You should learn from that, Doctor Peter Alden. If you can't play the game to this level, then don't invite me to the* kotra *board.* He stared at the wall. It looked back blankly, like an accusation. He fumbled in his pocket for the scarlet petal, but when he drew it out, it was in pieces.

Katherine Pulaski stretched out her legs and thought about what she had just been told. "Well," she said, "of course he'd deny it."

She was sitting safely in the Federation embassy,

where she had been since her collection earlier that day. The big skimmers that had descended on her had turned out not to have been sent by Garak's people, as she had feared, but had come direct from the embassy, after Alden alerted Federation security.

"In fact," said T'Rena, "he didn't deny anything. I was listening very closely. The castellan assured us that his best people were looking for you—and for Elima Antok. He neither confirmed nor denied that he was involved in your disappearances." T'Rena glanced at Alden, who was standing with his back to them, over by the window. Softly, she said, "This was not a wise move."

Pulaski looked at Alden too. "What do you mean?"

"Doctor Alden was of little assistance. I'm afraid to say that the castellan found him rather easy prey."

Pulaski, imagining how the scene must have unfolded, was furious. She knew that part of the reason for Alden leaving Starfleet Intelligence was that he'd been sent on one mission too many, that his nerve had nearly gone, and he'd been close to a breakdown. The castellan would surely know that too, if he'd taken the trouble to read Alden's file, and Pulaski doubted anyone came near Garak without him reading their file. He knew Alden's weaknesses, and he'd chosen to use them to his advantage. Pulaski knew she had been right not to trust Garak. "That lowdown, goddamn . . ." She called over to Alden. "Peter, don't beat yourself up."

Alden turned at the sound of his voice. He gave

a bright, rather brittle smile that Pulaski did not like at all. "I'm sorry," he said. "I made a mess of things. I went in pretending to be angry, and he made me angry."

"Hey." Pulaski got up and crossed over to him. "Stop it. You shouldn't have gone in there."

"An apology, Kitty? That makes everything worthwhile." Alden gave a thin smile. "The fact is, it was a high-risk strategy and it's blown up in our faces. And we're still none the wiser about the castellan's motives."

"I think we know," said Pulaski. "Discredit Lang at all costs."

"Why remove you? Why remove Antok?"

"I don't know how his mind works!" said Pulaski. "The man is one riddle after another! If he's framing Lang, then perhaps he was afraid that Antok would find out that the files had been doctored. As for me . . . You know what, I think he's just pissed with me."

Alden gave a snort of laughter.

"You're cheering up," said Pulaski. "Good."

"Kitty, you're one in a million," said Alden. "Do you think the castellan would risk an alliance with the Federation to which he's devoted years of his life by kidnapping you just because you gave him a hard time at a reception?"

"I'm told," Pulaski said, "that I have that effect on people. And it wasn't just the reception. I bad-mouthed him on a live 'cast."

"True," Alden conceded.

"I confess I'm struggling to understand why you were taken and then allowed to get away," said T'Rena.

"I don't have an answer to that," Pulaski said. "All I know is that it happened, and that the man who took me wanted to know why I was here on Cardassia Prime." She shook her head. "What could I say? I told the truth, but he didn't believe me. I don't know what he was getting at—did he think I was here with Starfleet Intelligence?"

"He doesn't know much about you if he thinks that," said Alden.

"I think I was a mistake," said Pulaski. "And that's why I was allowed to get away. You're right, Ambassador. Elima Antok is the key."

"She gave crucial evidence to the war crimes report," said T'Rena. "It could be connected to that."

"Or this ridiculous attempt to frame Lang," said Pulaski.

Alden looked at her with interest. "You think the files are faked?"

"I think they're absolute baloney," said Pulaski bluntly. "I'll stake my reputation on it that Lang is being framed."

"I'll take that bet," said Alden.

"You're on. But in the meantime," said Pulaski, "we're still no closer to finding Elima Antok." She frowned. "I don't generally take to people who drag me off in the middle of the night, but this guy was twitchy as hell. I don't like to think of her in his hands."

"For that young woman's sake," said T'Rena, "we should notify the authorities that you have been found, Doctor. They can surely garner information from the apartment where you were being held."

Pulaski shook her head. "I'd rather we did this ourselves for a while longer. The constabulary chief was appointed by Garak, wasn't she?"

T'Rena nodded. "Arati Mhevet. Garak appointed her to the position shortly after he became castellan."

"My understanding is that she's one of his people," said Alden.

Pulaski gave him a narrow look. "Your understanding, huh?"

"I've told you that I keep myself informed," said Alden. "It's not my fault if you only know what's happening at the hound-racing. I've been out and about on Cardassia Prime, and I've been listening to what people say. Arati Mhevet is one of Garak's people."

"She has by all accounts an excellent reputation," said T'Rena. "Resigned her post before the war when Meya Rejal ordered Dukat to open fire on a civilian demonstration in the capital. Came back after the war and played a vital part in reconstituting the constabularies. And she was very friendly to the Federation while we were here."

"All right," said Pulaski. "But does she have enough influence to pressure Garak?"

"I'm still not convinced that the castellan is behind

this," said T'Rena. "It might be that Garak has no idea of what's going on." She pursed her lips. "We cannot go back to him."

"Sorry," said Alden.

"Hey, mister," said Pulaski, "you did your best."

They fell into silence, each lost in thought, trying to find their way through the riddle.

"There might be another route to Garak," Alden said slowly, at last. "Ambassador, what do you know about Kelas Parmak?"

"He is the castellan's close friend," said T'Rena. "Probably one of his closest advisors—not officially, but certainly they are often together."

"Are they lovers?" said Pulaski.

"I don't know," said T'Rena. "I do know that Parmak was interrogated by the Obsidian Order in his youth, and that Garak may have been involved."

"Damn," muttered Alden, "this place is twisted."

"Peter," said Pulaski, "are you thinking of using Parmak to get to Garak?"

He shrugged.

"What do you have in mind, Doctor Alden?" said T'Rena.

"Just an approach," he said. "An informal approach."

"Oh, I bet Garak will love that," Pulaski said.

"The thought of offending Garak has not even crossed my mind," said Alden.

"You should move soon," said T'Rena. "Not just for Antok's sake, but if Garak *is* behind these disappearances, it won't be long before he knows that you've escaped, Doctor Pulaski. He might be hoping that he'll still be able to recapture you. Revealing yourself to Parmak loses us an advantage—"

Pulaski shook her head. "I'm not interested in playing games. Elima Antok is still out there, and she's in the hands of a nasty piece of work. I'd swap any theoretical advantage we might have over Garak if it means that we can get her home safe and sound."

Alden nodded. "Then let's approach Parmak," he said.

"If that causes trouble for Garak?" said T'Rena.

"Then he's earned it," said Alden.

Throughout his working day, Garak was accustomed to receiving messages from Kelas Parmak offering wry commentary on the news as it unfolded, most reliably whenever it was causing the castellan a headache. Parmak had been Garak's comfort for many years now, particularly after Garak had taken the momentous decision to step into the public life and run for castellan. Parmak, Garak knew, had not been entirely sure that deciding to take on executive power was a good choice for Garak, but with the decision made, his support had been unconditional, steadfast, and honest. Bashir, on learning that Garak was running for castellan, had written telling him to surround himself with good people, people who would be honest with him, and not afraid to tell him when he was wrong. Mhevet was one; Akret was another. Garak had hoped that Bashir might continue in that role, but that, it seemed, was not to be . . . But there was the other doctor in Garak's life—Kelas Parmak, patient and forgiving.

Yet today, of all days, Parmak had been silent. This was not unusual; Parmak had a thriving medical practice to attend to, and, in addition, he served on numerous public health committees and on the board of trustees of one of the capital's biggest hospitals. It was not that Parmak had nothing better to do than sit at home watching the 'casts and waiting for Garak to find time to play *kotra* and drink *kanar* with him. But something about his silence today troubled Garak. He knew that Parmak was not happy with how he had welcomed Pulaski, and he knew that Parmak did not understand his apparent lack of enthusiasm for Lang's elevation to chief academician. And then there was the complicating presence of Bashir . . .

Garak rubbed his hand across his eyes. Complication piled upon complication. Sometimes he wished that life could be simpler. Sometimes he thought wistfully of his tailor's shop, when his most pressing concern was how to cut cloth. Then he would shake himself. Being in that tailor's shop had nearly killed him. He'd had to blow it up to get some semblance of normality back to his life. "Get a grip," he commanded himself. "Get a grip."

The comm on the desk chimed. *"Sir,"* Akret said, a strange note of apology in her voice, *"Doctor Parmak is here."*

Garak was surprised. Parmak generally kept a

careful distance from Garak's physical office during the working day. An unplanned visit was unheard of. Garak sighed. He feared he was about to become the recipient of one of Parmak's gentle admonishments. He had the vaguest feeling that it was probably deserved, but then, he always felt that way.

The door opened, and Kelas came in, slow-moving and slightly stooped. Garak, looking up, seemed to see him properly for the first time in a while. He was shocked at how weary Kelas looked. He felt terribly guilty that he might be the cause. For all Garak's frustrations with his current job, for all that it caused him worry, and anxiety, and the occasional panic attack, Garak knew that the truth was that he thrived on it. He was good at being castellan, and he was doing well. But was that true for the people who were around him?

He hurried over from behind his desk. "My dear Kelas, are you quite well?"

"I'm fine, thank you, Elim," Parmak said. "I'm rather tired at the moment, and I'm also rather anxious."

Garak took Parmak's arm and led the doctor toward the comfortable seats. Forgoing his usual chair, he sat down on the sofa beside Parmak. "Can I get something sent in? Do you need a skimmer to take you home?"

Parmak shook his head. "No, no . . . That's not the issue—"

"Then what *is* the issue?" said Garak urgently,

ready to put all his weight behind whatever would make Parmak happy.

Parmak pressed his fingers against his eyes. "I know where Pulaski is."

Garak nearly fell off his chair. "Kelas, you never fail to surprise me. Where is she?"

"She's at the Federation embassy."

Garak stared at him. He was starting to get the feeling that he was being played, and he didn't like to find himself playing against Parmak. "I've just had T'Rena and Pulaski's colleague Alden here. Did they know where she was when they came?"

Parmak nodded. "I understand they were attempting to bluff you."

"To bluff me." Garak's voice was rather chilly. He was beginning to feel angry again.

"They were hoping that you might reveal whether or not you were involved—"

"They need," said Garak, "to stop thinking they can play me."

"They've lost trust in you," Parmak went on. "They are no longer certain of your motives."

"They didn't bother to ask!"

"I am also no longer certain of your motives, Elim," Parmak said softly. "I am also losing trust in you."

Garak felt the cold familiar bands of panic tightening around his chest. Shocked, he looked at Parmak—and he was horrified to see that the other man was trembling. "Kelas? What do you mean?"

"I don't know what you're doing. I don't know how far you're willing to go."

Parmak fell into silence. He was still shaking. Garak reached out to put his hand upon the other man's shoulder. To his great grief, he saw that Parmak had to struggle not to flinch. Garak removed his hand. He breathed deeply. Slowly, both he and Parmak began to relax again. Only when Parmak was still did Garak speak.

"Kelas," he said quietly. "My best friend, my truest friend. I do not deserve you, but I try—oh, how I try!—to be worthy of you. Look at me, please."

After a moment or two, Parmak looked at him.

"I have nothing to do with this," Garak said. "I am not involved in the disappearances of Katherine Pulaski and Elima Antok. This has nothing to do with me."

"Do you swear, Elim?"

"I swear to you, I swear upon everything that I hold dear—our friendship, the memory of Tora Ziyal, the ashes and the ruins of all of our poor people—that I have done *nothing* to harm them." *I swear upon the life of Julian Bashir*, he thought—but he kept that back.

Parmak looked steadily at him. "And what about Natima Lang?"

Garak's eyes narrowed. "What about Natima Lang?"

"You're not telling me everything there, are you, Elim?"

Slowly, Garak shook his head. "No," he said, "I'm not."

Parmak put his hands up to cover his face.

"But not because I've done anything wrong!" Garak burst out. "Kelas, please, listen to me! Believe me! I am not a monster!" *I am not my father*, he cried out silently, imploring the other man to hear, and to understand, and to have a little faith. *Believe me*, Garak begged. *I am not him. I am better than him.* "Kelas, please, I am working so hard . . ."

Now Parmak's hand was on his shoulder. "Deep breaths, Elim," he was murmuring. "Deep breaths."

Garak obeyed. "I swear," he said at last, "that I have done nothing wrong."

Parmak nodded. "All right," he said. "You've done nothing wrong. You did not order the kidnap of either Katherine Pulaski or Elima Antok, nor were you behind the threats that Antok received."

"That is correct. Absolutely, entirely, and utterly correct."

"And I am also going to believe—although you have not promised me either way—that you have nothing to do with this attempt to blacken Lang's name."

"It may not," said Garak scrupulously, "be untrue."

"Oh, Elim, please! Natima Lang agreeing to experiments on children?"

"It was a different world—"

"I know! I know what kind of world it was! I was there too! But Lang?"

"Who knows what compromises she had to make?" Garak said. "Her students put themselves on the line at her instigation, and she always came through for them. Do you know how many of her students the Order interrogated over the years? Not one. Not a single one. As soon as we made a move on them, they were gone, like that"—he snapped his fingers—"offworld, out of the Union. That woman's network was impenetrable, and it moved at warp speed. You don't do that without exchanging favors."

"You cannot dismantle the master's house with the master's tools," said Parmak.

Garak blinked. "That's . . . not a quotation I recognize."

"No?" Parmak gave a wry smile. "Look it up. You're not the only one who reads, you know."

Garak smiled back. "I have never underestimated you, Kelas."

"Was that why you were the one to interrogate me?" said Parmak.

And there they were, back to the matter that would always be between them. Bitterly, as he so often did, Garak regretted his past, which still came back to taint his dealings with the people who were most precious to him, most beloved.

"Yes," Garak said, and stood up. Slowly, he walked around the room. He could see red lights flashing on his desk, a thousand and one demands upon his time and his attention, none of which mattered as much as this. He poured *kanar* into two glasses and handed one to Parmak, who drank quickly. The doctor's hands were shaking again slightly, Garak noticed with great sadness. This confrontation was costing Parmak very dearly. Carefully, Garak sat down again beside him. He did not try to touch the other man.

"I'll contact Ambassador T'Rena," Garak said. "I'll say that you've brought their concerns to me, and that they should not worry. Katherine Pulaski has more to fear from herself than from me. And my very best people are looking for Elima Antok."

Parmak, blessedly, began to relax. "I'll speak to them for you," Parmak offered. "If you'd prefer."

"You're not my messenger," Garak said. "It's not appropriate for it to come from you, and—to be frank—it's not appropriate that they used you as a channel to me. Still," he said, "I'm glad that we've talked."

Parmak nodded. "So am I." He took another sip of *kanar*, then said, "And Lang?"

"Natima Lang," Garak said, "needs to start answering some questions."

Parmak nodded. The man was calmer now, happier—but Alden, Garak thought, had taken a cruel revenge.

The comm on Lang's desk had been going wild all day, red lights flashing and chimes ringing. She turned off the sound early on. All calls were currently being fielded by Servek and an experienced but harassed U of U press liaison. But the simple knowledge that she was currently the most talked-about person in the Union—and the thought of why—made work impossible. She had tried going back to Reta Ghemeny's thesis, but it was no use. Then she had tried simply to read, choosing texts that would relax rather than challenge her, but that did not work either. Her mind was inevitably drawn back to the terrible accusations being leveled against her, and most of all her thoughts were full of the twelve children concerned. Were they still alive? Were they still on Cardassia Prime? Did they know what had happened to them, what had been done to them? *Our crimes*, thought Lang, *our terrible crimes. Will we ever be free of them? Will we always find yet another unburied body?*

Despite Lang's stated preference, Servek had been clear that going to the house in the Perok district was out of the question. The press, she told Lang, knew that the house was hers and that she had been planning to go there, and were already camped on the doorstep. Lang wondered vaguely who had told them her plans, but realized she had been talking about them for some weeks. Anyone could have supplied the information—although it saddened her to think that a colleague would choose to speak to a journalist rather than protect her. Perhaps she should have given that interview to that young man after all. You never knew how you were storing up trouble for yourself. But the house was out of the question, and Servek, for whose quick decisions Lang was starting to find herself extremely grateful, had booked a flight for Lang offworld. There was a small resort in the Arawath system, expensive but discreet, where Lang could hide until this all blew over. All they had to do was get Lang to the spaceport, but even then it wasn't straightforward.

"I'm guessing," said Servek, "that there might even be people at the city spaceport. Your flight is going from Metenok."

Lang nodded. An old military base, now refitted as a small spaceport, and some distance from the capital. A much less likely starting point.

The day wore on. Lang paced her room. She felt trapped, frightened, like a creature stuck in a maze, an experiment of someone else's devising, or a character from the human author Kafka. This was not the first time she had been forced to leave Cardassia Prime in a hurry, but she had thought those days were over, and the fact that this was happening now, when she had believed that the Union was, if not wholly cured of sickness, then certainly well on the way to recovery, was shocking.

Who is doing this to me? Why am I being tormented in this way?

There was a tap on the door, and Servek, without waiting for her to answer, came in, wheeling a small case behind her.

"I sent someone to your house," she explained. "They've packed this for you. It should have everything you need. We were right not to send you there.

Half a dozen journalists from several different 'casts were sitting on the doorstep."

"Thank you," said Lang faintly.

"I hope we got everything," Servek went on. "There's always the replicator on the transport, I suppose . . ."

They stared at each other. Lang felt ashamed. She had not been generous to this woman, she thought; she had not wanted her here, and she had not gone out of her way to integrate her into her working life. But today, Servek had shown her why she had been on Therok's staff. She had kept a level head and helped Lang stay away from anything that might have caused her difficulty.

"The tickets are all booked," said Servek. "I got a good deal on the exchange, although it is rather late notice and I couldn't avoid a fee for that. But it won't break the bank. The resort is rather pricey too, but I think the press office has been persuaded that you should claim some of that back in expenses. Better for them to have you safely away from the press." She gave a knowing smile. "Oh, and there's a skimmer coming to collect you." She checked the chrono on the wall. "Well, it should be here by now. I asked the driver to go to the back of the next building. There are journalists out front hoping to catch you. But you'll be able to get away without attracting any attention. They'll work out eventually that you've gone, but with luck you'll be safely aboard the *Perek* before then."

Lang nodded. "Thank you," she said.

"It's what I'm here for," said Servek. She bustled across the room, found Lang's jacket, and helped her into it, surrendering the suitcase to Lang's care. "The resort has been instructed to block all calls," Servek said. "Once the 'casters work out you've left, they're going to try to track you down. But I'll start putting about a story that you're with friends up in the mountains. Really, Professor—don't take any calls."

She held the door open for Lang. They went through Servek's office and out into the corridor. One or two colleagues were hanging around, but they looked away with embarrassment as she passed. *Of course*, she thought, *they're afraid that there's something to all this. They must hold me in contempt.*

She almost cried at the thought of that, but, grimly, she gripped the handle of the case and marched with her head high to the main elevator. She went down to the lowest level, a basement level, coming out into the warren of corridors that connected the whole campus.

Beneath U of U was a busy underground complex, with *geleta* stops at various points, and the odd small eatery where students and staff could grab a bite to eat before dashing off to their next class, or sit with friends and colleagues and debate their most recent sessions. It was a clever addition to the campus, connecting all the disparate buildings and providing cover during the days when heat, cold, or dust made being outside unbearable. Today Lang was very glad for that cover. She dashed through the corridors and came up again into the next building, finding the back door where, as Servek had promised, a small private skimmer was waiting to collect her. The driver, a stocky male, took her case and opened the door for her. She fell back into her seat with relief.

Soon they were out onto the road cutting through the campus and leading to the main circular. The driver offered no conversation. Lang was grateful. She had enough to think about without having to make small talk. Anxiously, she checked tickets, travel documents, anything to keep her mind away from her situation. When she looked up again, they were on the city circular. They took the southwest exit and then struck north, heading out on the big road past the main spaceport and toward Metenok. Lang felt herself begin to relax. She watched the road go past for a while, and then opened Reta's thesis once more. Soon her eyes began to close.

The driver cleared his throat. Lang opened her eyes, unsure how much time had passed.

"Professor Lang," the driver said, sounding apologetic, "I'm afraid we're being followed."

Lang's heart sank. Journalists? The whole plan had relied on her getting away unnoticed. They would easily find out where she was going and follow her to Arawath.

"If you have any idea how to shake them off, please feel free," she said, and she was rewarded by a smile from the driver. He took the next exit off the boulevard and started winding through back roads.

"Any luck?" said Lang after a while.

"No," said the driver. "Whoever's driving that skimmer knows what they are doing."

They drove on, eventually hitting the northern edge of the city again. Soon they were weaving through Coranum. Lang checked the time. "We're going backward," she said. "I'm going to miss my flight."

The driver nodded. "It's up to you, Professor," he said. "We can stop and sort this out now, or we can turn around, head to Metenok, and deal with them there. But I won't be able to shake them off."

Lang, after a moment's thought, told him to pull over. The big black skimmer behind followed suit. As they waited for someone to come and speak to them, Lang said to the driver, "Why are you helping me?"

"I heard your talk," he said with a shrug. "The one about the enigma tales. I love enigma tales. The missus thinks they're rubbish. It's nice to have a comeback for once."

Saved by pulp literature, thought Lang wildly. There was a tap on the window, and she pressed the control to open it. A tall broad male in a nondescript dark suit leaned down to speak to her. She heard the driver mutter something under his breath.

"Apologies for disrupting your ride, Professor Lang," he said. "Perhaps you could step outside for a moment."

"Well, I am in rather a hurry," she said. "I have a flight to catch."

"Just for a moment."

"Can I ask on what authority?" Lang said.

The big man said, "Step outside, please, Professor Lang."

"You don't have to get out if you don't want, Professor," said the driver.

No, thought Lang, *but where would I go? They'll follow me wherever I go. This lie will follow me, wherever I go.* She opened the door and got out. She looked around, wondering if she could run, if there was anywhere to hide, but she did not think she would get far.

"This way," said the man, pointing toward the big skimmer. "It won't take long."

My dear Doctor—

From the university we move west into Barvonok, where the banks and businesses have their offices. Do you have places like this in your moneyless society? Like everywhere else, this district is not what it once was, and its tall and glossy towers were flattened along with everywhere else. It rebuilt quickly— money is resilient—but the nature of the district has changed substantially. The new Barvonok is home to the many news organizations that have sprung up since we have embarked upon our democratic project.

Of all the sacrifices I have made for Cardassia, and there have been many, allowing the emergence of a free press has to number amongst the most trying. How much easier life was when nobody dared say a word for fear the Order would come knocking at their door! I tell a lie, of course—keeping tabs on what everyone was doing and saying and reading and thinking consumed the waking hours of a great number of people, not to mention a significant amount of money in keeping our army of informers paid and happy. It is in fact much easier just to let people say what they think. Someone else, it turns out, will always be ready to take on the burden of telling them what a fool they are, and they are happy to do it for free.

Besides, I doubt even the Order could keep track of everything being churned out now. Newscasts, broadsheets, channel upon channel—there is too much. It keeps a lot of people very busy. Still, I foresee some difficulties ahead. The proliferation of material means that people might start to be-

come selective about what they consume and, if my instincts are correct, they are likely to read only that which confirms what they already know. This means they will never have their ideas tested. I worry that as a result, people will form tight groups around those who confirm their biases, mistrusting those whom they encounter who think differently. All of this might cause problems for our fledgling democracy. We are new at this game. We are still practicing. We are still learning.

I might set up a committee.

If you have any ideas, let me know.

Garak
[unsent]

Eight

A rati Mhevet was weary of corpses. She knew that this might beg the question of what she thought she was doing in her current job, but Mhevet was police through and through, and could not imagine herself doing anything else. She had long since resigned herself to the more distressing aspects of the job, although she did not have to like it, and from the depths of her being, she longed to live in a world without violent death. Whenever she was called out to one, she would find herself remembering a conversation she had had once with a man who had, at the time, been her people's ambassador to the Federation. *"There is a universe of wonders out there,"* he had said. *"And all I ever seem to see is small rooms and seedy alleyways."* Shortly after this conversation, Garak had become castellan. Mhevet reckoned he didn't see so many small rooms and seedy alleyways these days. So she had taken over responsibility for maintaining and extending the list of the small and seedy. "Bad canteens" had featured heavily once upon a time, although since her promotion to constabulary chief, she had seen fewer of these, swapping them for "ill-lit meeting rooms."

And, of course, there were the crime scenes. Once upon a time, not so long ago, the whole of the Cardassian Union had been one vast and suppurating crime scene, and all Mhevet and the other unlucky survivors did was bury bodies. She had thought at the time, about a year and a half into this nightmare, that there would be no end to it, that life would only ever be one long, endless funeral. She watched people come to terms with it in many different ways. Some cried all the time. Some went dead behind the eyes and never really recovered. Garak, she thought, still burned brightly from the memory of this time, as if the fire lit inside him during those days would never be extinguished. Sometimes she worried that would consume him. As for Mhevet: she had done what she always did. She got on with policing. And yet she never quite inured herself to what it meant when someone died, and it seemed to her that every untimely death these days was crueler. To have survived the Fire, for so long, and then to have one's life cut off seemed the most heartless tragedy.

The death was compounded by where the body had been found, dumped in the pond that surrounded the campus memorial. Sickening, thought Mhevet. One of the most heartbreaking massacres at the end of the war—the deaths of so many young

Cardassians who could have done so much to help in the reconstruction, and someone had put the body there. There were good reasons: it was private, and only a few people came by regularly. A violation. Mhevet was not religious, but she felt that some kind of taboo had been broken. Murder was bad enough. Soiling the campus memorial was vile. She would be glad to arrest the perpetrator, and she would be glad to see them imprisoned. Even if, as she feared might be the case, the murderer was Natima Lang.

The hunt for Lang was on, and the professor, for such a public figure, was proving oddly elusive. Mhevet had numerous teams out looking for her, and the professor's picture was all over the 'casts and the public screens. But so far, there had been no sign. It was as if she had been spirited away (and Mhevet was having all locations they searched checked for transporter signatures). She was not at her office on the campus, nor was she at her home in the Paldar sector. This stood dark and empty, although a few journalists were still lurking on the step in the hope of an exclusive. Getting permission to review security footage was a somewhat cumbersome process these days (the Cardassian people were understandably twitchy about surveillance and regulated the access thoroughly), and eventually their breakthrough came from good old-fashioned police work. A skimmer had been booked earlier that day from Lang's aide's desk, and one or two colleagues reported that they had seen Lang going through the building with a suitcase around the time the skimmer had been booked to arrive. There had been another sighting or two of Lang in the corridors that ran below the campus. Given that checks had already proven that she had not arrived at Metenok, and that Mhevet's people were waiting there, the driver of the skimmer was the best lead. A couple of officers found him taking his ease at a *geleta* house in North Torr.

"It was very strange," he told the officers when they asked. "A skimmer came after us—big thing, not cheap, out on the Metenok road. We turned back and it followed us all the way to the city, and then we had this slow, stately chase around Coranum—ridiculous, really, those roads are full of bumps, you can't get up to speed. When I said I wasn't going to be able to get away, she instructed me to pull over—this was up on the north heights—and the fancy skimmer stopped right behind us. Tinted windows. Looked like the kind of thing the Order would have. A big man got out—the kind of person you hire to punch people for you, but smart. Not showy. They talked for a while—no, I didn't hear what they were saying—and then Lang got into the skimmer. I was about to get out and make sure she was all right, and then the next thing I knew, the skimmer pulled out! Without paying! I was furious, I can tell you. I was about ready to chase after them, when a triple payment popped up on my account. Can't say fairer than that, so off I went."

And that was the last anyone had seen of Lang, getting into the kind of skimmer that the Order would have. Mhevet sighed. She had strong suspicions as to where Natima Lang was right now, and she was very unhappy about the conclusions she was drawing from all this. She sat for a while, thinking about her job and why she did it. To watch. To be vigilant. To never let anything like the Obsidian Order happen again. That was why she had joined the constabulary, and that was why, when the offer of this promotion had come, she had taken it. Remembering all this, Mhevet took heart, and reached for her private comm, entering a number known to only a handful of people throughout the quadrant. A voice familiar throughout the Union came through.

"Arati? Is that you?"

"Yes," she said. "It's me."

"Any word on Antok?"

"No, not yet. Sir, I hate to ask you this, but do you by any chance have any idea where I can find Natima Lang?"

There was a brief pause.

"Now why do you think that I would know that?"

"I don't know, sir. I don't know what's going on. I'm working on the assumption that we're all still on the same side—"

"Well, so am I, Arati, although I'm rather surprised to find that you feel the need to say it out loud."

"In that case, sir, I think it might be helpful for

you to know right now that Lang's aide has been murdered."

She heard him groan. *"Murdered."*

"Body dumped in the garden where the campus memorial stands."

He hissed in a breath. *"I see."*

"I think we should talk, sir."

"Yes," he said. *"I think you're right."*

With great trepidation, Lang climbed into the skimmer. The door sealed behind her. She looked around. It was as if she was enclosed in a box with dark tinted windows on all sides. She could just see the driver through the screen ahead, and the road outside, but to her left a jet-black screen divided her from the other passenger seat. Slowly, this divide began to lower, and she came face-to-face with Elim Garak.

He was not smiling. "Professor Lang," he said. "I gather you're going on vacation to Arawath. It's lovely there. I own a small house there myself. But perhaps before you leave you could do me the courtesy of speaking to me first?"

Lang briefly closed her eyes. All the fear that had accumulated over the past day was starting to turn into a deep and bitter fury. She knew she had done nothing wrong, nothing other than want a job that this man did not want her to have. She was being played with, toyed with, and she had done nothing to deserve this kind of treatment. But she was not easily cowed. She had run rings around the Obsidian Order for many years. She was happy to go around one more time.

"Are you in the custom," she said coldly, "of chasing prominent intellectuals across the city in your skimmer, Castellan? I shall have to write to my assemblyperson and tell her that they're not keeping you busy enough."

"I'm not in that habit, no," replied Garak. "But then you are *quite* exceptional." He looked past her, through the dark window. "Well done, by the way. You led us a fine dance. Whatever you're paying that driver, you should double it."

The driver, she thought. She fumbled for her personal comm in order to pay him, and perhaps she could send a message through him for Servek, to contact her nestor. This situation was clearly even more serious than she had realized.

"That won't work in here," said Garak.

"I beg your pardon."

"Your comm. It will be blocked. I like my privacy."

"Are you allowed to do that?"

He gave her a very cold stare. Then he tapped a few buttons on the armrest beside him. "Don't worry about the driver," he said. "I've picked up the tab."

"I was also going to contact my nestor."

"Oh yes? Let's hope it doesn't come to that."

Garak leaned forward and rapped on the window. The big skimmer pulled out onto the road, leaving

Lang's skimmer on the roadside. They sat in silence for a while, and then Garak said conversationally, "Have you heard from Quark recently?"

So he was going to play games with her first. "Not for a few months."

"Perhaps you should invite him to visit." His lips twitched. "Yes," he said. "That might be very amusing for us all."

"Castellan," she said. "I do not understand what is happening and I am very afraid. Must we play these games?"

"All right, no games. It might not console you entirely to hear that I too do not understand exactly what is happening. I am, however, not easily scared."

She opened her eyes to look at him. Had he ever been tasked to investigate her, she wondered. Had he read her files or tried to infiltrate her network? If so, she had defeated him. He had been exiled from Cardassia before she too was forced to leave. *I will not be afraid of you*, she thought.

"Tell me about Project Enigma," he said.

"I have no idea what it is!" she said. "I had heard *nothing* about it before this week!"

His blue eyes narrowed. "Are you quite sure?"

"What do you mean?"

"Ultimately, what I mean is—can you prove it?"

"Of course I can't prove it! I can only give my word that I know nothing about it."

"Be as accurate in your statements to me as you would be in your own work," he said softly. "Think back to when you first served on university commit-tees, and be scrupulous in what you assert to be the truth."

She thought carefully before offering a reply. She was starting to feel that this was less an interrogation, and more the start of the process of constructing her defense. "I served on a large number of committees before I fled Prime," she said after a while. She shook her head. "The truth is—I can't remember."

"Ah."

"I know that sometimes I agreed to decisions that sat badly. I supported—or did not obstruct—the removal of numerous texts. I did not prevent finan-cial support being removed from one or two trouble-some students. I'm not proud of any of that," she said.

"We all had compromises to make."

"But a project like this? Experiments on chil-dren?" She shook her head. "I'd remember that! But I don't. I don't remember. Therefore, I have to assume that I never saw anything about it. Could I have for-gotten? I don't think so. Not something like that. But that's not the same as proof, is it?"

"No," Garak said. "Not the ideal answer, but it's a start at least." He took a deep breath, and she had the distinct impression that he was greatly relieved. But then he pursed his lips and gave her a vexed look. "Might I suggest that running for the hills at the first sign of trouble was not the best way to communicate your innocence?"

She shook her head. "I don't know what I was thinking."

"Nor do I!"

"It was my aide's suggestion."

"Ah, yes, your aide," said Garak. "Do you know where she is?"

Lang looked at him in puzzlement. "I left her at my office. She packed my suitcase for me."

"Did you also know that somebody has been systematically deleting files from your archive?"

"I have been doing some housekeeping."

"Someone other than you."

Lang shook her head. "No, no, I didn't. Servek had access to them . . ."

"Did she? Well, when we find her, we'll ask her about that." He studied her. "Really," he said, "you've made the most frightful mess of all this."

"I know," Lang said, and put her hand to her brow. "It's been terrible. All of it—terrible. I thought I was going to be chief academician. I suppose I can forget that now."

"Well, it's certainly going to make it harder."

"What I don't understand," said Lang bitterly, "is your hostility toward me."

"My hostility toward you?"

"What have I *done* to you, Garak?" she burst out.

Garak looked at her in frank amazement. "Natima, what are you saying? I have no hostility toward you! I admire you greatly!"

"Then why are you so opposed to my taking on the role of chief academician?"

Garak didn't answer right away. He leaned back in his seat and studied her carefully. "Do you want the post so much?"

"Of course I do!" said Lang. "The university is my *home*! The place that has mattered most to me my entire life!"

"Perhaps," said Garak.

Lang stared at him. "What do you mean by that?"

"I mean . . . that places change. People change. You were away from Cardassia Prime for quite some time. Exiled. So was I. I cannot speak for anyone else, but I know that when I returned, I found that all that had once meant a great deal to me had been transformed. Remade." He looked at her curiously. "Did exile not have the same effect on you?"

"I . . . had not thought of it in that way," she said. "Of course, so much was gone . . ." She shook her head. "I don't believe I have an answer to that question." Lang gave a small laugh. "That hasn't happened in a while."

"I'm certainly flattered to think that I could challenge your thinking in that way." He smiled, leaned over, and patted her arm. "I think we should take you home."

"Home?"

"Yes, home—by which I mean your house here in the capital. Not some country retreat or hideaway on a distant system. Go home, walk past any journalists with your head held high, and then come out and make a statement. My people can help you write it—I strongly suggest you take me up on this. But, really, this has gone on long enough. You say you have nothing to hide, and I am prepared to believe you." He looked at her with pity. "I am not your enemy," he said. "Far from it. And I believe that these accusations are most likely to turn out to be baseless."

She gave a wry smile. "That is not quite a full statement of support."

"Well, I prefer to cover all the bases. Take me up on my offer," he said. "Go home and make your statement. Speak to your nestor. And then think carefully about what it is you really want."

The skimmer turned off the main circular and began to wind its way through Paldar, the residential district where Lang had her home. "A nice area," Garak said. "Recovering well."

"But not what it once was."

"None of us are what we once were," he said. "For which I am, daily, very grateful." They pulled up outside her house. "What a lovely home you have!" he exclaimed. "What a sensitive reconstruction!"

She looked out fearfully. "There's nobody here," she said. "Where have they all gone?"

He gave a sly smile. "I instructed my people to let out the information that you were heading for the spaceport. I imagine they've all gone over there. It's easy to put people off the scent, when you know how."

Lang laughed at that, at the thought of them all scurrying toward the spaceport while she was sailing back in the opposite direction. Smiling, he offered her his palm, and she pressed her own against it and felt oddly cheered that this man was so plainly on her side.

"I'm glad we're not enemies," she said.

"So am I," said Garak. "More than you know."

She heard a sudden chime from the comm on his armrest. "Forgive me," he said. "That noise means urgent. I should answer that. One never knows if one will find one's nation suddenly on the brink of war."

"I can hardly imagine."

He gave her a strange, bright look. "No? I'm sure you could, if you tried."

He raised the divider again to take the call in private. When he lowered it again, his face was completely changed. He was no longer friendly, but had schooled his expression to complete blandness.

"Castellan, is everything well?" she said, and then thought that perhaps that was an indiscreet question.

"I'm afraid not, Professor," he said. "There has been a rather unfortunate turn of events. We've found your aide."

"But surely that's good news?" said Lang. "We can get to the bottom of these wretched files and what's been happening with them."

"Alas no," said Garak. "She's dead. Murdered."

Lang raised her hand to cover her mouth.

"You understand," said Garak softly, "that this is very bad for you?"

"I understand," said Lang.

"It's imperative," said Garak. "That you do everything I ask, without delay."

And Natima Lang, nodding, found herself in the remarkable position of relying on a man who had, once upon a time, represented everything she most loathed and feared.

Garak leaned forward to speak to his driver. "To the residence, please. Not the official residence. My private residence. My home."

Mhevet had often visited the official residence, but she had never been to Garak's home in Coranum before. She knew—because he had told her—that it was built upon the ruins of what had been his father's mansion. His father, Enabran Tain, the former head of the Obsidian Order, once the most feared man in the Union, had attempted to wipe out the Founders, leading directly to their genocidal assault upon the Cardassian species. She wondered, as she drove her skimmer slowly through the haze up along the winding avenues of Coranum, why Garak would elect to build his home upon the ruins of that man's house. Was it to remind himself of his past? Tell himself that he had transcended it? Not for the first time, Mhevet thought that perhaps Garak's mind tended to the morbid.

Mhevet sighed. In her old life, before the war and

the Fire, she had no call to visit this part of the city, which had been home to the wealthiest and most powerful people in the Union. It wasn't that crimes weren't committed here—far from it—but it wasn't as easy to make anything stick. The kind of people who had lived in old Coranum had, on the whole, lived lives of complete impunity. The Jem'Hadar had put a stop to that. They had not discriminated. To be Cardassian was sufficient to merit extinction. And after that, in the new Cardassia, everything had changed. No crime would go unpunished; no criminal would think they were above the law. Not on her watch. No matter how eminent they were, and no matter what their past had been.

The security was lighter than at the official residence, but effective nonetheless, and Mhevet's skimmer was stopped several blocks away, and her clearances checked, before she was waved on. At the door of the house, a team of two bodyguards checked her credentials once again, and then one of these led her inside. It was a small place, almost humble, and it still had a rather makeshift air about it. Most people had rebuilt by now. But then, Garak had been away for some years on Earth before moving into the castellan's official residence. Still, she had expected something grander. He had never struck her as the kind of man to skimp upon his surroundings. Perhaps he found it soothing.

Garak was waiting for her in a small sitting room. This space was much more as she had expected, comfortable and tasteful. The lower walls were lined with bookcases, the upper sections with paintings. Garak was standing in front of a big window that looked out into a garden full of stone statues. Beyond was a view of the city at night.

"Arati," he said. He studied her carefully, and a small smile played across his lips. "It's nice to welcome you to my home at last."

"Sir," she said. "This isn't a visit. You know why I'm here. I'm looking for Natima Lang."

"Oh yes? And why do you think I would be able to help?"

Mhevet took up a formal stance, feet slightly apart, hands clasped behind her back. "Sir," she said, "a woman is dead. Natima Lang is the most immediate suspect. There is a clear motive—"

"Which is?" said Garak.

"Lang had given Servek access to her files. We know Servek had been tampering with them— perhaps on Lang's instruction. Lang murdered her to keep this secret—"

"Why?" said Garak. "Why do that?"

"I don't know," said Mhevet.

"No," said Garak. "You don't."

"I don't know because I haven't had the opportunity to interview Lang yet!" Mhevet said, not bothering to keep the irritation from her voice. "Perhaps Servek tried to blackmail her."

"Ah, I see we are already well into the realms of conjecture now."

"Which is where we will remain," Mhevet shot back, "until my people get to carry out their interview."

Garak didn't reply. He walked slowly toward her, away from the window, and sat down in a comfortable chair. He gestured to her to sit down in the chair opposite, but she remained standing. "As a matter of personal interest," Garak said, "do you believe that Natima Lang agreed to allow experiments to be conducted on children?"

"I have no idea. But I have reasonable grounds to suspect her."

"I see."

"Do you, sir?"

He shrugged.

"Do I have to spell this out for you, sir?"

Garak's expression was still, almost stony. Mhevet felt herself tremble and struggled to conceal it.

"By all means spell it out for me, Arati."

"Very well. You're obstructing a police investigation."

"And?"

"Sir," said Mhevet, "do you really want me to arrest you?"

Garak rose from his chair and slowly walked over until he was standing directly before her. They were about the same height. Garak looked directly into her eyes. "Say that again," he murmured. "I'm not sure I caught it."

"Yes, you did. But just in case I wasn't clear—I said, do you want me to arrest you?"

Something flickered behind Garak's eyes. "Would you really do that?"

"You bet your boots I would!"

They stood, face-to-face, staring at each other. After a moment, Mhevet thought she saw the faintest ghost of a smile upon the castellan's lips. She thought she caught something like pride.

Garak said, "And you'll be glad to hear that I find you completely convincing."

He turned away and walked back to the window. Mhevet was totally at a loss. What had all this been about?

"She's in the bedroom at the back," Garak said. "I think she was trying to rest, but if you're keen to talk to her now, then you should."

"I think that it's best all around if we resolve this as quickly as possible."

"I agree," said Garak. "But if you could remove her to the constabulary buildings discreetly, I'm sure she would appreciate it. I would too. Should the poor professor turn out to be innocent—as I am as sure as I can be that she will—it would be a great shame if the 'casts had footage on file of her being unceremoniously dragged from a police skimmer."

"I'm happy to oblige you on that, sir. My personal skimmer is outside, and we can enter HQ through a back door. Let me assure you too that I'm not in the habit of dragging anyone in or out of skimmers, be they professors or not."

Now he was definitely smiling. "No," he said, "I

don't imagine you are. You're direct, Arati, but you're not brutal. Merely efficient."

"Thank you, sir."

"No, Arati," he said softly, turning back to the window. "Thank *you*."

She left and went out to her skimmer to wait for Lang to appear. She gripped the controls with shaking hands. She had faced some pretty terrifying moments in her life—riots, marauding Jem'Hadar— but she hoped never again to have to face down the man with the most frightening reputation on Cardassia Prime. She tried to understand what had just happened—had it been a test? To see how far she'd assert herself, assert her authority over him? Mhevet shook her head. Couldn't they all just be a bit less, well, *Cardassian* about things? It would make life easier all around. Still, the threat to arrest him had done the trick—even if it was a test, he now knew how far she was willing to go. *And if I'm smothered in my sleep tonight,* she thought, *I'll know I've made a terrible mistake and that we really do have a monster at the top of our government.*

The front door opened. She saw the castellan, in silhouette, and another figure beside him—a tall woman with long hair. Lang. She and Garak exchanged a few words, and pressed palms, and then Lang came slowly down the steps and got into the back of Mhevet's skimmer.

"Don't worry, Professor Lang," Mhevet said as she rolled the skimmer forward and back out onto the road. "I'm sure we'll have this cleared up soon." She glanced over her shoulder at the weary woman sitting in the back. *Unless you're guilty*, she thought, *in which case, your problems are only just beginning.*

It was dark and the dust was rising. She drove carefully and slowly back to HQ. On arrival, Mhevet handed Lang over to Dhrok, one of her most experienced and trusted colleagues. She found some coffee, and then she went down to the interview room. Dhrok came out to speak to her.

"She's quite open that Servek had access to her files. But she denies knowing that Servek had been tampering with them. And of course she flat-out denies murdering her."

"What about Elima Antok?" Mhevet said.

"Not gotten there yet."

Mhevet nodded. "I think I'll come in for this." She followed Dhrok back into the room and sat to one side as Dhrok asked her whether she knew Elima Antok.

"I know her work, of course," said Lang. "And I know that it was significant to the war crimes report." She looked from Dhrok to Mhevet and back again. "Why are you asking me about Elima Antok? Is she in trouble?"

"Don't worry about that," said Dhrok. "Have you had any dealings with her, direct or otherwise?"

Lang shook her head. "I've read her books. Does that count?"

"I think," said Mhevet, "that we can consider

reading somebody's books to be a benign activity. Unless there was something particular in her work that you took exception to? Her area of study sometimes covered difficult material."

"I don't know why you're asking me about Elima Antok," Lang said, "but I thought she was a rising star and a credit to her profession. I was looking forward to her next book."

"For what it's worth," said Mhevet, "Antok was the one who discovered the files on Project Enigma. She's missing now."

Lang stared at her, and then put her head in her hands. "Oh, what a mess," she said. "What a terrible mess." She looked at Mhevet. "I wish I could help you. But I have no idea what is happening. I have no idea why I—or Antok—would be targeted in this way."

"Unless you *did* sign off on Project Enigma," said Mhevet. "Then everything becomes clear."

Lang shook her head. "But I didn't," she said simply. "I didn't."

Mhevet's personal comm chimed, and she went out to take the message. It was another of the investigators, looking harassed. "Antok's been found, boss," he said, "but there's a complication."

Mhevet went cold. "She's not dead."

"No, chief—"

"Don't give me surprises like that. What's the complication?"

The man's expression became almost comical. "You'd better come and see for yourself."

*   *   *

"This is all taking too *long*!"

Pulaski paced the room at the embassy. Alden, unruffled, continued reading from his padd. "What's the matter now, Kitty?"

"All I can think of is that poor young woman, at the mercy of that lunatic—isn't *anybody* going to do anything about it?"

"Garak has promised us that he's doing all that he can."

"Garak!" Pulaski scoffed.

"Parmak believes him." Alden glanced up at her. "I'm hardly well disposed toward Garak. But Doctor Parmak is completely trustworthy, and if he believes that Garak has nothing to do with this, then I believe him, and we should leave the city constabulary to get on with doing what they do best." He sighed. "It's not as if we can go wandering around looking for her ourselves."

Pulaski grunted and took up watch by the window. Night was falling, and in the bowl of the river valley below, an orange haze was filling the sky. "Smog," she muttered. "This poor damn planet."

After a while, Alden yawned, stretched, and stood. "I'm off to bed." He glanced at Pulaski, tense and tall by the window. "Can I suggest you do the same?"

"You can suggest."

"You're a woman with good sense. You know as well as I do that standing by a window and sulking isn't going to find Elima Antok."

"Maybe not," Pulaski said. "But it makes me feel like I'm doing *something*."

He shook his head and left the room. Pulaski gave him ten minutes and then turned purposefully away from the window and strode over to the comm on the desk. He was quite right: standing by a window and sulking wasn't going to find Antok, and she had no intention of doing it any longer. She punched through a message and, a bare ten minutes later, a very sleepy Metok Efheny appeared.

"Doctor Pulaski," he said. "Is everything all right?"

She gave him a toothy smile. "Everything's fine, Metok. But I need to go over to the campus."

He peered at her. She looked him up and down. Pulaski had the vaguest impression that underneath his jacket he was wearing pajamas. "Do you need to go and get changed?"

Efheny was back at the embassy in record time, fully dressed and carrying two masks, one of which he handed to her. Pulaski eyed hers suspiciously. "What's this for?"

"The first dust storm of the summer is due," Efheny said. "It'll be just our luck if it hits the city tonight, but the air quality was poorer today and I think it will get worse. And if it does—well, you won't be able to breathe without this." He showed her how it worked, helping her clasp it around her face and adjusting the straps and the filters until clean air was coming through. He put on his own mask. "Anyone with any sense," he said, his voice muffled, "wouldn't dream of going out tonight. The first storm is always a bad one."

"Nobody ever accused me of having sense," Pulaski said.

They went out of the embassy, and Pulaski almost regretted her decision to go out. The simmering, brooding heat fell like a blow across the face, and she gasped behind the mask, amazed at how quickly the weather had changed in the short time that she had been inside the embassy.

"Awful, isn't it?" Efheny said.

"Is it like this the *whole* summer?"

"It gets worse," Efheny said. "Hotter, for one thing. And the dust accumulates. Some days you can't see your hand in front of your face."

"Goddammit!"

"The summers are better than they used to be," he said. "The soil reclamation work up in the mountains is really starting to have an effect. Ten years ago—it felt like we were in darkness the whole summer. And masks were hard to come by."

Dante's Inferno. Pulaski shook her head. She'd known, intellectually, that postwar Cardassia had been a hard place, and—despite the small matter of her kidnap—she was already well disposed toward these talkative, combative people. But facing the dust for the first time—and knowing that this was a shadow of what had once plagued Cardassia Prime—

Katherine Pulaski at last fully understood the people of this world. She found that she completely admired them. They had guts, grit, and determination. To come through this hell, to keep on digging deeper into themselves to find the place where hope lived and to keep drawing from that well, to keep on trying and building and healing. That, she thought, was worthy of her respect.

"You people," she said to Efheny in wonderment. "You're tougher than a basket of snakes."

His eyes crinkled behind his mask. "Thank you, Doctor Pulaski."

He led her to the skimmer, and soon they were on their way to the campus. They used the clearances that had been arranged for her during her tour to get into one of the labs, and she quickly found the scanners that she needed.

"I know what will help us," said Pulaski as she worked. "Antok is part Bajoran." She saw Efheny's expression. "Don't look so surprised," she said. "It happened a lot. So we start by seeing how many people we can find who have at least some Bajoran DNA . . ." She started fiddling with controls. "Now, I suspect there are more people like her in the capital than perhaps most Cardassians like to admit—" She shot Efheny a stern look. "And look! Yes. Almost seven thousand."

"Seven *thousand*?" Efheny gasped.

"It's a lot, isn't it?" Pulaski said. "Well, that's what sexual slavery does." She glanced at Efheny, who didn't look happy. "Sorry to be so blunt. But I bet you can count on the fingers of one hand the number of Bajoran women who were happy to find their Cardassian masters had made them pregnant."

"I just didn't think it would be that many . . ."

"Makes you think, doesn't it?" said Pulaski dryly. "Let's start narrowing it down. We know she's female, we know her age . . ."

That still left her with almost a hundred women. But not all of these were a quarter Bajoran, and in one or two rare cases the DNA had come from a grandfather and not a grandmother. Soon they were down to about twenty leads, and Pulaski was able to discount some of these—they had not had children.

"All right," said Pulaski, when they were down to a dozen. "Here's where we have to start guessing, and I'll need your help. Here are my likely candidates, superimposed over a map of the city. I don't know this place, Metok, but you do. Where could you hide someone? Here?" She pointed to the northeast of the map.

"That's Coranum," said Efheny. "Big houses . . . Oh, I don't know! You could find somewhere to hide there, couldn't you? This is just guesswork!"

"It's the best we have," said Pulaski firmly.

"Weren't you found in one of those new apartments north of campus?" He pointed at the map. There was no red light there.

"Nope," said Pulaski. "He's moved on. Guess again."

"Then, I guess, down here," said Efheny, pointing toward the southeast. "That's the edge of North Torr . . ."

Pulaski nodded, recognizing the name of the district.

"And that"—Efheny drew his finger slightly north—"is Munda'ar. Industrial estates. Light industry, replicator plants. Storage and silos. A lot of warehouses."

They both looked at the red light blinking.

"That's not a very nice end of town," said Efheny anxiously.

"Well, that's where I'm going next," Pulaski said. She looked at him thoughtfully. "You don't have to come, you know."

Efheny squared his shoulders. "I was instructed to help you. So I'll help you."

"Good man! That's the spirit!" She downloaded the data into an ancient Cardassian tricorder.

Back outside, the dust had become markedly thicker, and the wind was rising. They got back gladly into the skimmer, moving it along slowly. Visibility was low. "Sensible people," said Efheny, "are indoors with their filtration systems maxed out."

"Who said scientists were sensible people?"

They drove slowly south and east. There was barely any traffic on the road, and those skimmers that were out were also crawling along. They crossed the Liberation Bridge, the river below an eerie orange, and headed slowly into East Torr. They heard the bell of a tram up ahead, and Efheny, peering out into the haze, slowed down the skimmer. The tram came out of nowhere, rattling past, and went on its way.

"We won't see many more of those," said Efheny. "They cancel services when the storms start. Most people hole up where they are, if it hits this bad."

They inched on through Torr. Pulaski saw dull lights behind sealed windows, but no people. The tenements grew narrower and taller, and eventually ended. They crossed another set of tramlines and then entered the industrial landscape of Munda'ar.

Pulaski was holding the tricorder. They were drawing very close to where the red icon was now. She could only hope it was Antok. They'd come on a long and wasted journey otherwise, and they would have to start all over again. Eventually, Efheny pulled up outside a squat dark warehouse. They both got out.

"Look," Efheny muttered hoarsely. "Someone's coming!"

Pulaski looked where he was pointing. A figure was coming toward them through the haze. *Damn*, thought Pulaski. *Should have gotten a phaser*.

But the figure had his hands up, palms facing out, showing that he too was unarmed. He came right up to them and stopped. From behind his mask, he said, "I knew you were going to pull a stunt like this, Kitty. Has anyone ever explained the Prime Directive to you?"

"Mister," she said, "I was violating the Prime Directive before you were even out of diapers."

Alden glared back at her through his visor. "So, have you found her?"

Pulaski smiled. "I think I have."

A phaser screamed. They dived for cover, and Pulaski said, "Now I *know* I've found her!"

My dear Doctor—

*Does anyone come to Cardassia Prime as a tourist? Perhaps—
as news filters out that we are no longer the quadrant's basket case, and that one is not likely to be confronted with the
sight of hungry children, or trip over corpses, or catch an
infectious waterborne disease—we may see an uptick in visitors. I think there are one or two, more adventurous than the
average traveler, who have already come. But they, surely,
stick to those areas where they can enjoy art and culture,
or perhaps go out into the countryside, where not all is dust
and famine, and can at times be grandly, violently beautiful.*

*We, however, shall move briefly off the beaten track, and
pass through Munda'ar. It is not the most pleasant area of
town, and unlikely to attract many visitors, but we shall pass
through nonetheless, on the way to somewhere else. This
was where the factories were, and the grain silos, and once
upon a time you could not hear yourself think in certain parts
of the area over the thump of the industrial replicators. Industry on Prime suffered along with everything else—you can't
produce much when most of you are dead and the rest of you
are hungry—but things are getting better.*

*I once said to someone that I had spent too much of
my life in small rooms and seedy alleyways. Now that I think
about it, I would also add industrial estates. There is something about these places—with buildings often unmanned for
large periods of time and toward the edge of cities—that
draws people like me to them. For good reason. They offer*

*concealment. They offer hideaways. I seem to have seen the
inside of a lot of these kinds of places.*

I definitely joined the wrong intelligence agency.

Garak
[unsent]

Nine

"It's coming from over there!" Alden cried. Pulaski saw that he had drawn a phaser and was holding it up, ready to fire.

"Where the *hell* are all these phasers coming from?" she said, aghast. "Peter, did you bring that with you?"

"Kitty, someone's shooting at us!" Alden hissed back. "We've got more to worry about than where I got a phaser on Cardassia Prime. Just be glad I've got one!" He grabbed her arm with his free hand and gestured ahead with the phaser. "*Look!*" he said. "Over there!"

Pulaski swung around just in time to see a dark figure dashing away through the haze. Alden began to give chase. "Come *on*, Metok!" she yelled, running after them, and she heard him hurrying behind her. There was a bright light ahead, high up and slightly blurry, and she realized that it was at the top of a big, dark warehouse. Alden had come to a halt in front of it and was rattling at the doors. "Blast resistance."

"Where did he go?" said Pulaski when she reached Alden. She too yanked at the doors, but they were firmly locked. "Dammit, where is he? Where's Antok?"

"All right, Kitty," said Alden. "Calm down."

"Calm down! She's in here, look!" She waved the tricorder at him. "If that was him we were just chasing, he knows that we've caught up with him. And who knows what he'll do to her?"

"Doctor Pulaski!" It was Efheny arriving, breathless and anxious. "We're not going to get in this way, so why don't we try the back? There might be a way in."

"Good idea," said Alden. "You two go that way," he gestured to the right-hand side of the building. "I'll go around to the left."

She thought of asking for that phaser, but he was gone and quickly lost in the haze and the gathering dust. She twitched at her mask, adjusting the filter, and followed Efheny as he set off.

They inched their way on. The wind was picking up, whistling down the narrow roads between the big buildings, lifting up and whirling the dust. Pulaski's affection for Cardassia was rapidly diminishing. She saw Efheny, an indistinct figure up ahead, come to a halt. He called back over his shoulder.

"Doctor Pulaski! I think I've found a way in!"

She came to join him. He was standing by a flight of metal steps and pointing up. She peered up the steps and thought she could make out a doorway there. An emergency exit, perhaps? Pulaski didn't care as long as it had been left open. She ran up the steps, Efheny closely behind, and tried the door, which opened with a creak.

"Good man!" she said, patting Efheny on the shoulder.

They came out into a dark stairwell. Pulaski led the way carefully, trying to keep quiet. They closed the door behind them, to keep out the wind and the dust, and they both shook off their masks with relief. Pulaski rubbed at her eyes until Efheny stopped her.

"It doesn't help," he said. "It only makes it worse."

She grunted her agreement and looked around, trying to get her bearings. They were at one end of a narrow corridor, at the far end of which was the light that they had seen outside: someone had left a lamp on in one of the offices. They walked along the corridor until they reached the office and peered inside. It was empty. They went in. The far wall was made of transparent aluminum, giving a good view down onto the warehouse floor.

"I wonder what they store here," said Efheny.

"Does it matter?" said Pulaski.

"I guess not," said Efheny. "As long as it's not combustible, toxic, or liable to burn on contact with skin."

"Huh," she said. He had a point. Perhaps she was glad she hadn't brought a phaser after all. She checked the tricorder—yes, Antok was still here. The ancient tricorder couldn't tell her where. She peered down into the dark warehouse, trying to see something that might help.

Suddenly, in the big open space below, lights came on at one end, sending long strips of illumination down through the warehouse. Dark stacks of packing crates and pieces of machinery cast long, weird shadows. She heard a muffled cry and then saw movement, and a Cardassian figure—her kidnapper, she guessed—dashed out from under cover.

Alden came from nowhere. He dived at the other man, grappling him to the ground. They fought like hounds.

"Is he okay?" said Efheny anxiously. "He looks like he might be in trouble."

If Pulaski was going to put money on anyone in this fight, she would put it on Alden, who was, she knew, fit and professionally trained. But the man who had held her hostage had had a fierce look about him—something desperate and slightly unhinged. She knew that he would fight on beyond reason.

"I guess it won't do any harm if we try to help," she said. She led Efheny back out of the office into the corridor, and they found the stairs leading down to the warehouse proper. She took these two at a time, Efheny close behind, and she came out through a set of double doors into the warehouse itself. And then she nearly fell flat on her face—something was lying on the floor in front of the doors.

She bent down, and her eyes widened in shock.

Not something—someone. Elima Antok, her hands and mouth bound, her eyes bright with terror.

"Oh, Elima, honey!" she whispered, bending down alongside her. "I'm so glad I've found you! Honey, it's going to okay. I promise everything's going to be okay!"

With Efheny's help, she released Antok's hands and feet. The young woman threw her arms around Pulaski's neck. "Oh, I hoped you were okay!" Antok whispered, her voice hoarse. "I hoped you'd get away and bring someone after me . . ."

Pulaski, soothing the other woman, took the opportunity to check her for injuries. Everything seemed okay—there'd be shock, of course, and that bastard had tied those ropes tight enough to leave marks, but nothing that a tissue regenerator wouldn't heal. The fright might take a little longer to recover from.

A phaser blasted out, echoing around the open space. Antok screamed. Pulaski, looking up, saw Efheny standing there, mouth open, an easy target.

"Metok, you damn fool, get down!" Pulaski yelled. He turned at the sound of her voice and, suddenly realizing his danger, fell to the ground. There was another blast from a phaser. Pulaski threw herself over Antok. Yet another shot. Then everything went very quiet.

After a moment or two, Pulaski risked moving. "Elima," she said, rolling over to check on the other woman. "Are you okay?"

Antok nodded. Efheny too, she saw, was fine, pressed back into the shadows.

But who had fired those shots? Had anyone been hit? Who was still out there?

Pulaski stood up and inched forward. "Peter?" she called in a hoarse, carrying whisper. "Peter! Are you okay?"

Then, suddenly, wide doors at the far end of the warehouse swung open, and blasting in from the outside came a wave of dust and the shrill sound of sirens, and she heard people calling out, yelling orders, and bright white spotlights shone inside. *The cavalry*, thought Pulaski. She stepped forward, and found herself looking down the barrel of a snub-nosed Cardassian disruptor. The big guy holding it was uniformed and wearing a helmet with a visor.

"I'm the honored guest," Pulaski said. "The bad guy is over there."

But she raised her hands just in case, not particularly keen on being the recipient of friendly fire, and she let him lead her out into the thick night air.

Outside, all was busy. There were skimmers, and more lights, and a great stirring of dust. Pulaski peered through this and saw Antok being led, stumbling, off toward one of the skimmers. Next she saw Efheny, taken off into another direction, his hands upon his head.

"Hey," she said to the officer with her, "leave him alone! He's not done anything wrong!"

She made to push past him and go over, but he blocked her. Not by restraining her—he wouldn't have dared do that—but by simply being big and in the way. "Doctor Pulaski," he said firmly, "it's time to go."

"But where is he?" she said. "Have you got him?"

"We've got him," he said. "Doctor Pulaski, this is all under control now. Please—come this way."

Reluctantly, still anxious about Antok and concerned for Efheny, Pulaski allowed him to direct her over to a larger skimmer. She found Alden already sitting in the back. He was covered in dust and there was a bruise forming around his eye.

"Sheesh," she said. "Let me take a look at that."

He leaned forward obediently and let her check him out. "You'll be fine," she said. "Though that'll look impressive in the morning."

"You should see the other guy."

"You got him, huh?"

He gave her a crooked smile. "Did you ever doubt me?"

She gave a caw of laughter and patted him on the arm. "Good job, mister."

He closed his eyes, sighed, and let his head fall back. "Kitty," he said.

"Yes?"

"Remind me never to go on vacation with you again."

The nerve of it. She looked out through the window, hoping to catch sight of the kidnapper, hoping to see with her own eyes that he was restrained, but the dust was too bad, and the skimmer pulled out, and she saw nothing more.

The skimmer purred steadily through the city. Pulaski tried to pick out landmarks, but the dust made it impossible.

"Hey," she said to Alden after a while, "do you think we're under arrest?"

He cracked open an eye. "I have no idea," he said. "What crimes do you think we committed?"

"I've not done anything," she said.

He thought about that. "Breaking and entering," he said.

"That emergency exit was unlocked," she said. "And I had good reason to think that Elima Antok was in trouble in there—I was right too."

"Breaking into the lab," he suggested.

"Nope," she said. "I had clearances. They invited me to use their equipment too, so don't think you can pin anything on me there."

He thought awhile longer. "How about being a damn nuisance?"

"I don't think there's a law about that."

"This is Cardassia," he said.

"Best legal system in the quadrant," she said. "Aren't you worried, though?"

"Worried about what?"

"Well, where did you find that phaser?" She looked at him suspiciously. "And how did you manage to turn up at the warehouse at exactly the same time as I did? Are you keeping tabs on me?"

"Kitty," he said, exasperated, "you were *kidnapped*. Would you rather I *wasn't* keeping tabs on you?"

"Huh. You haven't answered my question about the phaser."

He turned to look at her. "Funny thing about Cardassia Prime," he said. "There's all sorts of stuff just lying around."

"You're full of shit, Peter. Did you bring it with you?"

"I promise you that I didn't bring it with me."

"So where did you get it?"

He didn't answer. The skimmer eased up to a halt in front of a big building, and the officers in the front politely but firmly escorted them inside. They were led through various doors and down numerous corridors to a small room with some bad art on the walls. Some tea arrived. Then they were left to wait. Alden investigated the tea.

"I'll be mother," he said, and poured.

"I don't want any tea," grumbled Pulaski. "I'm sick of drinking damn tea."

"It's not possible to be sick of drinking tea," said Alden. "Besides, this is good stuff, Kitty—ettaberry. Helps soothe some of the effects of the dust."

Grudgingly, she took the cup from him, and, even more grudgingly, discovered that he was right, and that the brew was not only pleasant, but had a mild analgesic effect. She thought of quizzing him again about the phaser, but decided it probably wasn't a good idea inside a police station. She stared at the pictures on the wall—they really were horrible, big crude splashes of brown and orange—and worried about Efheny and Antok.

They waited. Time passed. They drank some more tea and waited awhile longer. Eventually, the door slid open. A Cardassian female, tall and on the youngish side of middle age, strode in. Her clothes were plain, but smart, but she looked as if she'd slept in them. No, thought Pulaski, she looked like she wished she'd had the chance to sleep in them. She went straight to the teapot and poured herself a cup, pulled a face when she tasted it (it must be cold by now), and then sat down. She eyed them both balefully.

"Doctor Pulaski, Doctor Alden," said, "I'm Arati Mhevet. I'm—"

"Chief of the city constabulary," said Alden.

"On top of your brief, eh, Peter?" Pulaski muttered.

"I told you I do my research," he murmured back.

"That's right," said Mhevet. "I'm in charge around here. I'm also furious."

"Me too," said Pulaski. "We've been sitting here for ages. I thought I was an honored guest of the Union—"

Mhevet's eyes flashed. "You're an absolute menace, is what you are! I should throw you in the cells for obstructing a police investigation!"

"Obstructing?" Pulaski snorted. "I found Antok,

and I found your kidnapper." She nodded at Alden. "He helped, I suppose."

"Keep me out of this," Alden muttered.

"You're already deep in it," Mhevet said. "That phaser didn't come out of nowhere. You're no longer in Starfleet, and outside the embassy grounds it's proscribed. Which means that either you brought that weapon here illegally, or you procured it illegally once you were here."

Alden shrugged. "It was lying around inside the warehouse," he said, which Pulaski knew was a lie—he'd been carrying it before they went inside. Still, she wasn't going to tell. "He'd already shot at us. It seemed prudent to make use of whatever was to hand to defend us."

"If you think I believe that, you're mistaking me for a fool," said Mhevet. "Nevertheless . . ." She didn't look very happy, Pulaski thought, which probably meant good news for her and Alden. "Nevertheless, your ambassador is very persuasive. And the castellan has put in a good word for you."

Pulaski's eyebrows shot up. "The castellan?"

"He thinks—now how did he put it—he thinks that 'on balance you add greatly to the general gaiety of life.'" Mhevet shook her head. "He says that kind of thing sometimes. My impression? You've amused him, Doctor Pulaski."

Alden covered a laugh. Pulaski pursed her lips. "Well, that's better than nothing, I suppose. But if I can be frank—"

Mhevet sighed. "Must you?"

"I think I will. Frankly, I don't care what you do, nor do I care what your castellan thinks of me."

"I'll make sure I mention that when I next see him," said Mhevet.

"Be sure you do. Anyway, what I do care about is what happens to that poor young man I dragged around the city with me."

Mhevet, a puzzled expression on her face, glanced at Alden.

"What?" Pulaski said. "No, not him! He can take care of himself."

"Thanks, I think," muttered Alden.

"I mean poor Efheny!" said Pulaski. "You know, he didn't ask to be assigned to me. He got stuck with the job, and he hung around to look after me even when I dragged him off into a storm in the middle of the night to get shot at. He was worried about me, looking out for me, and I don't want him to get into trouble for that. He just wouldn't let me go off on my own."

Mhevet was looking at her thoughtfully. "Well, I'm glad to see you think of the little people. No, we won't be pressing any charges against Efheny. I'm happy to assume that he didn't know exactly what he was getting himself into. But I hope . . . I *hope* that he's learned something from all this."

"Learned what?" said Pulaski.

"Not to go outside in dust storms," said Mhevet. She stood up. "There's a skimmer waiting to take you back to the embassy, where I understand your ambassador is hoping to speak to you."

"Ah," said Pulaski.

"And then you're welcome to return to the campus and continue with the program of events scheduled for you. If you could try," said Mhevet, a note of weary pleading in her voice, "please, *try* not to get involved in any sensitive debates, kidnapped, or intervene in any ongoing police investigations before you leave, I would be very grateful."

"I'll try," said Pulaski.

"Not long now before we're gone," said Alden.

"The countdown has started," said Mhevet. She led them out of the waiting room and back through to the front of the building, where she left them with another officer. "It's been interesting to meet you, Doctor Pulaski," she said. "Congratulations on the medal, by the way. I hope the ceremony goes well. I will be the first to say that you most definitely make an impact."

She was considerably less courteous, if that was possible, with Alden. She stood for a moment looking at him, arms folded, eyes narrow, and lips pursed, as if she wasn't sure about letting him go, but eventually she shook her head and went on her way.

"Hey, Peter," said Pulaski, nudging his arm, "looks like we got away with it."

"Seems so." Mhevet went through a set of double doors, and Alden breathed out. He turned to Pulaski and grinned. "We live to ride another day."

An officer emerged from a side door and, to Pulaski's immense relief, he was followed out by Efheny. "Metok!" she cried in delight. "Good to see you!"

Efheny walked over to join her. She took a good look at him, and to her alarm she saw that he was shaking. She turned to the officer accompanying him, ready to kick up a storm about police brutality, but then suddenly Efheny laughed out loud. He grabbed her hand.

"Doctor Pulaski! That was *amazing*! Can we do it again?"

Garak welcomed Mhevet into his office at the official residence with great relief. Whatever had come between them, he now fervently hoped was resolved. He was glad to see her; most of all, he was glad that his instincts about her had been correct. She was as courageous and as incorruptible as he had hoped. Sometimes, looking at the generations that came after him, Garak was humbled and ashamed. What a terrible inheritance they had received, people like Mhevet and Antok. How their world had been squandered; all that was left for them was ash and dust. And they had not given up, but had turned their hands to the task of reconstruction without complaint. They had not deserved their start in life, and all that Cardassia had become was down to their efforts. One day, this world would be theirs entirely. He could not think of better hands in which to leave it. He was so glad to have her back. He was proud of her, like a father with a daughter. He had missed her.

He was also enjoying her report immensely. Whenever Pulaski was mentioned, she collapsed into incoherence. "That woman!" she cried. "That bloody woman!"

"Do you know," said Garak, "when I heard that she was coming, I recalled that she had served on the *Enterprise.* So I sent a message to Jean-Luc Picard asking him for his impressions of her. And that is almost *exactly* what he said. You're in fine company, Arati."

She sank back in her chair. "She was in there like some kind of amateur sleuth! Like some aristocratic idiot prancing around an enigma tale. She said she had 'gotten impatient.' I'll give her impatient—"

Garak stifled his laughter. "But to give the good doctor her due, because of her efforts—"

The look Mhevet gave him was murderous.

"Or, perhaps, *despite* her efforts," Garak hastily amended, "we now have the murderer in custody. At least, that's what I have gleaned from your tirade."

Mhevet ran her hands through her hair. She looked tired. He wanted to press food on her. He wanted to tell her to go to bed and sleep. He wanted to tell her to take the day off and go home and take it easy. He would do none of these things, but the urge to protect her, to nurture her, was very strong. It was strange, this attachment. He had not thought that there was anything paternal about him. He had hardly had a good model, when it came to being fatherly. He felt timid and uncertain. He did not want to harm her in any way, and that, he supposed, what was counted. Tain could not have said the same.

"Yes," she said, "we have him."

"You don't sound very happy about that," Garak said. "I assume he is the murderer? Are we in fact able to prove that he killed Servek?"

"Well, yes," said Mhevet. "He confessed immediately."

"How extremely obliging of him," Garak said.

"He's been altogether very obliging. He told us that he added Lang's name to the files on Project Enigma, and that he sent the files to Antok to discover. He also threatened Antok in order to spur her into action—"

"Wait," said Garak, holding up a hand. "Do we know whether or not Project Enigma actually existed? Was the whole thing a fabrication by this man?"

"Now, that crossed my mind. I asked, but he's not telling."

Garak hissed softly to himself. That would, of course, have cleared Lang's name completely. But it seemed this man wanted that question mark to remain. "So not completely obliging, then?"

"No, but enough for us to put him away. He instructed Servek to tamper with Lang's archive so that it contained communications about Enigma.

Paid her. Servek then tried to blackmail him, so he killed her."

"What a charming pair," said Garak. "And has he at any point offered an explanation as to *why* he embarked upon this sequence of extremely questionable life choices?"

"No," said Mhevet, "he hasn't."

"How vexing," Garak said.

"Vexing isn't the word I'd use, sir, but it will do. He just won't be drawn. He admits to the kidnappings, but he won't say why."

"So you have means and opportunity, but no motive?"

Mhevet leaned back in the chair. "Why does anyone commit murder?"

Garak tilted his head. "Was that a rhetorical question, or do you want an answer?"

"That," said Mhevet, "depends on whether or not you want me to arrest you."

Garak smiled demurely. "I was, of course, only going to attempt an explanation based on what I've read."

"Well," said Mhevet, "I don't claim to be as, er, *well-read* as you, boss, so if you do come up with anything, let me know. In the meantime, we're checking out everything—connections to ultranationalists, possible personal grudges against Lang, history of anti-Bajoran activity, connections to the military on Bajor. The problem is that his records are rather scant."

"That's not unusual," Garak pointed out. "Not much came through the Fire."

"I know that," Mhevet said. "But there should be more, surely? We were all stamped and filed and registered a thousand times over by Starfleet. Admission to a refugee camp, ration cards, evidence of inoculations, burial details. We've all got files as long as our arms, haven't we? Everyone who survived has all of that. What about employment history? Has he been living hand to mouth all these years?" She shook her head. "It's not right. He should have left some mark on the world."

"Some people," said Garak, "are good at concealing their histories."

They looked directly at each other. "Something will turn up," said Mhevet.

"I'm sure you'll tell me," Garak said. "If you find something."

"I will, sir," she promised.

They were still looking at each other, but Garak was glad to realize that there was no fear on either side, only honesty, a shared conception of the past, and a desire for a better future. "Good," Garak said softly. "I'm glad about that. I'm glad you're watching, Arati."

"I won't give up, sir," she said. "It matters too much."

"And if I was at any point not clear," Garak said, "I would rather that you erred on the side of caution."

She smiled at him fondly, like a daughter to a father. "I'll remember that, sir."

"In the meantime," Garak said, "perhaps you could let poor Natima Lang go? It seems that she is guilty of nothing more than taking bad advice." He pondered this. "Of course," he murmured, "that can be fatal, in some cases. She'll need to keep an eye on that."

"Already in hand, sir," Mhevet said.

Garak got up from his seat and wandered over to his desk to admire the vase of spring flowers there. Akret had done a beautiful job with the arrangement. There really was no end to her talents. "I wonder," said Garak, "if I might speak to the young man you're holding in custody?"

Mhevet burst out laughing. "Are you kidding me?"

Garak was offended. "I am most certainly not!"

"Why do you think I'd let you near him? On what grounds are you authorized to speak to him?"

"I am—"

"Yes, I know, you're the castellan of the Cardassian Union. You're not a police investigator, and you have no business being in an interview room with a murder suspect. Honestly, sir, do you want a clever nestor to get him acquitted on a technicality?"

Garak hissed in frustration.

"Checks and balances, sir. You signed up for it."

Garak shook his head. "But why Lang?" he said, burning with frustration. "I still don't understand about Lang. Why target Natima Lang?"

"I don't understand that either," said Mhevet. "I know you're not telling me everything, sir."

"You're right," Garak muttered, "I'm not."

"And I'm not going to press you. I'm going to trust you."

"I'm glad about that. But I still have many questions of my own." His eyes gleamed. "Please can I speak to him? Just for a minute or two?"

Mhevet stood up and stretched. "No."

"Please?"

"No."

Natima Lang stood in the street, blinking. It must be the dust, she told herself. The dust was getting in her eyes. She rubbed at them, trying to clear her vision, and then slipped on the mask that she had been given, tightening the straps and pushing up the visor. She was glad for the mask in a way that she had never thought she would be: it gave her some cover, hiding her away from prying eyes and holo-cameras. The officers, appreciating her worries, had taken her to a side door, where it was quiet, and one of them was waiting with her as protection while the skimmer came around for her.

Everything had resolved itself very suddenly. One minute she had been a murder suspect, subjected to questioning from the most senior police offer in the city. Then Mhevet had suddenly been called away, and the interview had terminated. Lang had been asked to wait. She knew that she did not have to remain—she had not been arrested—but she couldn't face going outside again with all this hanging over her. She had waited several hours. There had been a sudden bustle of activity, then deep quiet, and then more activity. Eventually, Mhevet returned.

"I'm glad to say that we've made an arrest, Professor Lang. The man concerned has confessed to the kidnap of Doctor Antok and Doctor Pulaski, and the murder of your aide. He's also admitted tampering with your files."

Lang bowed her head. At length, she said, "Does this mean I'm free to go?"

"You were always free to go," Mhevet said. "Although we appreciated your patience in waiting all this time. I've arranged for a skimmer to take you back to Paldar."

"Thank you." Lang felt awkward, uncertain, as if there was some formality yet to be completed, but of which she was unaware. "Is that really everything?"

"Not quite," said Mhevet. "Would you be willing to look at some images?"

"Of course," said Lang faintly.

Mhevet pulled out a padd and pushed it across to her. "This is the man we've arrested. Do you recognize him?"

Lang studied the face closely. "I'm sorry, no."

"It might have been years ago, before you defected."

She stared at the face, trying to find something there that was familiar. She shook her head. "I have never met this man," she said.

Mhevet put the padd away. "Ah well," she said. "There might have been something. If you do remember anything, please, let me know." She pulled out her contact info and passed it over. "He's gone to some lengths to frame you, Professor Lang. I'd like to know why. I imagine you'd like to know too."

Lang took her details and stood up. Mhevet held the door open for her, and, as Lang passed through, Mhevet said, "The castellan sends his regards. He wonders whether you could make an appointment to see him at your earliest availability."

"Do you usually help the castellan with his diary?" Lang said.

"I'm here to serve," Mhevet replied. She offered her palm for Lang to press, and then surrendered her to the care of her officers and strode off briskly down the corridor.

And now Lang stood outside, in the dust, waiting to go home. She felt a tap on her arm, and she jumped. Her hand shot up to cover her face, to prevent anyone taking images of her; ridiculous with the mask in place. She wondered how long it would take before she no longer felt she had to hide herself away. She took a deep breath and turned to find herself looking at a young woman, slight and finely boned, with her mask pushed up on top of her head and a rather distracted expression.

"I'm so sorry to disturb you," the young woman said. "You're Professor Lang, aren't you? Natima Lang?" She suddenly sobbed. "Oh! Oh, I'm so sorry!"

Lang, startled by the young woman's distress,

pushed her own mask away. "My dear, are you all right?" she said. "Can I help you?"

"I'm fine, I'm fine. I just wanted to apologize."

Suddenly, Lang recognized her. She had seen her speak on the 'casts, and she had seen her give evidence to the war crimes committee. This was Elima Antok. This was the person who had nearly destroyed her reputation. She went very still. She was not entirely sure what to say to her.

However, Antok had plenty to say. "I doubted you. I shouldn't have done that. I am so, so sorry."

Lang, turning, had a quick word with the officer waiting nearby, and then she grasped the young woman's arm and led her over to a nearby *geleta* stop. It was small, only a pit stop for officers at constabulary HQ on their way to work, but there were a few seats inside. Lang settled Antok in one of these and went to get two small cups of *gelat*. "Now," she said, making the young woman take a sip or two of the hot, bitter, life-giving drink. "Tell me everything."

"It's my fault," Antok said. "I found the files. I gave them to a journalist friend. I should have known better. I should have known that you wouldn't do anything like that! Natima Lang, of all people!"

Lang sighed. How she wished she could be angry— but she couldn't. Antok's distress was so plain, and her remorse palpable. "My dear young woman, as I understand it, a threat was made against you!"

"But you! Natima Lang! Our finest, most consistent dissident voice! Our *conscience*!"

Lang felt naturally gratified, but she also felt considerably embarrassed. "There were many people involved in the dissident movement, Elima. I was lucky to have platforms outside of Cardassia that protected me from the Order. Many other people took risks far greater than I did, and very few of them lived to enjoy the freedom we have now."

"But you!"

"You found compelling evidence. You did what was right when confronted with that evidence. And look! Everything has turned out for the best! The culprit has been found, and the files, it transpires, have been tampered with."

Antok nodded and drank some more of the hot *gelat*. She was starting to look less distressed. "I remember exactly where I was when I first read your writing."

Lang smiled. People often told her the story of their first encounter with her works.

"I was a student," Antok said, "just after Meya Rejal came to power, and all your books became available again. I shared an attic with four other students from U of U. We had a reading group. Every week, ten of us crowded into our attic and pored over your books. None of them made it through the Fire. Only me . . ." She held back a sob. "We thought we were on the verge of something, back then. We thought we were going to be able to be a democracy at last. We all said, you know, that if you hadn't had to flee, if you'd been here when Rejal took power, then maybe she would have held course. Our whole history would have been completely different, if you'd been there. No Dukat, no Dominion. No Fire—"

Lang gave a rueful smile. "Doctor Antok, you attribute too much to me. I should have returned when the civilian government took power, you're right. But the truth was, I was afraid. It's one of my greatest regrets. I should have been here." She shook her head. "But you are too good a historian to suggest that one person can change events. Collectively, we change events. I could not have held back the Jem'Hadar."

"I'm so ashamed that I doubted you. That I've thrown your reputation into question."

"I think . . ." said Lang slowly, "that that's why you were chosen to find the files, you know. Because of your voice."

"What do you mean?" said Antok.

"I've read your work. You're fearless. Honest. Brave."

Antok shook her head. "Oh, if only you knew! I'm not brave! Not really!"

Lang clasped her hand. "You're braver than you know." They sat for a while together, not talking, but comforting each other nonetheless. At last Lang said, "I have a skimmer coming," she said. "Can I take you somewhere?"

"I want to go home," said Antok. "I want to see my children." She fumbled in her pocket and drew out an earring, which she clipped on. Suddenly, her fine bones came into focus, showed exactly who she was, showed the history that had brought her into being, that had brought her here.

"See," said Lang, placing her hand upon the other woman's face. "Fearless." She smiled. "The future is in good hands."

My dear Doctor—

I have saved the best till last. We are now crossing the river, and soon we will be in Torr, the real heart of the city. Yes, there were once fine homes in Coranum, and flashy towers in Barvonok, and everyone in Tarlak is busy, but Torr is where most of us live.

The people here are not rich, and the homes are not magnificent. Often they were cramped, dirty, and over-crowded. There was real poverty here before the war, a lack of water, and sickness too. Cardassia was not kind, at that time, to the weak. I do not mean to romanticize this area, and indeed we did our best not to re-create the problems of the past when we rebuilt. But it seems to me that every stone of Torr has been made to count, and every space within harbors life. Children play, and people smile. Here, more than anywhere else, I see how and why we managed to survive.

I don't get to visit this part of town as much as I once did. When I was younger, I used to wander around here all the time, whenever I had some rare free time. I felt at ease here, at home, and most of all I felt that I had been able, blessedly, to lose myself entirely in the crowd. Immersing myself in the whole, disappearing myself, I got what I most craved. Anonymity. Freedom.

Now . . . Well, my face is too familiar. I wouldn't get more than two steps.

I still love this place.
I wish I could persuade you to come and see.

Garak
[unsent]

Ten

The clatter of teacups signaled that yet another decorous meeting between a head of state and the ambassador of his chief ally was under way. Pulaski glanced at the Vulcan and the Cardassian covertly under her eyelids. Did they like all this decorum? Did it help? She personally loathed it and all its ceremony: the careful positioning of the crockery, the turning of the scones counterclockwise. Or had she made that one up? Whatever, the whole damn thing set her teeth on edge. There was no honesty to it, no openness. She looked at the castellan, who smiled at her brightly. Would he sit here drinking tea while deciding whether or not to go to war? Had he sat and drunk tea just before starting an interrogation, or just after? Why couldn't they just get on with things?

The castellan's smile had become less bright and more contemplative. He turned away from her, and to Ambassador T'Rena. "I'm hoping," Garak said, "that we can put the events of the past few days behind us, and reestablish a relationship based on amity and trust. I sincerely hope"—here he gave Pulaski a somewhat steely look, which she shot right back, thank you very much, mister—"that neither of you believes, any longer, that I had a hand in your kidnapping, Doctor Pulaski, nor in the kidnap of our esteemed Doctor Antok. Neither have I been attempting to discredit Professor Lang."

T'Rena nodded her agreement. "For my part, Castellan, I'd like to assure you that there will be no further commentary upon Cardassian affairs—"

Pulaski shifted in her chair.

"Nor," concluded T'Rena, "will there be any more unscheduled interruptions of your working day."

If Garak had any decency, Pulaski thought, he'd be looking pretty damn chagrined right about now. Instead he simply said, "And how is Doctor Alden?"

Not coming anywhere near you again, thought Pulaski. "He's fine," she said. "He's gone to an exhibition over in Torr. Bajoran-Cardassian art."

"I wondered if he might," said Garak. "He'll see some fine work over there. Well!" he said, and beamed at them both. "I am so glad that we have normalized relations between us once again."

"I'd like to know who had the knives out for Lang," said Pulaski. "That guy you've got in custody—did he say why he got Servek to try to frame her?"

"I don't know," said Garak. "And I don't like not knowing."

"Hate it when someone gets one over on you?" said Pulaski.

"I most certainly do," said Garak. "Because that means that there is an agenda at work that is not plain to me. I do not like surprises. Surprises are never good."

"Nobody ever threw you a birthday party, huh?"

Garak looked appalled. "Thankfully not. But I'll be frank with you, Doctor Pulaski, since you do me the courtesy. I didn't see this business with Lang coming. You know I am keen for someone else to take up the appointment at U of U."

"I know," said Pulaski, "and I just don't understand why. Lang's marvelous—"

"I don't disagree," Garak replied. "Natima Lang is an exceptional candidate of great merit. She seems an ideal choice."

"But?" said Pulaski. "The ambassador said that she thought you wanted someone younger to take over. That you wanted to put people in appointments like this before sending them on to bigger jobs."

"That's part of it," Garak said.

"Well, what more are you after?" Pulaski said with rough impatience.

Garak gave a rather canny smile. "Doctor Pulaski, do you really think that I would reveal all of my secrets to you?"

"Huh," said Pulaski. She didn't think much of that as an answer. "But you don't believe she had anything to do with it? You know," she said, "the more I think about it, the less I believe there was even such a thing as Project Enigma. That the whole business was cooked up by this guy you're holding."

So she'd gotten that far, Garak thought. The jury was still out on that, as far as he was concerned, and he could not forget Lang's own quiet fear that she could not with perfect certainty deny that she had signed the minutes put before her. He sighed quietly to himself. With so much lost, and records so sparse, he doubted they would ever get to the bottom of it. They could try to trace the children, he supposed, but what would be gained by that? They had been very small when they had been taken, some no more than babies. Why force upon them a history they had never known, a sorrow they had never felt? Cardassian history was enough to bear already.

"We know that these files were tampered with recently," he said. "There's very little we can say about their truth. But Natima Lang?" He shook his head. "She was the only innocent one among us at the top on Cardassia Prime. Even her prose style is faultless." He smiled. "Perhaps we should not be surprised by that. All the workings of her mind are revealed to us. She has nothing to hide."

And if she does? Garak wondered. *Then I might be about to make a big mistake. But I must trust my instincts here. Lang did not do this thing. She has nothing to fear from the past—unlike many of us.* He bit the inside of his lip. *Still, something here does not yet add up . . .*

The gentle clatter of a teacup brought him back to himself. He looked at Pulaski. "You wanted to see Julian."

She leaned forward in her chair, ready to fight her case. "I know you don't want me to see him," she said. "But I'm his colleague. A fellow doctor. I'd even go so far as to claim him as a friend. Sure, we weren't bosom buddies, but I still want to see him—"

Garak raised his hand in gentle rebuke. "If you'll let me finish," he said, "I was going to say that I have arranged a visit for later today."

"Oh," she said. "Well, that's great. Thank you."

He smiled at her. "Picard was right about you," he said. "Completely right."

She laughed out loud. "I dread to think!"

No university skimmer took Pulaski over to the castellan's residence that afternoon: instead a great dark official skimmer arrived, courtesy of the castellan himself. She laughed when she saw it, and decided to take it as a gesture from Garak that while they might never be friends, they were no longer enemies.

"Hey, Metok," she said. He was goggling at the sight of the huge skimmer, and she knew he was desperate for a ride and a peek inside the residence. "You coming?"

He looked at her with undying love. She could get used to that.

"Come on," she said. "I don't know if the invitation said plus one, but I'm willing to push my luck one more time."

He didn't need telling twice and jumped inside the skimmer. They spent a happy few minutes playing with all the buttons and watching the screens shoot up and down, and then, at the driver's insistence, making free with the small stash of refreshments. They quickly left the campus behind, but as they wove out toward Tarlak, they became snarled in traffic coming up from the river. Eventually, they ground to a halt. Pulaski, peering out of the tinted window, saw streams of pedestrians coming past.

"I wonder what's going on. Was there anything on the 'casts this morning, Metok?"

Efheny, rather shamefacedly, had to admit he hadn't been watching. Pulaski was delighted. "Keep at it!" she cried. "You'll soon break the habit! And you'll be a happier man all around."

Their pace continued to be slow, but the driver made steady enough progress. They got their answer to what was causing the delay when at last they pulled into Assembly Square. They could hear amplified voices making speeches, and the skimmer had to halt again, very suddenly, to allow a parade to pass by. But this was no celebration—it was somber, and steady, and the men and women were marching with great pride and dignity. They were all in uniform.

"Now this isn't something I've seen a while," the driver muttered. Pulaski, lowering the window and poking her head out for a better look, saw that many of the people marching were carrying banners and placards:

WE SUPPORT OUR MILITARY
VETERANS OF THE FOURTH ORDER
AGAINST PROSECUTIONS
TO PROTECT AND SERVE!!! NOT IMPRISONED!!

And on and on in this vein. This was a demonstration against potential prosecutions for war crimes, Pulaski realized, and, more generally, in support of the Cardassian military. She had to admit that it gave her the shivers. The uniform had changed significantly since the days of the Dominion War, but there was still something unnerving about seeing so many Cardassians marching together.

She glanced at Efheny, still and alert beside her. It was bad enough watching as a human, but what must this sight be like for the average Cardassian? It was—what?—fifteen years since Dukat had seized control, and the Jem'Hadar had been marching through the streets of the city. Efheny must remember that. He must remember what came after, and he can't have been very old.

"Hell of a show, huh?" she said.

He nodded.

She peered out of the window. Someone was passing out scarlet flowers. "What are they, Metok?"

"They're called *perek*," he said. "We send them when people have died. They're used in our burials."

"What a crowd. A reminder of bad times?"

"It's more complicated than that," he said. "The sad thing is that we were all excited when Dukat came back. It seemed like one great party. Parades and banners. Bigger than this—there were a lot more of us then, of course. You know, I wasn't really very old. I remember being excited to go along to one of the parades. And the other thing I remember was that the shops were full of things to eat again—Dominion goods, flooding in because we were now members. There'd been pretty thin pickings before then—did you know that?"

Pulaski nodded. She'd known about the humanitarian crisis on Cardassia Prime in the last days of Meya Rejal's rule, and had even looked into how she could help, but the borders had been firmly closed.

"I remember thinking how great it was," Efheny said. "My oldest brother signed up—Dukat's Draft, they called it. I thought he looked grand in his uniform . . ." His voice trailed away.

He surely would have died, Pulaski thought. There had been a huge rate of attrition among the soldiers serving alongside the Jem'Hadar: they had been easy targets when the Founder gave her order to exterminate the Cardassians. She hoped it had at least been quick.

"How did you escape, Metok? Can I ask that? Is it okay to ask that?"

"Yes, it's fine. We all did that, once upon a time.

Particularly here in the city. 'However did you escape?' Like we wanted to touch each other's luck." He shrugged. "It wasn't very complicated. I was quite small for my age. My mother realized what was happening and told me to run. There was a big public screen at the end of the road, and there was a space behind it for maintenance. The door had broken off, so I climbed inside and hid. When everything went quiet, I came out again." He had a distant look in his eye. "That was the easy part, really. Everything that came after was harder."

She pondered all that must lie behind that. She imagined that his mother hadn't been there when he went back home. She suspected his home hadn't been there. She knew what life had been like here after the Fire, as they called it: the privation; the lack of food, water, and shelter; the disease. She reached out, with great tenderness, and squeezed his hand.

He smiled at her fondly. "A few years ago, I think I would have been frightened by this," he said, nodding out at the parade. "Soldiers out on the street again. But I'm not afraid. They have a right to be here, don't they? They have a right to stand in public and let us know what they think. The difference is—I have that right too. And the other difference is—they're not going to try and force their beliefs on me."

"I'm sorry I've caused so much trouble for you, Metok," she said.

"Trouble?"

"Wrecking your itinerary. Dragging you off into a dust storm to get shot at and arrested."

"When you put it like that, I suppose it has been rather chaotic," said Efheny. "But I've loved every moment of it, Doctor Pulaski. It's all been huge fun. I hope you'll come and visit us again."

She smiled at him. "I'd like that."

"But really, there's no need to say sorry to me. I've had the time of my life. Besides," he said, lowering his voice and leaning in toward her, "I took your tip on Riddle Runner on the 10:52 at Orlehny. I've made a small fortune."

Pulaski roared with laughter. "Oh, good man!"

He grinned back at her. "There is a favor that you could do for me."

"Name it. Anything."

"There's going to be a vigil later, at the campus memorial. For the victims of the Occupation. For the victims of all wars. Could you come along?"

She leaned over and offered him her palm. He pressed his young hand against her older one, and then she wrapped her fingers around his. "I'd be honored."

Bashir was sitting in a chair by the window, staring out, unmoving. *Damn*, Pulaski thought, crossing the room and kneeling down beside him, *this is even worse than I imagined.*

She was a doctor, and she was there to offer hope when none could be seen. Despair was not in her nature. Pulaski was one of nature's battlers, and she used her intelligence to find solutions. But most of all, she was here to see her friend, and she was here to see what she could do for him.

She leaned back on her heels. "Hey, Julian," she said. "It's Kate Pulaski. Sorry to be your first visitor. But I was passing this way, and I thought I'd come by and say hello."

She lifted up his hand, but it was limp within her grasp, and it fell back down upon his lap when she let go. She pulled out her medical tricorder and did a few tests—shone a light in his eyes, which stayed unblinking; tested a few reflexes, which were dulled—and then she sighed and sat down in the chair beside him. She shook her head.

Bashir had been special. Pulaski knew that this was in part an effect of his genetic enhancements, but it had not simply been that. The intelligence, the grace, the physical beauty, perhaps, but that had not been the sum of Julian Bashir. What had impressed itself most upon Pulaski was his moral core, and that was Bashir's own. It owed nothing to any creator; it was a system of considered ethics and a deep well of personal courage that had informed all his choices. *Do no harm* was a good rule to live by, but *Do good with everything you have*? That was a great deal better, particularly when you had the gifts of Julian Bashir.

None of that was there now. It had all gone. Julian Bashir was a hollow man.

So now they had to fill him up again.

She cleared her throat, and then began to talk in a conversational tone. The idea was to give him stimulus, to make him feel secure enough to return. The voices of friends helped, and she would do in lieu of anyone else. She'd bet her medal that he would recognize the voice of Kate Pulaski. "You won't believe why I'm here," she said. "They're pinning a medal on me. Distinguished Impact Medal. Well, you know me. I like to make an impact. I can't think of anyone more deserving."

She observed him for a moment. Nothing. She hadn't expected anything, to be honest; she'd only been here two minutes and, besides, she wasn't really the person for the job. But she was friendly, and familiar, and they had to start somewhere if they were ever going to claw anything back.

"I'll tell you something, Julian, this is an *amazing* planet. Don't tell your friend the castellan I said that, mind you—we haven't exactly taken to each other. No, that's not quite true. I think we've taken to each other very well. But I think he's a crook, and he thinks I'm a pest. Which is fair enough. I *am* a pest. Still, he's sharp as a laser, isn't he? I wonder what he'll do next. He can't stay castellan forever."

Nothing. But this was only the start. There was a great deal of work to be done here, and she may as well be the one to get going.

"So I met the castellan, and I've been wined and dined, and I've watched a lot of hound-racing. Altogether, I've been having a fine old time. Well, apart from the kidnap—I'll come back to that. It got kind of hairy at one point. But this city! This world! I wish I'd known. I wish I'd come here during the reconstruction. There would have been good work to do here. I have to say that I'm surprised you didn't come here sooner. Still, you're here now, and you should know what a fine place is it. The people are gutsy, they're funny, they're strong and brave, and they're doing their damnedest to put behind them some of the worst mistakes I've seen a culture make, and one of the worse comeuppances it's been a people's misfortune to suffer. The dust is up now, Julian, but you should see this place in the spring. You should see what they've built already, and what they're building. They could have given up, Julian, but they didn't. They were down to nothing, absolutely nothing, and they got back up again."

She went on in this vein for some time, just talking to him, telling him her observations of this strange and inspirational world, hoping that something would get through. She told him the sights she'd seen; the facilities she'd visited; she told him about her exploits across the past few days, making them funny, a kind of escapade. She told him about Natima Lang, and Elima Antok, and her admiration for both women. She told him about the hound-racing, and the food, and the dust, and her encounter with the fourth estate. She told him about flowers she'd noticed, and fashions she'd seen, and about the sound the trams made rattling their way down to Torr.

"You should see it all, Julian," she said. "You should see it all."

The door to the room opened. Pulaski looked around to see Efheny, an apologetic look on his face. "I'm sorry," he said, "but it's time to go."

"Two more minutes," she said. He nodded and went back out.

She picked up the parcel she had brought with her. "Hey," she said. "I've got to go now. I hope it's been good to see me. But I brought you a present. Well, it's not really from me. Several of your friends got together and found this, and when they heard I was coming they asked me to bring it with me. I hope there's no injunction on importing livestock. I think I got away with it."

He was hardly going to unwrap the gift, so she pulled at the paper, revealing the small brown bear inside. She reached for Bashir's hand again, lifting it and pressing it against the toy, in case the touch stirred some memory. She pressed it against his cheek too, so he could catch the scent. Smell and memory were closely intertwined; smells took you back to places more than anything else. Then she put the bear upon the windowsill, half looking out at the city, half looking back at Bashir. She smiled at it; this little guy had been loved, she saw, and someone had done some stitching that would make a surgeon proud. She reached out and rubbed its ears.

"He's an old soldier, isn't he?" she said. "He's been through some wars. We've all been through some wars." She stooped and kissed her lost friend gently on the brow. "Come back, Julian," she said. "We miss you."

Pulaski stood in the garden, holding a candle, and looked around. Efheny had explained the campus memorial in some detail, and the ambassador's briefing document had supplied the rest. At Efheny's instigation, they had gotten here early, and she was glad that they had: the garden was small, and people were backed up beyond the hedge into the spaces all around.

The mood was somber, but oddly positive. There were a lot of children. She spied a few Bajoran earrings here and there. Someone handed her a white *meya* lily, the symbol for peace. The speeches were brief and respectful. Some people talked about their Bajoran grandmothers; others, older, spoke about their mothers. There were one or two prayers to the Prophets. This history was still very much alive.

There was a quiet rustle all around, and suddenly the space was filled with armed men. Under the old regime, this would have been the prelude to arrests. Not now. They were here simply to keep watch and to protect their charge. People peered around, hoping to catch a glimpse of him. He came out from the shadows, wearing a plain but beautifully made black suit. On his shoulder were pinned two small flowers: scarlet *perek* and white *meya*. He stood for a while, gravely, hands clasped behind his back, looking around the assembled crowd. The word quickly passed around: *The castellan is here. The castellan is here.*

One of the organizers came forward, and he and Garak exchanged a few quiet words. At first Garak shook his head, but after some quiet but impassioned pressure from the organizer, he nodded, reluctantly, and stepped forward.

"Our friend has asked me to say a few words," he said. "We are here to honor our dead. We lost so many of our best and brightest, our finest minds, our promise—and there were so many that sometimes I cannot bear the weight of their numbers."

A murmur of agreement, quiet but strong, passed around.

"But standing here tonight, I realize how far we have come. Here is everything I hoped for from our new Cardassia. Here we stand together, peacefully and without fear. We remember our past, honor our dead, we look to the future, and we hope." He smiled around at the crowd, sadly, fondly, like a father who knows that soon he must let go. "So much promise," he said. "You fill Cardassia with hope."

He stepped back. There was no applause, that was not suitable for the occasion, but the murmuring of the crowd was approving. They liked what he had said. Garak breathed out, and let others step forward to speak. He became aware that someone had come to stand beside him, and turned to see Pulaski.

"Doctor Pulaski," he said. "You've come to honor our dead."

"Efheny invited me. How could I say no?" She gave him a small smile. "I know we've not exactly hit it off, you and I, so what you might not have gathered over the past few days is how much I admire this world and its people. I don't think I've ever met people so dogged and so brave. And these youngsters . . ." She looked around and whistled softly. "What a legacy. How proud you all must be."

He too looked around, and he smiled. "They are everything that I could have hoped for, and more."

They stood in companionable silence for a while, watching as people came and laid flowers around the edge of the pool where the monument stood. Then Garak said, "And how was he, Doctor? Were you satisfied with how we are caring for him?"

"Oh, that was never in doubt," said Pulaski. "But, you know—I thought he looked lonely, Castellan. I thought he looked like he could do with a friend."

"That's your professional diagnosis," he said.

She nodded. "He just needs to see a friendly face. He needs to hear a friendly voice."

"I understand," said Garak. He turned to go, his security team falling into place around him. As he left, Pulaski saw Lang arrive. She wore a long white coat, with fur around the neck, and she was holding her head up high. She and the castellan saw each other, and he moved toward her. People didn't miss it, Pulaski saw. They didn't miss the castellan publicly greeting the professor. Looking at them she thought that they must be about the same age. They must have lived parallel lives under the old regime, but how different their paths had been. History had its own designs for them, and now they stood together.

She watched them press their palms together. Garak said something, and Lang nodded. They moved apart. Later, that image would come back to Pulaski again and again: the man dressed in black, walking away into darkness, the woman in white moving forward to greet the people gathered.

After the vigil, Garak directed his driver to take him up to Coranum. He sent a message to Parmak to say that he was going back to his house to collect some books. He could, of course, have simply had an aide do this for him, but that was not the point. He wanted to be back in his home for a while, to be himself—whatever that was—and not be the castellan, if only for a little time. He knew his security team wasn't happy, but he thought he'd earned it. The past few days had been a trial in ways he had not anticipated.

He went into his sitting room. He lowered the lights, trying to make the space comfortable and comforting, but he could not settle. He prowled the room, looking for distractions. The absences seemed very strong tonight: Ziyal, Damar, Ghemor. He had found that he could not remember the sound of Ziyal's voice. She was slipping away. Would this happen with Bashir, he wondered? Would he slip away, too, like everyone else?

Garak shook himself and tried not to think of Bashir, sitting in his chair on the other side of the city, motionless and empty. Wearily, his mind drifted to the war crimes report, and he began to fret over what might come next. Nobody was immune, he had promised. But there had to be evidence. There had to be a case. How carefully had the person he had once been disposed of the evidence? How well had he concealed his crimes? Probably extremely carefully, Garak guessed. Still, someone was bound to go looking. What a coup it would be, to claim his head! Would they find anything? Would he be relieved if they didn't, or would he regret it? Did he want to be punished? He had been to prison before, for his attempt to wipe out the Founders. Six months in a holding cell on DS9. Garak thought that was a rather perfunctory sentence for attempted genocide, but then, Captain Sisko did have his funny human ways.

He wandered about the room, looking for Sayak's book, thinking that he could take the chance at last to start reading it, but he realized with some frustration that he had left it back at the official residence. Would he ever get a chance to read it? Life was so busy these days; there was so much to do. That was one benefit of incarceration. He could catch up on his reading. And he would no longer be plagued with intelligence reports, policy documents, files documenting experiments on children.

Garak came to rest looking out of the window. His garden lay in darkness, but he could just make out the shapes of the monuments that he had built years ago, when Cardassia was at her nadir, and his grief was unspeakably vast. After his exile he had come back here, to the ruin of his father's house, and slowly, from the rubble, built these towers of stone. He had needed to be building something. The thugs of the Directorate, the first batch of tyrants and demagogues that Garak had fought off since the end of the war, had seen his work and tried to knock the stones down. Garak and Parmak and Alon Ghemor had defeated them and raised the monuments again. Ghemor had become castellan, and he had been murdered. Cardassia had done that to many leaders over the long years of its bloody history. Garak was still standing, bruised but unbeaten, with Parmak, the solid ground upon which Garak stood.

Garak closed his eyes. When he opened them again and looked out, he became aware that someone was standing out among the stones. Garak was not afraid. He would prefer not to have strangers wandering around his garden, but the transparent aluminum was reinforced. His security team would soon remove them, whoever they were. He peered once again at the figure, standing motionless in the night. Then his eyes adjusted. He realized that what he was seeing was a reflection. This person was not outside. This person was in the room, behind him.

Garak didn't panic. He didn't, in general, panic

about assassins. For years before he took on this job, even when his kingdom had been no bigger than a shop, he had gone about his daily business assuming that assassins might be on their way. Garak had made many enemies across the years. He thought of this permanent state of watchfulness as an occupational hazard—although, admittedly, that was more often the case for heads of state than for tailors. Still, he was resigned to it; he didn't have to like it, however. In fact, he took it rather personally. Slowly, without wanting to startle, he put his left hand against the window, palm flat and fingers splayed out. His right hand he slid unobtrusively around, coming to rest out of sight upon his stomach.

His visitor, perhaps responding to the movement, moved forward. Garak let him come. He guessed that this person, whoever it was, wanted to speak to him; otherwise he would already be dead. *Let him come close,* thought Garak. *Let him come as close as he wants.* Garak kept his body relaxed, projecting unawareness, drawing the visitor nearer and nearer. At last he could hear his breath, ragged and a little anxious. This was not, Garak thought, a professional killer. Fine. Garak would prefer to be the only professional killer in the room.

The man came to a halt behind him. Garak tilted his head to one side. "Hello, Telek," he said quietly.

He watched in the window as the gul started at his voice. "How did you know it was me?"

"I saw you in the window," Garak said. He lifted

his left hand and rapped his knuckles against the glass. It distracted Telek, just for a moment, but long enough. As Telek looked over at the window, Garak drew a small type-1 phaser from his pocket, twisted around, and shoved the gun forcefully into Telek's gut. Telek looked down and recoiled. A simple enough trick, but effective.

Garak sighed. "How many times to I have to tell people that they shouldn't play a player?"

Telek closed his eyes. "Go on, then," he said. "Get it done."

"Get what done?"

"Kill me."

Garak felt irritated more than anything else. Too many people these days watched bad holo-dramas. Garak was by no means averse to popular culture, quite the contrary, but he did wish that people were a little more selective in what they took away from it. "Don't be ridiculous," he said. "I've no interest in killing you. I am, however, quite keen to talk to you, and you seem to have gone to some lengths to come to talk to me. So let's talk. I'd like you to move over to that chair—slowly, please—sit down, and put your hands on your knees where I can see them."

Telek obeyed to the letter. Garak sat down opposite, stretching out his legs in front of him and crossing them at the ankles. He looked ready for a pleasant fireside chat, apart from the phaser, propped up in front of him, pointing directly at Telek's chest.

"Does Legate Renel know you're here?" said Garak.

Telek stared at him, so Garak reciprocated. After a moment, Telek looked away. "No."

"Good. At least one of you is showing some sense. I'll assume this isn't an official visit on behalf of your colleagues in the military, so perhaps you could tell me why you're here. It's very late, and I was intending to go to bed soon."

Telek glared at him.

"You know, this is a fairly extravagant way of getting an appointment with me," Garak said. "One liable to leave you open to prosecution. There are much easier ways to come and see me. You could quite easily have contacted my secretary. I'm sensitive to your worries, and I thought you knew that my door is open. All of this means I have to assume that the reason you're here tonight is not something you want to address with me in an official setting—"

"What right do you have to rake all this up?" burst out Telek.

Good, thought Garak, *all that mindless chatter has had the desired effect and driven Telek to talk.*

"Everyone suffered on Bajor, you know!" Telek said. "We did too! Children of officers murdered, wives and mothers! The Resistance didn't just target our soldiers, you know—they came after our families!"

Nor had the Cardassian military targeted only their counterparts. It had seen every single Bajoran as an enemy, or an enemy in the making. No wonder the Bajorans had not discriminated.

"I know what it was like on Bajor," Garak said. "Some suffered a great deal more than others."

"You know nothing about it!" Telek shot back.

Well, thought Garak, there was something here, something he had not yet quite understood. Garak's mind, as sharp as it had ever been, full and busy, began to shift around data, seeking patterns, seeking meaning. Garak had a vast bank of information stored in his head, and he trusted his intuition completely. He found himself thinking of Bashir, his secrets, he found himself thinking of recent reading, and he pondered what secrets a Cardassian might want to keep.

"Did it hurt?" Garak said suddenly.

Telek looked at him in shock.

"There must have been injections, drugs," Garak went on. "Nausea. Very frightening for a child. I had water fever once as a child. Quite a bad case. I thought I was going to die. I'll never forget how that felt. Did you think that you were going to die?"

Telek was trembling. Good. He pressed on.

"Did they tell you that you were sick? That you needed treatment? You weren't sick, were you? They were the sick ones. Trying to cleanse that part of you. But you can't wipe away history like that. Something always breaks through."

Garak leaned forward, putting himself within the other man's personal space. His expression was

kindly, a little sorrowful. *I am your friend*, he signaled, not entirely truthfully. *You can confide in me.*
He kept his hand tight on the phaser.

"Who did it to you, Telek?" he said softly. "Was it
family? Was it your father?"

"He . . . There was a Bajoran woman."

You mean your mother, Garak thought, but he
kept that one in reserve for when he needed it, even
as he pitied this man.

"A Bajoran woman," Telek said again. "A child . . .
A half-Bajoran child would have ruined him. But
there were no other children. It was . . . It was difficult for him."

"And then a child did come along," Garak said.
"But wasn't quite what was needed."

"It didn't hurt very much," Telek said. "I was only
sick for a year, maybe a little more. My father would
say, all the time, how much I was wanted. How much
he had wanted me."

Well, he had wanted something, Garak thought.
Telek's father had not wanted the child he got. And
that hurt, as Garak had cause to know; yes, that hurt
very badly.

"When I got better, I came home," Telek said. "I
came back here to Cardassia."

But the memories were still there. Of a Bajoran
woman. Of being sick. Of being treated and tweaked,
and given therapy, until he matched the fantasy of a
son that his father held. *Poor Telek*, Garak thought.
Had he known, or had recent events helped him put

the pieces together? Telek's father must have learned about the gene therapy and given permission for it to be tried on his son.

"We all suffered on Bajor!" Telek said, and choked back a sob. "You have no right to do this!"

Calmly, Garak rested his hand upon the other man's knee. "Ssh," he soothed as the weeping began, untrammeled. "Everything will be fine."

He glanced briefly behind the other man's shoulder, to where two of his bodyguards, alert and guilty-faced, were now standing, ready to move in. He consoled the other man for a while, and then carefully withdrew, allowing his guards to take Telek away. "Be gentle," he murmured. "Be gentle."

When Telek was removed, Garak stood and walked back to his window. He heard a discreet but firm cough behind him and turned to see the head of his security team.

"We've called a skimmer to take him—well, where should we take him, sir?"

"He's not well," said Garak, "but he's not safe. Get a doctor. Get a diagnosis." He was trembling a little, he realized. *Get him away from me.*

The other man was watching him closely. "Perhaps, sir," he said, not without compassion, "you might remember why it was that we moved you to the official residence."

"I remember," Garak said. "I promise I'll be good in future."

"Thank you, sir," he said, and left.

Garak realized that he was still holding the phaser. He slipped it back into his pocket, for he would no doubt need it again one day, and then he rested his head against the cool of the window. *My poor Julian,* he thought. He let himself tremble for a while, allowing his body to process the shock. He might have allowed himself some tears then, too, in the dark while nobody could see, for all that had been lost, for all that he had done; for everyone that he had harmed.

Everyone that he had been unable to save.

My dear Kelas—

I'm coming home.

Elim
[sent]

Eleven

On arriving home from the vigil, Natima Lang did not, as had been her custom in recent years, immediately turn on the rolling news. She picked up a book, went to her own bed, in her own home, and was soon fast asleep. The following morning, she rose early and was ready for the big official skimmer when it arrived. She sat down comfortably in the back. She could get used to this.

The castellan, who looked extremely bright for someone who, she suspected, had already been hard at work for some hours, welcomed her cheerfully. They ate breakfast together in a beautifully appointed private dining room. The spring sunshine glowed off the white walls and the yellow, white, and pale green furnishings.

"How lovely!" she said.

"I would prefer to have you come back to my home," he said. "Sadly, after a rather unfortunate incident, I am forbidden from going home. Another exile! Maybe one day. Maybe not. Former castellans are targets as much as current ones." He studied her. "I mention this in the spirit of complete openness."

That final remark confused her, but she left it. Castellan Garak often said odd things, as if one got sudden glimpses of the multiple schemes running through his mind. They ate well and drank numerous cups of hot *gelat*. Their conversation ranged widely: the vigil the previous day; her current work on enigma tales. As she had expected, he was both widely read in the form and remarkably conversant with current scholarship.

"But have you read the new Sayak yet?" she said. "There are a few surprises there that you will enjoy. Personally, I think it's her best."

Garak sighed. "Over the past week I have done no more than look hungrily at that book," he said. "What's the point of an advance copy if it just sits there gathering dust? Never mind. This is the path I chose, and I must follow it to its conclusion." He was about to pour himself another cup of *gelat*, and then tutted and held back. "My aide doesn't allow me more than three cups," he explained. "She says it makes me impossible."

Lang poured him another one anyway. "Live dangerously."

He laughed, and then studied her sharply. "I was sorry to hear you decided you are no longer willing to be considered for the post of chief academician."

"You'll forgive me if I say that that was not the impression I was given!"

"Yes, I would like Ventok to take the post," he agreed. "I think he'd be rather good at it, don't you?"

Lang picked at the remains of an *ikri* bun, pushing her fingertip through the dust of icing on her plate. "He will be a fine leader. He's a good man and very energetic."

"Why have you decided to give up?"

She looked around the room. There was a fine painting on the wall behind Garak, depicting a city on Earth. "Is that Paris?" she said.

"Yes, it is. I imagine you'll visit one day. You've not answered my question."

"Well," she said, "I'm not sure that my future lies on Cardassia Prime."

He shook his head briskly. "Nonsense. You're one of our leading public figures."

"I don't see how that can continue—"

"It shall," he said firmly. "It must." He pursed his lips. "Really, Natima, what would you do in retirement?"

"Travel. Write the next book."

"Charming plans. I hope for something similar. Reading rather than writing. What will you write about?"

"Truth," she said, "and reconciliation."

"No small topic," he said. "Perhaps you need more material before starting work." He picked up a sweet pastry and tore it apart. "Are you worried about your reputation?"

She nodded. "After this . . . What credibility do I have?"

"Don't be ridiculous," Garak said. "What do you think my reputation is?"

She looked at him directly. "You are rumored to have been a killer. A torturer."

"Yes," agreed Garak. "I was all those things."

"A soldier, and a patriot."

"Those too."

"And, perhaps, a penitent?"

He smiled. "I'd like to think so. So many of us were so very guilty in those days. Our whole way of life forced us into it." He took a small bite of the pastry. His manners were almost dainty. "Why am I telling you this?" he said. "You knew it. You diagnosed it. You wrote about it in your book. *The Ending of the Never-Ending Sacrifice*."

"Some of us," she said pointedly, "were considerably guiltier than others."

"You are not telling me anything that I do not know."

She looked back at the painting. Paris did look very beautiful. All light and glass. "When did you read my book? While you were in the Order?"

"I did read a great deal of your work at the time. But that particular book I didn't read until I went into exile."

"A little late for it to be useful, then," she said tartly.

"Not given my subsequent career. You talk about guilt, Natima, but the point is that some of us—you, not the least—were considerably more innocent than others. The people of Cardassia accept me as castellan because they have understood the work that needs to be done to secure our future, and because I am a reminder of the uncomfortable truths of our past. But the time is coming when the past will no longer have such a hold on us. You'll find the castellanship is not an easy task—"

She stopped him. "The *castellanship*?"

He gave an impatient tut. "What else? You can do it. I believe you might even enjoy it." He paused. "Of course, you'd have to persuade the Cardassian people of that. We are a democracy now. For better or worse."

Lang pondered this future for a while. Then, very softly, she said, "The problem is that I'm not sure. I'm not sure whether I was responsible or not. I don't remember. I was under so much pressure at the time, concealing so much. I was on that Committee. Did I sign something, allow something, without knowing?"

He looked at her with great compassion. "Don't torment yourself needlessly. But don't make the same mistakes again."

"What mistakes?"

"Don't run. Fight! Get the right people around you. Let them in and keep them in, and if they ever stop telling you when you're making mistakes, remind them of their job." Garak added, "I have a fine team. They all greatly admire you, and I imagine they'll jump at the chance of working with you."

She looked at him dryly. She thought she understood, now, his careful distance from her over the past few months and the past week in particular. They had been vetting her. "This all sounds as if it's decided."

A small smile played around his lips. "Do you *really* want retirement? You were going to be Tekeny Ghemor's successor, once upon a time! Why not mine?"

"There is," said Lang, "the small matter of an election."

Garak waved his hand. "Oh, that's the *fun* bit. Really, I haven't enjoyed myself as much in years. Being cheered. Having people chant your name. It's marvelous! You'll love every second." He became deadly serious. "But then the election day is over— and what comes next? There is nobody in the Union who has thought as deeply about that as you, Natima, nobody who has prepared so long and so hard for this. A university?" He snapped his fingers, dismissing the project as unworthy. "Leave that to Ventok. There's the whole Union out there, Natima. You can—and you should—be the one to shape it."

She began to believe him. Elim Garak really was a most persuasive man.

Elima Antok's day began more gently, but was no less momentous for her. The reunion with her family had been tender and loving. The boys were vaguely aware that something very serious had happened, and that their mother had perhaps been in some danger, but the unexpected trip to the country, the arrival of the officers sent to protect them, and the numerous rides they had taken in police skimmers had gone a long way to leave them with the impression that they had been part of an exciting holo-drama. They were glad to see their mother, of course, but mostly were just full of their adventures of the past few days.

The previous night she and Mikor had talked for a very long time about what they should do. "I am with you whatever you choose," he said. "I love you and our children. I will support whatever choice you make."

So she made it. She would carry on with her work, and the next few days were busy speaking on the 'casts, defending the Carnis report, and saying what needed to be done to achieve justice. As for herself, Antok was no longer content to hide away.

"I am who I am," she said to Mikor. "And for the first time in my life, I am not afraid to say that in public. And I think . . . I think that people are ready to understand. I think that they are able to do what's needed to show us we are safe here, accepted here."

He nodded. "I think you're right."

Breakfast over, she called out to the boys. "Hey. Let's go for a walk."

They jumped off their seats. Evrek, the older, looked at her curiously. "Are you going to wear that outside, Ma?"

She tugged gently at her earring. "Is that okay with you?"

"Sure," he said, and shrugged, and moved on. She and Mikor shared a smile above their heads. *See?* he seemed to be saying. *No problem.*

She wasn't sure, yet, whether that was true, but she was ready to take the risk. "Come on," she said. "We're going to temple."

The boys sighed.

"And then there'll be *ikri* buns," she promised, to great cheers. They went out onto the street. Most people hurried past without a second glance. Every so often someone noticed the earring. Most of them smiled.

Here we are. Part of your history. Part of your heritage. We are here, and we are not going away.

Garak left the meeting with Lang feeling more upbeat than he had in some time. Mhevet was waiting for him in his office, and he greeted her cheerfully. "Good morning, good morning!"

"You're in a good mood," she said. She sat by his desk, leafing through a book that he had left there.

"The future," he said, "looks unusually rosy." He saw what she was holding and said, "Do you like enigma tales?"

"I've not read many," she confessed. "Are these any good?"

"I can't say," said Garak with some irritation. "I haven't had a chance to read them."

"This is quite a busy job, sir."

He took his seat behind his desk. "I know. But I do miss reading. I guess the day will come again when I have time on my hands." He stared at the book. "I suppose they must seem silly compared to what you do every day. I played a holosuite game about spies once. It was ludicrous."

"It's partly that, but also . . ." Mhevet put the book back down on his desk. "I don't really read much fiction."

He fell back in his seat.

"I don't understand the appeal—all those made-up places and people. There are enough real places and people in the universe. I'll never get the chance to see or meet most of them. Why add made-up ones to the mix?"

Garak was shaking his head. "I didn't know you felt that way," he said, his voice mournful. "I would never have promoted you if I'd known you felt that way."

"I'm sure we'll carry on somehow," Mhevet said equably.

Akret put her head around the door. "The legate is here."

"He's early," Garak said. He turned to Mhevet. "Do you mind?"

She nodded and stood up. "I'll wait outside."

Garak remained sitting while Legate Renel was brought in, and gestured for him to sit down. He skipped the formalities. "You've heard about Telek?"

"I heard he wasn't well," Renel replied.

"No, not well at all. He broke into my home and attempted to . . . I'm not sure, exactly. Dissuade me from taking action that I thought was right."

Renel's jaw dropped.

"He wasn't armed, thank goodness. Or else he wouldn't be in the hospital now. He'd be in prison. Did you put him up to it?"

"What? No!"

"Good," Garak said, although he'd known that. "You listen to me, Renel—now you have a choice. You can play this as dirty as you like. I'm not going to fight on those terms. So go ahead. Do your worst! Attack me, vilify me, dig up whatever you can and make it stick. Who knows what you'll find! When I said that nobody would be above the law, I meant it. But *never* come into this room again and threaten the castellan. Those days are gone. They're not coming back. You have no power over me that I recognize."

He turned to his computer. *Dismissed*.

"Garak—"

Garak looked up, a surprised expression on his face, as if to say, *Are you still here?*

"Castellan Garak, I did nothing. I most certainly did not ask Telek to threaten you—"

"I am extremely glad to hear that."

"But you're not going to bully me into giving up this fight," Renel said, shaking his head. "These prosecutions are unfair—"

"You are free, Legate, to do whatever you think is right. As I am. That is the joy of our new Cardassia."

He looked back at his padd and pretended to be busy. Eventually, he heard Renel stand and leave. Mhevet slipped back into the office and took her seat.

"The legate looked as if someone had set him on fire," she said.

"I merely expressed myself warmly," Garak said. "I can't help it if he has a thin skin."

"No more suggestions of the military showing its displeasure?"

"I sincerely hope I will never hear such a thing said again," said Garak. "Not as long as I hold this office." He thought about that. "Not *ever*."

"Do you want us to arrest Telek?"

Garak shook his head. "He's a victim here too. And he had to suffer a conversation with me."

"I hope you didn't do your worst."

"By no stretch of the imagination did I do my worst. But he's not the man he was, and I don't imagine he'll be returning to his post in a hurry." Garak sighed. "Poor man. It's sad to see someone blighted in their prime." His eyes prickled suddenly. He rubbed at them, and was glad when Mhevet's personal comm chimed, so that she was no longer focused on him.

"Sorry," she said. "I should take this."

"By all means." He busied himself while she took the message, and when she turned back to him, he was able to face her with equanimity.

"News," she said.

"Oh good," he deadpanned. "I adore news."

"The man we arrested is human."

Garak sat back in his chair. "Now, that I wasn't expecting."

"He's also gone."

Garak shook his head. "And I was having such a good day." He reached for his comm. "Akret, could you get me Ambassador T'Rena, please?"

"Shall I go?" said Mhevet.

"No. You don't want to miss this. Ambassador!" he said brightly. "And how are you today?"

"Very well. Is there a problem, Castellan?"

"Yes. I'd like him back, please."

"I'm afraid, Castellan, that I don't know what you mean—"

"Oh, please! You know exactly who I mean. Your operative!"

"Castellan, I do not know what you're talking about."

He frowned. He could very well imagine that they would not have consulted the ambassador. They would have done what they wanted and left her able to deny it. It had happened to him, once or twice, when he was an ambassador. He hadn't liked it then, and he liked it even less now. "The man who took Pulaski and Antok, and killed Lang's aide. He was human. And he has been removed from our custody."

"I see. But if there are failings in your police security, why are you speaking to me?"

"Oh come on! Starfleet Intelligence has taken him, for whatever reason—"

"I am unable to do anything about that."

"I want him back," said Garak. "I want him tried under Cardassian law—"

"I understand that your own people believe that he was unstable. Unwell."

"Nevertheless, he has committed crimes here— kidnap, of a Cardassian citizen, as well as a Federation citizen. Murder—of a Cardassian citizen. I am not happy, Ambassador."

"No," she said. *"I'm sure you're not. But now that you are at last concerning yourself with the fallout of your actions during the Occupation, perhaps you'll allow the Federation to deal with ours."*

Touché, he thought. Mhevet, across the desk, was mouthing, *Ouch.*

"I am not unsympathetic to your position," T'Rena said unexpectedly, and Garak listened closely. *"Intelligence agencies do have a tendency to take initiative where perhaps they should not. I imagine you know more about that than I do."*

He took that on the chin. If she was offering him some tidbits of information, he was prepared to swallow the pious reprimand that came with it.

"I understand . . ." she said, *"that this individual had been on Cardassia for some time. Our man in your dissident movement at the university. I believe"*—she raised an eyebrow—*"that he was tasked with pushing forward Natima Lang as a possible head of state."*

That was ironic, thought Garak, given how far he'd gone trying to discredit her.

"Beyond that I can tell you no more than that he

*has been here throughout your most recent and rather
dramatic history, and that his survival was unknown
until recently. I doubt he has enjoyed the past fifteen
or so years, and I suspect he went rogue some time ago.
This,"* she said pointedly, *"is, of course, conjecture on
my part."*

So they'd found him out and gotten him back.
How reluctant he was, Garak would probably never
know. He would have to be grateful with these
crumbs. "Thank you," he said.

"One last thing, Castellan," she said. *"I do not
appreciate diplomacy to be warped by the activities of
other government entities. But they have acted, and now
we must live with that. We have had rather a rocky
start. I hope this is the end of that. I look forward to
speaking to you next week about the Carnis report, Castellan. Good day."*

She cut the comm.

"Well," said Mhevet. "Starfleet Intelligence ran
rings around us."

"Don't," said Garak, putting his head in his
hands. "Don't."

"Sorry."

"And now I have to go and watch someone put a
medal on Katherine Pulaski."

Mhevet stood up. "Some days are better than
others, sir."

Pulaski enjoyed receiving her medal, of course, but she
was ready now to go home. One last evening among

her Cardassian friends, and then she and Alden would be leaving. She'd come back, she thought as she lay down on the bed. She liked it here. *Besides*, she thought as she fell asleep, *it would annoy Garak.*

She woke in the dead of night, instantly alert. Someone was in the room with her. She sat up and saw a figure sitting by the bed. She peered through the darkness.

"Doctor Pulaski. May we talk?"

"This is starting to get ridiculous," she said. "Don't you boys need to sleep?"

The light came on, and, to her surprise, Pulaski saw that her visitor was human. "I'm guessing you're not with the Cardassian secret service," she said. "Are you one of ours?"

"Well done, Doctor," he said. "Not much gets past you, does it?"

"A lot gets past me. Why are you here? What do you want? Why couldn't we just have a breakfast meeting?"

He smiled and shook his head.

"All right," she said grudgingly. "I'll stop asking questions. As long as you give me some answers. What's your interest in all this?"

"Your kidnapper is one of ours—"

"He's from Starfleet Intelligence? I could take that personally, you know."

"It would be more accurate to say that he *was* from Starfleet Intelligence. He was in deep cover before the war. Embedded within the dissident movement—"

"I thought we supported the dissident movement," said Pulaski.

"We supported parts of it. Part of what our man was doing was investigating whether Natima Lang was a credible leader for a democratic Cardassia. Of course, we never got the chance to find out. Lang defected, Dukat took power, and that was that."

"And your agent has been stuck here ever since?"

"We lost track of him until the start of this, when he came to our attention again."

"I bet you're popular with him," Pulaski said.

Her visitor looked rather strained. "No."

"I should think not," she said. "Stuck here during the Fire. What he must have gone through. And all the time waiting for a pickup that never came."

"It was impossible here after the war," he said. "One lost agent? No chance. We assumed he died."

"Poor guy," she murmured. Then, "You know, I should tell the castellan," she said. "He wants to know why Lang was being targeted. A shame, for some scheme cooked up by a bunch of spooks who think they're serving Federation interests."

"What?" He stared at her. "We're not targeting Natima Lang."

"You're *not* trying to discredit her?"

"Why would we want to do that? She's a force for good—pro-democracy and pro-Federation." His voice became testy. "We don't want a destabilizing demagogue running Cardassia! We don't want another war!"

"Then who targeted her?"

"Something our man cooked up on his own, I think. Maybe all that time he spent inside the dissident movement inoculated him against her. Maybe he knows things about her that we don't. He was undercover as a student for a while. Perhaps she gave him a bad grade."

"That's not good enough."

"It will have to do," said the visitor. "If there was any evidence of wrongdoing on Lang's part, I doubt it exists now."

No, thought Pulaski, *you'll have made sure of that.* And what would be gained from insisting he come clean about some transgression on Lang's part? She liked the woman; she had no desire to harm her. The whole thing could be a fabrication, created by the traumatized mind of an agent who had spent too long undercover.

"All right," she said. "We'll leave it."

"Anyway, chiefly, I wanted to thank you. We wanted our agent brought back, and you've done that for us."

"I think you'll find he's in the custody of the Cardassian constabulary," Pulaski said. "He'll probably tell them the truth about his activities here before the war." She saw her visitor's smile, and she stopped. "He's not in Cardassian custody any longer, is he?"

"It would be immoral to leave him at the mercy of the Cardassian legal system."

"It's been reformed," Pulaski said, through gritted teeth, but the agent just smiled, and dematerialized.

"Damn!" she cried out into the darkness. "I *hate* spooks!"

Before the move to the official residence, Garak would spend his evenings gardening. Even in the high dust seasons—particularly then—he would be outside, persuading his garden to stay alive. He was, after all, a persuasive man. One of his secret complaints about the official residence was that there was no garden here, or not one suitable for puttering. He flicked through a padd and put it down.

Parmak looked up from his book. "Have you started on the Sayak yet?"

"Of course not. Haven't read a word. I have been too busy proving to people that I have not turned into some kind of monster." He jabbed at the padd. "Turned back into some kind of monster."

"Poor you," said Parmak, without a shred of pity in his voice. "You could start it now, if you really wanted. Put down that padd, pick up the book, and start reading. You're the power here, remember?"

"These reports don't read themselves."

"Sometimes I think you find things to keep yourself busy," Parmak said. "Rather than do the things you need to be doing."

"What do you mean by that?"

"I think you know," Parmak said agreeably, and

then changed the subject. "Have you heard Elima Antok at all on the 'casts?"

Garak studied him for a moment, and then let the conversation continue on its new course. "No. Has she been impressive?"

"Very. Marvelous work defending Carnis."

"Well," said Garak, "the signs are that she's tapping into the public mood. Particularly among the young." Or that was what their information told them: the young people—who felt they had nothing to be ashamed of, who didn't want to be citizens of a nation that hadn't come to terms with its past—wanted to be able to travel, go out and be part of the quadrant. "But even those of us who were present—well, some of us—think that these wounds cannot be left untended any longer."

"So the work goes ahead." Parmak nodded. "Good, good."

"I'm meeting with representatives from Bajor next week to begin negotiating how we go about it. Trials here, or extraditions and trials there. Or trials somewhere else in the Federation, perhaps, to satisfy all sides."

"It will be worth it, won't it?" said Parmak. "It won't cause more harm?"

"It will cause pain to many people," said Garak. "Not least the victims, when they have to give evidence. But what was done on Bajor cannot remain unaddressed. Not if we are ever to be admitted—" He stopped himself, as if he thought he had suddenly gone too far. But he could get nothing past Parmak, who was always listening, and who pounced at once.

"Admitted, Elim? Admitted to what?"

"What do you think? To the Federation, of course."

If Parmak was surprised, he gave no visible sign. He closed his book and put it down on his lap. "So that's the next plan, is it?"

"It's *a* plan. I'm not sure it will happen in my lifetime."

"All we've worked for. A reconstructed and free Cardassia—do you think people would want membership of the Federation?"

Garak shrugged. "I don't know."

"And what about what we learned about how the Federation worked. About how it was set up. Thirty-one. Uraei."

"Have we been any better, with our Obsidian Order?" Garak sighed. "I believe we have something to offer, Kelas. Cardassians—we have something unique. Which empire has looked so boldly into its own darkness? Which empire has striven so hard to redeem itself? The humans?" He tilted his head. "Perhaps."

"You are besotted with that species," Parmak said dryly.

"I admire them for how far they've come. But in one respect they fail. They continue to be convinced of their superiority. But not us." Garak shook his head. "We will never—I hope—tell ourselves such lies again. And perhaps that is what we have to offer."

"It's a bold vision. Do you think you can sell it to the Cardassian people?"

"I have no idea. I have no idea if they will want it—and we have years of work yet. I might not be there. I might be . . ." He smiled. "Altogether elsewhere." He looked out of the window, at the day, ending. "We are a democracy now. It's not for me to say. But the choice—the choice must be there."

Parmak was nodding slowly. "Well," he said, "you will have my support, as ever."

"Thank you."

They fell into a quiet, companionable silence. Garak felt himself relax for the first time in weeks. He opened up his padd and began to write.

"Still," said Parmak, "and speaking as a medical doctor, you would do more concrete good right now by going upstairs and visiting Bashir, rather than writing him letters that you never send."

And Garak, who knew when he was defeated, sighed, and closed the padd, and did what he was told.

Cardassia Prime retreated slowly into the distance. Pulaski, standing at an observation port, and in a rare moment of sentimentality unusual for her, raised her palm in farewell.

"Good-bye, Cardassia!" a voice cried out happily behind her. "Good-bye, good-bye, until we meet again!"

She turned to see Enek Therok lumbering toward her. "I didn't know you were on this flight," she said.

"My first trip away in some time," he said. "Retirement will sit very well with me, I think." He beamed at her. "Thank you for all your efforts on my behalf during your visit, Doctor. I have been extremely grateful." He gave her a broad and knowing wink.

Pulaski was baffled. "I only gave a lecture," she said. And caused an interstellar incident, but that was par for the course.

"Oh, you did so much more than that. Tricky times ahead on Cardassia for those of us who found themselves on the front line in the old days. We're none of us entirely sure whether we'll find ourselves suddenly on the wrong side of history." He shook his head. "Most unfair. These young people today don't understand the world we lived in, the compromises we had to make. It's all very well to judge with hindsight, but it's very different from how it was. Still"— he gave her another wink—"your people have made good on their promises."

"My people."

"But then, I did do a lot at the time."

Pulaski thought she was beginning to understand. Her people. Starfleet Intelligence. A man like Therok would have been useful to them once upon a time, well placed to pass on information, well placed to advance their agenda. But he had certainly not been clean. And that would not reflect well on them.

"Difficult times," she agreed. "Like living in a riddle wrapped in an enigma."

He smiled and shook his head, as if to say that he wasn't going to fall for that. "I have no regrets," he said. "I did what I was asked, and I saved a lot of lives."

And prospered from it, she thought. Had he been the one to sign off on Project Enigma? She could imagine the justifications he would come up with: better with good Cardassian families than living as orphans on Bajor. It was always possible to come up with justifications. "Well," she said, "it's all turned out for the best in the end, hasn't it? For you, and for Cardassia."

"'For Cardassia!'" he cried, and laughed, and went on his way.

She went straight off to find Alden, who was resting in his cabin. "All right, mister, time to start talking."

"Kitty," said Alden, rolling up from his supine position to sit on the side of the bed. "It's always a pleasure to see you."

"What did you do?" she said. "How did you get him away?"

"I have no idea what you're talking about—"

"The agent, dammit! Starfleet Intel's man on Cardassia Prime!"

"Ah," said Alden, rubbing at his cheek. He was unshaven, and it gave him a faintly roguish look. "I was wondering whether you'd work any of it out."

"Were you sent here to get him? Goddammit, Peter, if I found out you used me—"

He held up his hands. "Kitty, I promise you, it was nothing like that. I didn't come along intending to get involved. But just after we arrived—the first day, you were busy—I was contacted by Starfleet Intelligence and asked to help."

"To *help*?" She stared at him. "To kidnap Elima Antok? To murder that aide?"

"No, none of that, quite the contrary. The agent—they were worried he was out of control. And they were right. He'd been undercover too long; he was making bad decisions, hasty and irrational. They asked me to track him down and bring him back."

"And you said yes."

"I said yes."

She thought awhile. "You didn't come to help us, did you, at the warehouse. You were after him."

"Well, I was there to help too."

"Is that when you gave him the transponder?"

He looked down at the ground.

"Come on, spit it out!" she said.

"I put a transponder on him, with a delayed recall. I don't think he wanted to leave, although he's surely better in our hands."

"Peter, he *murdered* someone!"

"My understanding is that she agreed to help him tamper with Lang's files, and then she tried to blackmail him—"

"That's no excuse for murder!"

"No, it's not," he said calmly. "He won't get away with murder."

"You mean he'll be tried?" said Pulaski. "In an open court?"

"No—"

"Of course not. So what? Court-martial?"

"Well, he'll need a psych evaluation first. And if he's well enough, then, yes, a court-martial would be in order."

"Not open."

"Kitty," Alden said, exasperated, "these things have to be held behind closed doors. There might be other agents on Prime who could be endangered if this was conducted in public."

"I'm glad we're carrying on the time-honored tradition of spying on our allies."

"Or, if you prefer, there might be people who spied on the Cardassians before they became our allies who might end up with covers blown and attract retribution."

She thought of Therok. "Or people we worked with whose reputations might not stand up to scrutiny."

"These were brave people, Kitty! They don't deserve your scorn! They put themselves in danger—for the sake of the safety of ordinary Federation citizens—"

"Yes, but you love it, don't you? The intrigue, the secrets, the risks. The riddles wrapped in enigmas— you love everything about it."

"I promise you I do not."

Pulaski snorted.

"That's why I left, Kitty."

"And then jumped back into the fray at the first call!"

"He was a colleague—"

"He *killed* someone! He shot me! I'm a damn colleague too!"

"He was in trouble . . ." He put his head in his hands. "Kitty, please, that could have been me, on Bajor, or on Ab-Tzenketh . . ."

Pulaski restrained herself and listened. She knew he had been undercover on both places. Bajor during the Occupation. Ab-Tzenketh . . . well, the whole place sounded like one giant prison camp. It had been a bad time for him.

"I nearly lost my mind on Ab-Tzenketh, you know," Alden said. "I thought I was never going to get away. That I'd spend the rest of my life a slave to the Autarch . . . I began to believe everything they said—that he was a god, that I was there to serve him, that I was lucky to have left the Federation and found myself there. But someone came and got me out. Someone *saved* me, Kitty. I'm paying that back."

"But you *left*, Peter. You knew that it was doing you harm! That's why you joined us on the *Athene Donald*. Why you went back to your research—"

"When they ask, you can't say no."

"You *can* say no. Try it! Say it! Say no!"

"If not me, then who? Someone less careful?

Someone less kind? I can't escape my past, Kitty. Those experiences made me who I am. I can only live with the consequences. He's safe. He's under guard. He's had a bad time. They'll take care of him. We always take care of our own."

"Sounds like you're not so much paying it back as paying it forward, Peter."

He shrugged. "Who knows? Perhaps one day I'll need their help again. Need someone to look out for me. Take care of me."

She reached out to touch his hand. "Dammit, man. You have those friends already. You have them elsewhere. They used you, Peter. They shouldn't ask you to play the game again."

"Once a player, always a player," he said. "Ask the castellan, next time you see him."

The castellan of the Cardassian Union sat alone in his office. Not even Ziyal's picture was there to guide him—or distract him. Sometimes, Garak thought, one did not need a confessor. One needed simply to sit and examine one's conscience alone.

He pondered the events of the past few days: the interruptions that Pulaski had provided; the complications with Lang; the relationship with T'Rena; the worries of the Carnis report, and where it might lead . . . *I did nothing wrong*, he thought, and marveled at the sensation. Innocence. He had often wondered what that might feel like. Now he knew. He had committed no murders, he had framed nobody, and he had broken no laws . . . And he had lost nothing. In fact, everything had turned out as he hoped. Natima Lang was cleared, and he had laid the groundwork with her to persuade her to become his successor. A working relationship had been established with the new Federation ambassador. And the final, necessary act of contrition, which would allow Cardassians to hold up their heads with pride across the quadrant, was now under way.

He had lost nothing, and yet he felt utterly defeated. Crimes had been committed: murder, kidnap, and the attempt to blacken the name of one of the best people that Cardassia had ever produced. He was not able to punish. But he could, perhaps, warn.

Opening his personal comm, he wrote the following message.

Dear Doctor Alden—

I trust that your time on my homeworld proved productive. I believe it did. I hope you will not find it forward of me to offer you some advice. I have played the game for a very long time, and I have seen most of the possible outcomes. You may have won today, but you are not the man you were, and I have seen what the future might hold for you. My advice is this—

Get out of this business as soon as you can. When nobody is seen to be innocent, nobody wins. And the guilt, Doc-

*tor Alden—the guilt is addictive. The game destroys. Some
of us make it through. But not all.*

Yours in pursuit of peace,
Elim Garak

He sent the message. He imagined it crossing the
darkness that lay between them, imagined it reach-
ing this young man and him reading it. He hoped it
would have some effect. He wished it would, but he
doubted that it could. Most of all he wished somebody had sent a message like that to him when he had
been younger. He doubted he would have paid any
attention to it either. Still, you had to try.

He picked up the book on his desk and went
upstairs.

The room was very pleasant and very calm. There
were *meya* lilies in a vase upon the table, and the first
pinks and purples of the sunset were beginning to
paint the walls. He walked over to the window and
picked up the bear that was sitting there.

"Hello, Kukalaka," he said. "I wonder how you
got here. Did Pulaski smuggle you over the border? I
don't mind. Perhaps I'll make you a citizen."

He turned to look at last at Bashir, who was sitting staring out of the window. He stood for a while
looking at his friend's unmoving form. Bashir's eyes
were open but unseeing. There was nothing there of
the vibrant, brilliant man that Garak had known, no
sign of the sharp and humane intelligence that had

animated the doctor. All that had made this man Bashir—*Julian*—was gone, and Garak did not know if it could ever be retrieved.

Slowly, heavily, Garak sat down in the chair beside Bashir. *This*, he thought, *this is the ultimate cost of all our games and schemes and enigmas; this is where we end up, locked in prisons of our own making, alone, without hope of a key . . .*

"My dear Doctor," he said. "It's good to see you. It was always good to see you."

He put the bear down on Bashir's lap. Then he held up the book that he had brought with him. "Enigma tales," he said. "I don't recall now whether I ever pressed these on you before. Kelas is insisting that I take a break and read them. Kelas Parmak, do you remember? My doctor, and my friend. I have been blessed with the friendship of many good doctors during my life. Still, I don't know when he thinks I'm supposed to find the time to read."

Garak stopped, his voice suddenly catching in his throat. He put the book down, stood up, and came to kneel beside Bashir's chair. He lifted up Bashir's hand—it was limp and unresponsive—and brought it to rest upon Kukalaka's head. Then—gently, tentatively—he reached to brush his fingers against Bashir's cheek.

"*Julian*," he whispered. "*Come back to me.*"

But there was no reply. There might never be a reply.

Garak sat back down in his chair and picked up

the book again. "I'll find the time," he said softly. "I promise." For Garak was a patient man, and had played many long games throughout his long life. And if this was to be yet another waiting game— then Garak was reconciled to being a player. He would play this game for however long it took, and he would win.

The sun was setting, the light bronzing Bashir's face. He looked the picture of health: a man in his prime. Garak couldn't bear to see. He opened the book and bent over it. He cleared his throat and began to read out loud.

"Tale One," he said. "*'Auto-da-fé.'*"

His eyes were fixed on the page. So he did not see Julian's fingers twitch, and reach out for a second to stroke the little creature tucked within his hand, before coming, once again, to their placid, empty rest. Garak, unknowing, read on, savoring Sayak's words and her deftness of touch, and the joy of a fiction in which innocence was not only possible but brought reward. At length, the sun set on the capital. The restless wind stirred the dust. Garak read on as if his life hung in the balance, read on into the darkness.

ACKNOWLEDGMENTS

My love and thanks as ever to Matthew, who gave me the space and support I needed to complete this book. Big hugs for Verity, who doesn't mind too much when Mummy has to do her tippy-tapping writing, and has become quite interested in the exploits of Mister Garak.

Huge thanks to Dave Mack for the sneak peek of *Section 31—Control*, for answering my questions, and for Kukalaka. It's a privilege to work with you, sir.

Thank you to Margaret Clark, who helped launch this book again when it looked like it wasn't going to fly, and has been such an enthusiastic supporter of my vision for Cardassia. Thank you also (and to my anonymous copyeditor!) for spotting the Briticisms.

My grateful thanks to the Librarian of Newnham College, Cambridge, who gave me permission to work there. Thank you to all the library staff, who welcomed me every time I visited, and were so supportive as I chased the deadline.

This book is dedicated to my friend Ina Rae Hark, who read my first attempts at writing, and, with infinite skill and patience, walked me through writing my first novel. This book, and all my other books, would not exist without her. Thank you, Ina!

ABOUT THE AUTHOR

Una McCormack is the author of six previous *Star Trek* novels: *The Lotus Flower* (part of *The Worlds of Star Trek: Deep Space Nine*), *Hollow Men*, *The Never-Ending Sacrifice*, *Brinkmanship*, *The Missing*, and the *New York Times* bestseller *The Fall: The Crimson Shadow*. She is also the author of three *Doctor Who* novels from BBC Books, *The King's Dragon*, *The Way Through the Woods*, and *Royal Blood*. She has written numerous short stories and audio dramas.

She lives in Cambridge, England, with her partner of many years, Matthew, and their daughter, Verity.